"Quit treating me like a child, Mason.

"If I want to stay, I'll stay."

"You will not," he warned her.

"Will, too."

"Lou—"

"Mason—"

They stood toe-to-toe, glaring at each other for a long moment. Drawing in a deep breath, Lou said, "You can't make me leave."

"I can't make you leave?" he asked in a deceptively quiet voice. "Is that a dare, Lou? That sounds like one to me."

"Mason—"

Before she could say anything more, he hooked one arm around her waist and hefted her up over his shoulder. He wrapped his other arm around her legs at the knees and clapped a hand soundly over her bottom. Then, ignoring the cheers and jeers of the audience they'd garnered among the dancers, and refusing to acknowledge Lou's colorful protests, Mason carried out his loudly objecting burden.

Dear Reader,

Welcome to Silhouette **Special Edition** . . . welcome to romance. Each month, Silhouette **Special Edition** publishes six novels with you in mind—stories of love and life, tales that you can identify with—romance with that little "something special" added in.

April has some wonderful stories in store for you. Lindsay McKenna's powerful saga that is set in Vietnam during the '60s—MOMENTS OF GLORY—concludes with *Off Limits,* Alexandra Vance and Jim McKenzie's story. And Elizabeth Bevarly returns with *Up Close,* a wonderful, witty tale that features characters you first met in her book, *Close Range* (Silhouette **Special Edition** #590).

Rounding out this month are more stories by some of your favorite authors: Celeste Hamilton, Sarah Temple, Jennifer Mikels and Phyllis Halldorson. Don't let April showers get you down. Curl up with good books—and Silhouette **Special Edition** has six!—and celebrate love Silhouette **Special Edition**-style.

In each Silhouette **Special Edition** novel, we're dedicated to bringing you the romances that you dream about— stories that will delight as well as bring a tear to the eye. And that's what Silhouette **Special Edition** is all about— special books by special authors for special readers!

I hope you enjoy this book and all of the stories to come!

Sincerely,

Tara Gavin
Senior Editor
Silhouette Books

ELIZABETH BEVARLY
Up Close

Silhouette Special Edition

Published by Silhouette Books New York

America's Publisher of Contemporary Romance

For my cousin, Lisa.
I saved a book with a mommy in it for you.

SILHOUETTE BOOKS
300 East 42nd St., New York, N.Y. 10017

UP CLOSE

Copyright © 1992 by Elizabeth Bevarly

ISBN: 0-373-09737-9

First Silhouette Books printing April 1992

ELIZABETH BEVARLY,

an honors graduate of the University of Louisville, achieved her dream of writing full-time before she even turned thirty! At heart, she is also an avid voyager who once helped navigate a friend's thirty-five-foot sailboat across the Bermuda Triangle. "I really love to travel," says this self-avowed beach bum. "To me, it's the best education a person can give herself." Her dream is to one day have her own sailboat, a beautifully renovated older model forty-two footer, and to enjoy the freedom and tranquillity seafaring can bring.

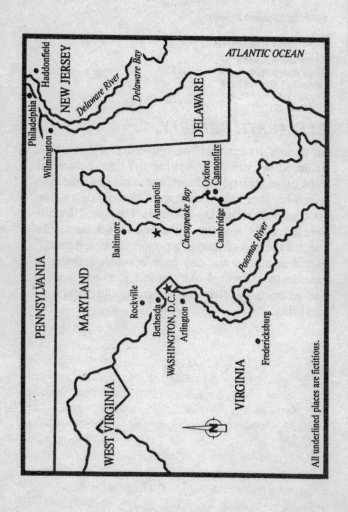

Prologue

He still couldn't get over the change in her. As Mason Thorne sat in the fourth row of the big auditorium studying the young woman who stood at the podium on the stage before him, he simply couldn't believe how much different she seemed now from the frightened, insecure girl who had entered his office at the newspaper nearly five years ago. Back then, Halouise Lofton had been all of nineteen years old, lucky to have received a complete education in a community where most never finished sixth grade, all the while, living in utter fear of losing her family, her integrity and her life. With only a twinge of guilt or regret, he reminded himself that thanks to him, her family was in fact effectively lost to her now, most of them locked up in federal penitentiaries scattered throughout the eastern part of the country. But during all the events that had transpired—the arrests, the publicity, the trials—Lou Lofton had somehow managed to maintain her integrity all on her own.

And as for her life, Mason had seen to it personally that Lou had received everything she would ever need to be happy—a college education, a nice place to live in Georgetown and a job she would begin next week. And as long as he was there to help her along, he knew that she would continue to be just fine. Today Lou was addressing her class at American University's graduation ceremony, and she would soon be receiving the degree in journalism she'd worked so hard to obtain. She was going to be a tremendous asset to the *Capitol Standard.* It was the least Mason could do for the kid who'd saved his life.

He realized with a start that after today, she would be out running in the rat race like the rest of them; she would pick up her life in an entirely different position from which she'd left it to go to school and head forward with every bit of speed she possessed. Mason realized that it should comfort him to know that he had been instrumental in getting Lou back on track. That he ought to consider his debt to her paid and focus on his own future now. Yet something within him recoiled at the thought of turning her loose to face the world alone. There was still so much she didn't know about, so many things that someone who'd grown up sheltered and cloistered in the mountains of West Virginia couldn't possibly understand.

Despite the undeniable maturity she'd achieved as a result of her university studies and her move to Washington, D.C., Mason knew Lou was nonetheless still very naive about life. He could hear it in the way she spoke, her voice soft and lilting, carrying only a trace now of the mountain-hollow accent that had once been so thick in her speech. He could see it in her face, too, almost angelic in its appearance, framed by a light brown halo of hair that had once been lank and lifeless, but was now shiny and boyishly cut in what she assured him was the latest rage. For Mason, it only acted to enhance his protective instincts, because instead of achieving the chic, sophisticated look she'd sought with the style, her short haircut only drew that much more attention to the brown eyes that reflected such an unmistakable innocence, eyes that were so dark and compelling, a man had to hold on to himself to keep from drowning in them.

Running two big hands through his own pale blond hair in frustration, Mason realized with little surprise that, college graduate and working-woman status aside, there was no way he was going to be able to let Lou out of his sight. Deep down, he knew that nothing had really changed. Sure, she might look as though she knew what she was doing, and in her mind, she was no doubt very confident that she was ready to take on the world. Maybe she thought he was fooled by the way she pretended to know exactly what she was doing. But Lou Lofton needed watching over. And Mason Thorne was just the guy to do it.

Chapter One

So this is Mason's idea of a promotion, Lou thought as she let her gaze wander around the elegant ballroom of the Sonoran Embassy. Rubbing elbows with the rich and political, observing the social ritual of the dinner party, which was such an integral part of international diplomacy. Being a newswoman, she was naturally impressed by the caliber and position of the people surrounding her. However, instead of attending the reception for General Papitou as a journalist covering the political and international implications of his visit to Washington, Lou was unfortunately here as a reporter for "The Social Scene" section of the *Capitol Standard*. Her mission was not to interview the diplomats and politicians about their opinions on world affairs as her gut reaction dictated she do, but to stealthily procure a guest list and menu, and to describe the gowns and uniforms that were of such vital national concern.

It helped little to remind herself that until two weeks ago, she had been assisting Henrietta for her "Helpful Household Hints" column. Lou's assignments during her first year at the newspaper had consisted of such pivotal issues as the limitless uses for baking soda and hot topics of controversy such as whether beef stock or beef bouillon made a better foundation for roast gravy. She had covered culinary incursions and household insurrections and had been virtually responsible for the spring-cleaning of the nation's capital. Why, the first lady herself had written Lou not long ago, thanking her for that helpful hint about the use of pennyroyal oil as a natural flea repellent, a practice that had been common knowledge in Lou's hometown. It was a dubious honor at best. But when she had complained to Mason, asking him to help her get into a more respectable, more gratifying area of reporting, this was all he'd been able to come up with.

Lou sighed theatrically and sipped her champagne, smoothing a hand over her sleeveless black cocktail dress before pushing a pale brown lock of hair that refused to behave back from her forehead. She shouldn't have to rely on Mason for everything, she told herself. But where would she be without him? How could she have known when she walked into his office at the paper six years ago that things would turn out as they had? When she'd been growing up in the mountains, her life had been completely mapped out from day one. She would marry Amos Hollis, the storekeeper's son and one of Hack's Crossing's most eligible bachelors, then she would have lots and lots of babies, be a grandmother by the time she was forty and die of exhaustion before she turned sixty. That was how it had been for her mother and for her grandmother. It was how things were in her hometown. At least, that's how they had been until the day Steven Destri had arrived in Hack's Crossing, driving his big luxury car. After that, everything had changed.

Pushing the thoughts of her past away, Lou began to walk casually around the room, observing the guests and eavesdropping on conversations. She tried to avoid memories of anything that had come before Mason had entered her life. Or rather, before she had entered his. She only wished that their initial meeting could have been under different circumstances. As it stood now, Mason felt responsible for her because he thought it was his fault that she'd been left without a family. And she was utterly indebted to him because he'd taken charge of her life and enabled her to become what she was today. There were times when she told herself she almost resented him for that. But more often than not, Lou accepted the fact that she couldn't resent Mason if she tried. She'd probably fallen in love with him the day she'd found him bound and beaten up by her brothers.

"Excuse me."

A lightly accented male voice behind her interrupted her thoughts, and Lou turned to find herself staring into one of the handsomest faces she'd ever seen. The stranger was young, not much older than her twenty-five years, with eyes the color of strong coffee and hair as black as the night outside.

"Yes?" she replied cordially with a warm smile.

Immediately, the man smiled back. "I hope I am not interrupting you. You seemed to be thinking about something—or perhaps...someone—and I could not help hoping it might be me."

Very suave, Lou thought, stifling the urge to giggle. As usual, she was helpless to stop herself from comparing this man to Mason, whose own approach to a woman would be bold and straightforward. Why was every man she met subject to such a comparison? she demanded of herself. Why couldn't she just once come into contact with a member of the opposite sex without instantly considering him lacking in some way?

"I was thinking about something else," she told the man evasively, trying to let him down gently. "I'm sorry."

"But not some*one* else," he replied smoothly, still smiling, rushing on before she could contradict him. "I will just have to try harder. My name is Albert," he introduced himself further, dropping the sound of the *t* in his name to give it the French pronunciation. He extended his right hand formally. "Albert Michaud."

Taking his hand gracefully, Lou responded politely, "My name is Halouise Lofton. Are you an attaché here at the embassy?"

Albert shook his head. "I am one of the guests invited here from Sonora with General Papitou. You have heard of it?"

Lou had to bite her lip to prevent a smile. What was it about her that seemed to make men view her as naive and ill informed? she wondered. Affecting a bland expression, she asked conversationally, "The Caribbean island nation that just a few months ago experienced a bloodless coup and put General Marco Papitou in power? The one that has been overseen by a fascist dictatorship under Lucius Senegal for twenty-two years and by his equally fascist and dictatorial father for thirty-seven years before that? The island that until recently headed the list of countries notorious for human-rights violations? Is that the Sonora to which you are referring?"

Albert had the decency to look sheepish. "American women," he said softly with a smile, "they keep themselves very well informed. Yes, that is the Sonora to which I was referring. Although many, many changes have occurred since General Papitou came into office. We will even be having our first democratic vote in only two weeks."

"There are those who would argue the precise democracy of the upcoming election," Lou remarked pointedly after an idle sip of her champagne, recalling that Mason was one of them.

"No, no, no," Albert denied, shaking his dark head in vigorous denial. "You could not be more mistaken. I myself am very close to the general, and he is a most honorable man."

"I see," Lou replied politely. "I must have been misinformed."

"Indeed you must."

Albert apparently relaxed at her acquiescence, and Lou took a moment to size up her new companion, not surprised to find herself viewing him as a potential source for newsworthy information. She almost chuckled out loud at the realization that she had finally escaped from Mason's supervision long enough to meet a very handsome, sophisticated man, and now the only interest she could summon for him was as a possible source. Why should she be surprised? It had always been that way since meeting Mason. Still, Albert looked like a decent enough guy, if she could wade through the smarminess long enough to get him to talk. It might be very handy to know someone who was "very close" to a political leader like General Papitou, whom the world was still watching carefully, waiting to see if he would be an improvement over his predecessor or, as some suspected, even worse.

"Mr. Michaud," Lou requested softly, trying out her rarely used feminine wiles, hoping they weren't as ineffective now as they seemed to be when she used them on Mason. "Would you be so kind as to get me another glass of champagne?"

Her companion smiled with limitless charm and tipped his head to her in deference. "Miss Lofton, I shall be happy to."

Lou watched him retreat toward the bar at one end of the room, thoughts swirling around in her mind with fury. Albert Michaud might just be her ticket to the one place on earth she really wanted to work, she realized suddenly—the newsroom of the *Capitol Standard*. No more baking-soda brigade, no more society tidbits. Conveniently forgetting about her assignment to cover the embassy reception, Lou's brain quickly jumped track and headed off in a new direction. She reassured herself by recalling that she had a copy of the guest list and menu in her purse and had made agonizingly detailed notes of the fashions immediately after arriving. She'd be filing the story she'd been assigned to cover. But nobody had said she couldn't pursue a hot tip if the opportunity presented itself.

When Albert returned armed with champagne and a tiny plate full of canapés, Lou offered him what she hoped was a winning smile, then batted her eyelashes in what she had heard was a flirtatious manner. "Now, Albert," she murmured in a low voice that she had been assured by a magazine article would entice men in a second. "Tell me more about what you do for a living. It sounds *so* very interesting."

* * *

"You want to do *what?*" Mason tossed his pencil angrily onto his desk in the newsroom, rising slowly to loom over and glower thunderously at Lou.

"Mason, it will be perfect," she assured him shakily. Even knowing him as well as she did, sometimes she was still completely intimidated by the tall, solid strength in him. Sometimes? she asked herself reticently. Try all the time. Taking a deep breath, she hastily pointed out, "Albert will be a great source for a piece I want to do about what's going on down on Sonora. Between the coup and the upcoming elections, there must be a wonderful story in there. I want to be the one to write it."

"Oh, he'll be the perfect source all right," Mason agreed. "And it will make a wonderful story. For someone else, Lou. Not for you."

Lou glared back at Mason with all her might, tamping down the desire to wrap her fingers around his throat and squeeze as hard as she could. Not because she didn't feel like killing him at the moment, but because she knew her slight hands were too small to master the muscular column sufficiently to strangle him. He'd have her flat on her back in no time. And as often as she had indulged in such a fantasy, at the moment, the image took on an entirely different meaning.

"Look..." she began again as her heart kicked up an erratic pace at the idea of wrestling with Mason. Trying to assert herself as a reporter and a woman, knowing full well that she failed miserably at both where he was concerned, she plunged ahead nonetheless. "I appreciate your getting me off the baking-soda brigade, but this society stuff is even worse. It's no place for a newshound like me. I should be out on the front lines covering world events. My instincts and talents are being wasted in the pages of 'The Social Scene.' Dissecting celebrity guest lists and hunting up menus is *not* my idea of investigative reporting."

Mason had to forcibly control his desire to smile at her. God, Lou was adorable. He loved how her West Virginia accent always got a little stronger whenever she was particularly emotional. It was the perfect complement to the way her brown eyes flashed with fire in a face that was just too sweet to be anything other than innocent and calm. What a wonderful little bundle of contradictions she was. And now she wanted to be a newshound. Well, wasn't that just the cutest thing?

"'Henrietta's Helpful Household Hints' is a perfectly respectable column," Mason told her. "And so is 'The Social Scene.' Both of them are quite possibly the most widely read parts of the paper. You should consider it an honor to be part of teams like that. Besides," he added mischievously, "that little tip you came up with about putting candlesticks into the freezer to remove stubborn wax came in the nick of time. Saved my hide when I had Tracy over the night after Audrey. Don't want to leave any of those telltale signs of previous adventures, you know."

No, I don't know, Lou wanted to say. And listening to Mason describe his exploits with women when she had a serious problem on her hands only made her more frustrated. Why did he always revert to such adolescent tactics when she was trying to make him take her seriously? And why, after all these years, did it still hurt so much to hear him talk about his girlfriends in such a fond, appreciative tone of voice?

"Mason," she began again patiently, "I have been with the paper for over a year now, and I'm still not working in the newsroom. I have a nose for news—"

"And a very nice nose it is, too. Freckles and all."

"—And you know how well I can handle myself in a crisis situation," she concluded, ignoring his comment. "I could be a big asset to, say... the Central America desk."

That certainly brought Mason forward. "That's my beat, Lou. And I don't need any help."

Lou tried to quell the heat she felt rising into her cheeks at the disapproval that clouded his pale blue eyes. "Mason—"

"Look, why don't you just bide your time with 'The Social Scene' for now, honing your skills and getting a feel for things?"

"Because I *hate* working on 'The Social Scene,'" she told him. "Staking out the White House to get the goods on how the first lady runs the First Kitchen and what she serves to the First Guests isn't what I went to school for four years to learn to cover."

"Hey, you never know who you might run into at these little affairs," Mason reminded her. "I understand Mel Gibson and Pia Zadora were at the White House last month. Not as a couple, of course, but still..."

Lou intensified her glare.

Mason feigned confusion. "I thought you liked Mel Gibson."

"I like his movies just fine," she said, through clenched teeth, ceding the point, her voice growing in strength and volume as she continued. "But I don't lose any sleep at night over what kind of pâté he likes on his Sociables!"

Mason lifted his hands palm up in surrender. "Fine. So the Mel Gibson diet is not a major concern for you. But this is the best I can do right now, Lou. If you don't like working with Henrietta, and 'The Social Scene' doesn't suit your needs, then you're stuck. I don't know what to tell you."

Lou expelled a frustrated breath she'd been unaware of holding and rubbed at an ache in her forehead. "I want to work at one of the news desks."

Mason gazed at her intently. Like hell she was going to work at one of the news desks. He wasn't about to see her put into any kind of risk such a position might bring about. She'd been through enough of that. "So do a lot of other people on staff," he replied evenly. "You'll have to get in line."

Narrowing her eyes and setting her jaw, Lou returned caustically, "Then consider me in line."

With a silent salute, Mason dismissed her, then sat down to work on the story he'd abandoned as soon as she'd approached his desk.

Knowing there was little chance of changing his mind in his present mood, Lou pivoted with a swish of her flowered skirt and exited the newsroom. It was lunchtime anyway, she told herself. After she had fortified herself with a bite to eat, she could regroup and attack Mason again. She retrieved her lunch from the refrigerator in the break room and headed outside to walk the three blocks that would take her to the Mall. It was wonderfully warm for late March, and the promise of spring hung heavy in the air. Soon the trees along the Mall would be full green with leaves and the cherry blossoms would burst out in pink and white along the Tidal Basin.

If someone had told Lou as an adolescent that she
would ultimately be a college graduate living and
working in a city like Washington, she would have
doubled up in hysterical laughter. Her life now was as
far removed from her origins as it would be had she
been abducted by a UFO and carried to a distant gal-
axy. It startled her now to recall everything that had
occurred since her family became involved with Steven
Destri. There were times when she awoke in the morning surprised to find herself in her tiny Georgetown
apartment, times when she still felt like the lonely,
frightened teenager who had left Hack's Crossing behind. Through it all, Mason had stood beside her, and
helped her to get the life that had been utterly blown
apart back into some semblance of order.

She supposed it was only natural that she would continue to feel such a relentless fascination with and attraction to the man who had been her savior and
became her guardian six years ago. Surely it was nothing but the adolescent infatuation she'd always felt for
Mason that caused her to continue viewing him in such
an ideally heroic way. Eventually, she would be able to
put everything in the past behind her where it belonged
and make a clean break from him. She told herself she
was certain of that. But despite her incessant reassurances to herself that she would be just fine, Lou still
went to sleep on far too many nights feeling frightened
and alone.

As she sat on the Mall watching the people go by, she
felt the tension in her body ease. The wind tossed her
short hair about playfully, reminding her, as it inevitably did when she was outside enjoying a sunny afternoon, of her uncle and brothers locked up in Lorton
Prison. Nowadays, she felt absolutely no emotion for

them whatsoever. When she was growing up, they had all terrified her, brutes and bullies every last one of them, just as most of the Lofton men were. After their trials for crimes ranging from narcotics possession and trafficking to complicity to murder, Lou had remained awake most nights, fearful of the nightmares they dominated in her sleep. She reminded herself that they were just thugs who had gotten what they deserved, and since they were all serving consecutive sentences that totalled more years than they had left in their lifetimes, there was no way they'd ever see the light of a day of freedom again. Still, Lou couldn't forget that they were her blood kin, too, and her remorse that she would never be able to completely disassociate herself from them continued to trouble her from time to time.

After she finished the last of her lunch and packed her things neatly back into her bag, Lou wandered down C Street toward the newspaper offices and tried not to dwell on the thoughts and memories that grew more and more vague as the days went by. She had a new life now, thanks to Mason. And a new project, thanks to Albert Michaud. No matter what Mason said about her position at the paper, he couldn't stop her from seeing someone socially. And if seeing Albert socially meant she picked up little snippets of information that might find their way into her diary, well, that was nothing unusual, was it? Lots of people kept journals of their daily experiences, didn't they? True, perhaps most of them didn't record what might potentially amount to state secrets, but then, Lou Lofton wasn't just anyone, was she? She'd been trained to be a journalist—an investigative reporter—and she would do whatever was necessary to assure her story was newsworthy and accurate. That meant having sources and contacts. And she'd just established her first one—Albert Michaud. Tonight, she'd be seeing him for dinner, and there was no way Mason could interfere. She'd show him who had a very nice, freckled nose for news. And if things worked out the way she planned, she thought smugly, she'd be rubbing *his* nose in it.

. Dammit, where is she? Mason wondered wildly as he listened to the chirp of Lou's phone ringing at the other end of the line for the twenty-sixth time. It was ten o'clock on a Wednesday night, and there was nowhere on earth he could imagine she would be. Her social life was inextricably tied to his; she never went anywhere without him. Every Thursday, they ate dinner together at her apartment, every Tuesday, he took her out to eat, and one weekend a month, they made the drive across Chesapeake Bay to visit his sister and brother-in-law in Cannonfire, a tiny coastal community in Maryland. Along with the occasional lunch together in the newsroom or on the Mall, Mason was certain that their schedule as a couple constituted the totality of Lou's personal social agenda. She didn't seem to have any interest in acquiring boyfriends, or even girlfriends for that matter, and she was always home on weeknights when he called her. So where the hell was she tonight?

Maybe he should go over to her apartment just to make sure everything was okay, Mason thought. Naturally, he wasn't worried about her or anything because it was probably nothing. But her phone might be out of order and she'd want to know about that, wouldn't she? He guessed he could call the phone company to find out if such was the case, but, hey, who trusted the phone company these days? No, it would be best if he just drove over real quick to discover the source of the trouble. Maybe he could even repair it for her. Lou loved it when he helped her out like that. He had to face it, he told himself. Lou needed him.

In a lot of ways, she reminded him of his kid sister. Emily had gotten in over her head more than once in her life, having to rely on Mason to bail her out again. The most serious occasion had occurred about six years ago, and had been what ultimately brought Lou into his life. Of course, Mason supposed he had only himself to blame for Emily's predicament then, because it had been he who'd gotten himself kidnapped by the very men he was investigating for a story, inadvertently leading them to her as a result. But Emily was the one who'd taken it upon herself to hire a private detective to find him, Mason reminded himself. That part was her own fault and had caused her as much trouble as anything he could have wreaked. Never mind that she and Mick Dante, P.I., had wound up falling madly in love and living happily ever after in Cannonfire. And never mind that there was also a little Dante on the way now. That was all beside the point. The point was that Emily had needed Mason to keep an eye on her and get her out of scrapes. Now she had a husband to do that for her.

Which was very convenient, Mason told himself, because lately, Lou had required that particular service from him. That's how it had been virtually since the day they'd met. He deftly chose to ignore the fact that it had been Lou who rescued him from the stickiest situation he'd ever landed in. Instead, he focused on the numerous occasions when he'd helped her with her algebra and sociology, and he recalled all the creepy guys he'd had to chase off to keep her out of trouble.

Lifting his wrist to inspect his watch, Mason also focused on the time and the fact that the woman he was supposed to be keeping an eye on was currently suspiciously incommunicado. And for the life of him, he couldn't figure out why. Yeah, he thought, placing the phone back in its cradle on the fifty-second ring, it might be for the best to go over to her place and check it out. Just to make sure her phone was working all right.

But when he arrived at Lou's front door a half hour later and tapped softly three times, he received no answer. He rapped again, more loudly this time, but no sound greeted him from the other side.

"Lou," he called out quietly. "It's me, Mason. Are you home?"

What a stupid question, a little voice in the back of his head taunted him. Of course she wasn't home. She was out. *Out,* the voice repeated adamantly. And she didn't take you with her.

"Come on, Lou, open up," Mason cajoled, telling himself that she was probably in the shower and couldn't hear him. It was about the time she usually started getting ready for bed, after all. But still he knocked, and still he received no response.

That does it, he thought finally. Reaching into a pocket of his jeans, he extracted the keys that Lou didn't know he possessed and unlocked her front door. It was an unbelievable invasion of privacy, he knew, and she could probably have him arrested for it if she put her mind to it. But Lou would never do that. This was for her own good. She'd understand. In fact, she'd probably be grateful.

Mason quietly closed the door behind him and glanced around the room. Nothing was out of place or seemed to have been tampered with. To be honest, he'd never seen her studio apartment looking so squeaky

clean and neat. Not that Lou was a slob or anything,
but that comfortable lived-in look that he always enjoyed about the place had been replaced by a just-
washed-and-waxed appearance that gave him the impression she was preparing to entertain royalty. From
his vantage point just inside the front door, Mason
could view Lou's home in its entirety. The jewel-toned
throw pillows that usually haphazardly dotted the
claret-colored sofa were now lined up like soldiers
awaiting orders. The numerous plants spilling from the
bookshelves almost looked as if they'd actually been
combed. He noted absently that there was a new emerald green bedspread draped over the mattress and box
springs on the floor in the corner of the raised plat-
form that constituted her bedroom. Her black cat,
Roscoe, snoozed in the window seat beyond, unconcerned by Mason's presence. And beside the closet-sized
kitchen, her minuscule table sported a new cloth printed
with roses. Good God, there were even fresh flowers in
a vase at the center.

Frowning, Mason wondered what Lou was up to.
Clearly, she was indeed out—without him, his inconvenient voice reminded. But where? He removed his
jacket and tossed it with intentional familiarity over the
green-and-burgundy striped club chair, then headed to
the kitchen for a beer. Lou always kept a six-pack in the
refrigerator for him. The cold swig did little to soothe
his frayed nerves and calm his suspicions, however. If
she wasn't home by eleven, he thought ominously, he
was calling the cops.

It was actually 10:58 when he called the police, but it
wouldn't have mattered anyway, because at eleven-
thirty there was still no sign of Lou. It didn't help Mason's black mood that the policeman who'd answered

the phone had said there was nothing they could do
until she'd been missing for twenty-four hours. After
verbally thrashing the desk sergeant for showing so little concern about a kid from West Virginia who was
naive and trusting and in constant need of supervision
to keep her safe, Mason had slammed the receiver into
its cradle and gone for another beer.

Now it was past midnight, and Lou still wasn't home.
Mason was just swallowing the last of his third beer and
had his finger on the dial to call the first of many hospitals when he heard footsteps in the hall outside the
front door. Hastily, he rose from his slumped position
on the sofa, smoothed the wrinkles from his jeans and
stuffed the loose tails of his blue chambray shirt back
into his waistband. As an afterthought, he ran his hands
through his hair in an attempt to hide the fact that he
had been clenching great handfuls of it in frustration
throughout the evening. While he listened to the footsteps draw nearer, he prepared himself to do battle with
Lou, to insist that she sit down and tell him exactly
where she'd gone and what she'd been doing. He intended to ask her in no uncertain terms what she could
possibly have been thinking to cause him such worry.
And he expected to give her a very stern talking-to so
that she would never, ever do something like this again.

However, what Mason wasn't prepared for as he listened to the scrape of her key in the lock, what he didn't
expect, was the fact that Lou wasn't alone when she
came home. As the front door swung open and he heard
a low chuckle such as none he'd ever known Lou to utter, Mason opened his mouth to voice a list of serious
demands, only to snap it shut again at the sight of the
man with Lou. The couple entering the apartment
looked as surprised and annoyed as Mason felt, and it

was a long moment before he fully understood the implications of the scene presented to him. Immediately, he knew that the man with Lou was Albert Michaud, and the knowledge that she had so blatantly ignored his warning to stay away from the Sonoran turned Mason's foul mood bitter. Then right on the heels of that shocking realization came another, equally disturbing one. Lou looked... incredible.

She was wearing red. Knee-jerking, heart-stopping red in the form of a tiny, curve-hugging dress that would raise the dead in a rainstorm. He couldn't recall a time when he'd seen her wear anything other than the shapeless, baggy clothes students seemed to prefer, in pale pastels or discreet darks. This new version of Lou Lofton was more than a little unsettling. The kid from West Virginia had turned out to be one red-hot tomata.

"Mason, what are you doing here?" he heard her ask from what seemed like a million miles away.

For a long time, he didn't—couldn't—answer her, but could only stare at the lightly made-up features beneath the boyishly cut hair that inexplicably added to her feminine appeal. All Mason could think was, Wow, and all he wanted to do was explore every inch of what little her dress didn't reveal.

Shocked by the realization that he was desiring carnal knowledge of a woman who was little more than a girl, Mason could only stammer, "Uh... Wh-what?"

"Halouise, do you know this person?" the man standing beside her asked.

Mason forced himself to stop ogling Lou long enough to focus his attention on the man in the charcoal suit that was her—the word stuck in his throat to even think it—date. Albert Michaud wasn't as tall as he was, Mason noted with smug pride. Nor was the other man's slim build anything like his own. And he had dark hair and eyes instead of the blond and blue that Mason himself claimed. At first, the recognition of their differences reassured Mason. Then he recalled that Lou had never put on a little red dress like that for *his* benefit. Maybe she preferred the slim, dark and handsome type. Boy, did that come as a surprise. Then giving himself a good mental shaking, Mason told himself that it was all beside the point.

"Who the hell are you?" he demanded of the newcomer, already knowing the answer but wanting the other man to be on the defensive.

But Michaud evidently wasn't one to be easily intimidated. "I could ask the same question of you," he announced crisply before taking a step in front of Lou, as if shielding her from harm.

Mason smiled grimly at the gesture. He'd show Michaud who needed protecting before the night was through. "Lou, tell him who I am," he instructed her with only a slight glance in her direction.

Lou sighed dramatically and rolled her eyes toward the ceiling, as if in a silent plea for patience. "Albert, this is Mason."

The other man's expression became calm and his body relaxed. "Oh, this is the one."

Lou nodded in what seemed to be resignation.

Mason watched the exchange through narrowed eyes. "What the hell is that supposed to mean?"

"Oh, Mason, stop swearing," Lou chided him. "It makes you sound like some kind of swaggering stud."

He drew his eyebrows down in confusion. "I thought I was some kind of swaggering stud."

She shook her head at him hopelessly. "Only sometimes. At the moment, you're more like a swaggering fool. Albert," she added, turning to the man at her side, taking his hands in hers. "I'm sorry the evening had to end this way. Let me make it up to you. I'll cook dinner here tomorrow night for us. How will that be?"

"Tomorrow?" Mason interrupted. "But tomorrow's Thursday. You always cook dinner for me on Thursday."

Lou glared at him and whispered through gritted teeth," You'll have to fend for yourself this time."

Albert ignored the exchange, focusing instead on Lou, Mason noted, and oozing his charm all over her. Mason felt his stomach lurch at the other man's ingratiating expression.

"I will bring the wine," Albert offered. "Red or white?"

Lou turned to smile back at her escort almost shyly, in a manner Mason had never observed from her before. "Oh, bring both," she gushed impulsively before standing on tiptoe to brush her lips chastely over Albert's cheek.

A great fist clenched Mason's insides and squeezed hard as he watched Lou kiss Michaud with such obvious fondness. Finally, he decided he couldn't stand it any longer and opted for a more aggressive attack.

"You're Albert Michaud, aren't you?" he asked the other man coolly. "Cloying diplomat and all around friend to fascist dictators?"

Albert's smile fell as he turned his attention to Mason. "I beg your pardon?"

Mason took a step closer before cautioning evenly, "If I ever see you with Lou again, I'll have INS all over you like flies on a sweaty horse's rump."

"Mason," Lou pleaded with him. "Please don't try to start any trouble."

"Listen up, Michaud," Mason continued, ignoring her petition. "Maybe you can fool little girls like Lou into believing you're some respectable diplomat, but I know all about Marco Papitou's little private terrorist army." He took three more steps forward and thrust his fingers against Albert's chest. "Don't come near her again or you'll have to deal with me."

"Mason," Lou tried again. This time both men ignored her.

"The Immigration and Naturalization Service cannot touch me," Albert announced to Mason calmly. "A very nice little benefit known as diplomatic immunity. And as for you, I am, how they say, shaking in my foots."

"Boots," Lou corrected him softly.

"Yes, that is it," Albert agreed. "Shaking in my boots."

Mason smiled ferally at them both. "Yeah, well if either one of you pushes me too far, we'll see who's shaking in what, won't we?"

"Albert, you'd better go," Lou suggested tactfully, opening the door behind them. "It's getting late."

Albert nodded stiffly to Mason, then turned to face Lou once more. "I had a very nice time tonight, and I look forward to tomorrow evening." He lifted her fingers to his lips, then brushed her palm softly with a kiss. "Adieu," he murmured quietly.

"Good night."

Lou closed the door behind him with a quiet *click* that sounded ominous in the otherwise silent room, then pivoted quickly to scowl at Mason. Before he could utter a word of accusation, she settled her hands on her hips and challenged, "Just what was the meaning of all that?"

"You tell me," he countered.

"I'm not the one who's obligated to make explanations here, and you know it. What are you doing waiting up for me in my apartment, and how did you get in?"

Gazing down at the floor in embarrassment, Mason felt himself succumbing to the tone of her voice and pulled a key ring reluctantly from his pocket. Lifting two keys for her inspection, he kept his eyes lowered and mumbled, "I...uh...I sort of have keys to your apartment."

When he gathered the nerve to look up at her again, Lou was still glowering at him, but had crossed her arms defensively over her abdomen. The gestured pulled the dress more tightly over her breasts, and Mason was abruptly aware of a flaming heat in his midsection that scrambled his nerves and made his blood go zinging through his veins with wild irregularity. What was going on? he wondered crazily. When had Lou become such a...such a...*woman?*

"Mason, I think it's time we had a little talk," she said quietly after a moment.

He latched on to her announcement like a lifeline, trying to dispel the other disturbing thoughts that were clouding his mind. "Yeah, you're damned right we need to talk. First and foremost, what was going through your head to be dating a guy like Michaud? And second of all, where do you get off kissing terrorists goodnight? And thirdly, where in the hell did you get that dress?"

"This isn't just about me, Mason," she replied smoothly, ignoring his outburst. "This involves both of us."

She approached him slowly, her red high heels scraping softly across the hardwood floor. When she was scant inches away, he could smell the scent of her perfume, something spicy and sophisticated and completely inappropriate for a young girl like herself. Still, he couldn't help but notice it was kind of nice. Very alluring. Almost . . . sexy. When she seated herself on the sofa and patted the cushion beside her in invitation, it did nothing to slow the delirium fast overcoming Mason's brain.

"Sit down," Lou instructed him when he remained standing. "This could take a while."

Mason obeyed, perching himself on the very edge of the couch at the other end. God help him, but when she'd voiced her belief that what was to follow might take a while, a big part of Mason had hoped it would take all night. And it wasn't a little talk he had on his mind, either. But it did indeed involve both of them.

Chapter Two

Lou looked at Mason for a long time before she spoke. What on earth was he doing here at this time of night? She could understand his anger toward her for developing a source after he'd forbidden her to do so, but to find him waiting for her here in her apartment this way... It seemed like a bit of an overreaction. Her evening with Albert had been perfectly harmless. They'd had dinner at a very popular Dupont Circle restaurant, then they'd gone dancing in an extremely crowded nightclub less than three blocks away from her home. She'd only been alone with him during the short trips in the car. Why would Mason imply that she was in any danger with Albert? And what difference did it make if she'd given her date a quick, meaningless peck goodnight? And when had her wardrobe become such a big concern for him? As she continued to stare at the man seated with his head lowered in chagrin, staring at the fingers twisted together in his lap, a steady throbbing began in the back of Lou's brain. Men were so confusing. One man in particular.

"Mason, what are you doing here?" she repeated when he still hadn't answered her question. "And how did you come by the keys?"

Several moments passed before Mason responded, and when he finally did, it was only to mumble something Lou didn't understand.

"What?" she asked softly.

Mason looked up at her quickly, his expression clearly exasperated. "I said I was worried about you."

That was no surprise, Lou thought sadly. Mason always worried about her. Worried the way a big brother would be concerned about his little sister. Lou had never embraced any illusions about what had happened to Mason after his sister, Emily, had married. The two siblings had always been very, very close, neither of them getting along with their parents, both of them driven together because they'd had nowhere else to turn. Mason had set himself up as Emily's protector, probably from the day she was born, whether she wanted or needed one or not. And now that she was married, Mason considered it his place to step down and let her husband, Mick, take over the position. As a result, he'd transferred all of his protective instincts and brotherly feelings onto Lou. It was a simple enough matter to understand. She had learned all about transference like that in her Psych 101 class at the university.

She supposed she should be flattered and comforted that Mason did care for her so much. But it was awfully difficult to feel good about the fact that he couldn't see past the Halouise Lofton she'd been six years ago to the one she was now—the one who could give him so much more than he wanted or was willing to take. Logically, she knew there was no way he would ever be able to offer her the love she craved so desperately from him, but emotionally... Well, Lou had never really been able to help herself where her feelings for Mason were concerned. Over the years, as she'd matured, her adolescent crush on him had expanded into a full-blown case of womanly love, and she had found herself indulging freely in fantasies that he would someday see past the scared little kid from Hack's Crossing and come to love her as a woman who had adult emotions and needs like his own. Instead, Mason had settled Lou right into Emily's place—unconcerned about whether or not she found it comfortable—where he could assure himself that he was watching over her and keeping her out of harm's way, just as he had done for his sister for so many years.

"And the keys?" Lou requested again as she rubbed away an ache at the base of her skull.

"That weekend you and Emily spent together at Ocean City," Mason replied hollowly. "You asked me to pick up your mail and feed Roscoe, remember?"

"You had a copy of the keys made," she guessed. "Oh, Mason, why didn't you just tell me you wanted a set for yourself? I would have given them to you."

Mason shrugged, flexing his fingers open in surrender, but said nothing.

Sighing in frustration at his uncommunicativeness, Lou toed off both of her red high heels, and they dropped to the floor with a gentle *thump-thump*. The sound brought Mason's attention to her shoes, and abruptly, he seemed to recall the original subject matter of their conversation. All at once, he sat up straight at the other end of the couch and glared at her ferociously.

"What were you thinking about to be going out with Michaud tonight?" he demanded with new intensity.

Suddenly, Lou found herself on the defensive and wondered what had happened to put her there. Then she remembered she was with Mason, and that meant she was seldom in control.

"I told you at work yesterday," she said softly, trying to regain some semblance of the assertiveness she felt fleeing now that she and Mason were back in their usual roles—he the commander, she the acceder. "He could be a good source of information about what's happening on Sonora. It could make a great news story."

"I agreed with you, if you'll recall, Lou. I also explained that we're putting a more seasoned reporter on any story about Sonora that might arise."

"But *I'm* the one who established the contact," she objected.

"And I appreciate that. But you're not ready to tackle a story like this. We'll put Atwater on it."

"Charlie Atwater?" Lou sputtered. "That bore? He couldn't write a timely story about a garden slug."

"He was covering Caribbean events before you were wiping your own nose," Mason reminded her. "Maybe his reporting is a little dry, but he gets the job done."

"Dammit, Mason, this is *my* story."

"Watch your language," he chided her.

Lou made two angry fists and rose from the couch to pace restlessly around the small room. In the window seat, Roscoe seemed to sense her uneasiness and skulked silently to the floor.

"Mason," she began, trying to keep her temper from flaring like a torch. "You can't keep telling me what to do. I will not stop seeing Albert. Besides being a potential news source, he's a perfectly nice man and very interesting to talk to."

"But—"

"Look," Lou said, interrupting him before he could object, "I don't know what you were trying to insinuate when you referred to General Papitou's 'private terrorist army,' but I can assure you that whatever it is, if it even exists, Albert has no part in it."

Mason, too, stood then, towering over Lou by nearly a foot. He took several deliberate steps toward her, stopping when only scant inches separated them. Forced to tip her head back to gaze into his eyes, eyes so light blue they sometimes seemed almost transparent, Lou felt her pulse run wild at the expression of undisguised concern that clouded them.

"Lou, you have no idea what you're up against here," Mason warned her in a quiet, steady voice. "What's going on in Sonora isn't anything like what you've encountered for 'Helpful Hints' or 'The Social Scene.' There's still a war going on down there for the most part, with daily bursts of gunfire from either Senegal's loyalists or Papitou's guerrillas. There are even a handful of independent factions that have yet to identify their demands."

Lou's heartbeat skittered about erratically as Mason lifted a hand to gently brush her bangs back from her forehead, letting it slide back over her hair to the curve of her skull before skimming down to curl his fingers softly around her nape.

"This isn't a story for you, Halouise," he told her quietly. "People like Michaud and Papitou eat little girls like you for breakfast."

Her eyes never left his as she pointed out in an unsteady whisper, "Mason, I'm not a little girl anymore."

For long moments, he didn't speak, but only studied her face as if seeing it for the first time. The fingers at her nape shifted a little, then she felt the gentle brush of his thumb along the line of her jaw. Her eyelids fluttered closed, and Lou realized with very little surprise that she wanted more than anything in the world for Mason to kiss her. She even felt her lips part slightly, as if in preparation for receiving what she so desperately wanted him to give.

Mason wasn't sure what kind of madness was causing him to touch Lou the way he was doing now, but upon feeling how soft and warm her skin was, it was as if a match had been set to his heart, and he didn't want to let her go just yet. Something in her had changed somewhere along the line, he realized suddenly. He wasn't sure what or how or when, but there was something about Lou that was . . . different.

Brushing his thumb softly over a high cheek bone, he decided it wasn't the cosmetics making her eyes seem so huge, and therefore so haunted, that had made him want to reach out to her. Letting his gaze roam down over her neck and shoulders to settle on the small cleft between her breasts that was barely visible above the scooped neckline of her dress, Mason felt his heart skip a couple of beats, but knew it wasn't the little red dress, either, that had brought out his desire to be closer to Lou. It was something else, he realized. But for the life of him, he wasn't sure what.

"No, I don't suppose you are a little girl anymore, Lou," he finally murmured before looking at her face once again. To say he was startled by her expression would have been to rudely understate his reaction. When he fully comprehended the implications of the eyes closed in expectation and the lips parted slightly in invitation, Mason realized dazedly that he'd have to be a dead man not to see the signals Lou was sending his way. Good God, she wanted him to kiss her!

As if a fire alarm went off right next to his ear, Mason leapt away from Lou with all the speed and grace of a retreating elephant. Before he tumbled backward over the club chair, his arms flailed out wildly, the left one toppling a floor lamp while the right took out a ceramic vase that fell harmlessly onto the sofa. Roscoe, who had been uneasily curled up under the chair, came screeching out just as Mason tried to right himself, and both man and cat went careening forward, the latter avoiding the former's big feet only in the nick of time before escaping to the kitchen. Mason, unfortunately, did not fare so well and wound up face first in the throw pillows that were indeed now haphazardly scattered on the couch.

"Mason!" Lou shouted at the sudden chaos. After realizing that the cat was involved in the mishap, too, she cried out Roscoe's name as well, then scurried to the kitchen after him, crooning peaceful reassurances to the animal.

When he was finally able to extricate himself from his cramped landing position and sit on the sofa like a normal human being, Mason shook his head soundly and wondered what in the hell had just happened. Looking toward the kitchen to see Lou's lovely, red-clad bottom sticking out from beneath the table where she was trying to soothe Roscoe's ruffled fur helped Mason calm down not at all. Rubbing a hand roughly over his cheek as if trying to dispel the memory of Lou's silky warm skin, he stood resolutely, quite confident that it was time for him to leave. Then he sat down again just as resolutely, quite confident that he should stay and hash this out with Lou. When his gaze wandered involuntarily toward the table again, only to observe Lou's tempting little backside wiggling out from beneath it, Mason quickly glanced away and stood once more.

"I've got to get out of here," he muttered under his breath.

Finally, Lou stood with Roscoe in her arms and faced Mason with an expression that was clearly puzzled. "What?" she asked quickly, sounding a little out of breath.

Just don't look at her, Mason instructed himself. Look at your shoes, your hands, anything. But not *her*. Yet he was helpless to stop himself. When he glanced up again, it was to find that Lou's little red dress had become even smaller, thanks to the way the clingy skirt had ridden up over her thighs after her struggle with Roscoe. Mason had never noticed before how long Lou's legs were. Long and lean and supple and—

"I've got to go," he repeated. "Right now. I'll see you at work in the morning."

And with that, he turned and marched to the front door, opening it, exiting and closing it again without once looking back. In the middle of her apartment, Lou stood alone with her cat, shaking her head in disbelief, feeling annoyed, irritated and confused as hell.

Several hours later, Lou sat wide awake in her window seat beside the bed, still annoyed, still irritated and still confused as hell. Staring down at the dark, deserted street outside, she wondered what had happened between Mason and herself tonight. Although she'd had a surprisingly nice time with Albert, Lou knew there was no way she'd feel for him a fraction of the emotions stirred in her by the looming specter of Mason Thorne. What was it about Mason that kept her so utterly enthralled? Why couldn't she just face the fact that no amount of wishing was going to make him feel any differently about her? She had to get on with her life. And that meant getting involved with men. Other men. Men who weren't Mason.

As she often did at night when she couldn't sleep, Lou found herself wondering what it would be like to be involved in a normal relationship with a man. Any man, really, but there was always one in particular who monopolized her visions of what such a future might hold. There had been a boy in college with whom she had tried to establish a relationship. She smiled now to remember it. Jeffrey had been as shy and reserved as she had been then, however, and after fumbling through the most basic of experimentations and explorations, they'd both realized that neither was what the other really needed to be happy.

She wished things could have been different between them, truly she did. She'd wanted more than anything to feel passion and yearning and desire for a man who would ache for her in the same way. But every time she and Jeffrey had been together for even a kiss, it had been impossible for Lou to keep from comparing him to Mason and wondering how it would differ between the two men. That had just been the first of many such episodes. Every time Lou met a man, she immediately began sizing him up in relation to Mason. Try as she might to stop the reaction, by now it was as if the practice were instinctive, something she'd been born with and was helpless to change. As a result, her experience with men was limited at best.

Maybe that was why Mason wasn't attracted to her. He always went for the flashy, glitzy type of woman, the kind with big hair, long nails and lots of makeup. Hopelessly, Lou realized she didn't stand a chance. Women like that had something else that no amount of hair teasing, manicures or cosmetics could provide. They had *experience.* They knew how to do things. Things that Lou had only read about in books and was quite certain she would never be able to master herself. Sex sounded like it could get pretty complicated. There were just too many things a person had to remember.

Roscoe joined her in the window seat with a muffled *Prrrt,* then curled up in her lap with loving informality to go back to sleep. Absently, Lou stroked his black fur and rubbed under his chin, smiling at the regular thrumming of his purr box that always soothed her. Tonight, however, even Roscoe's familiar warmth couldn't put her thoughts to rest. Because tonight, she realized suddenly, something between her and Mason had changed. She wasn't sure what or whether it was good or bad, but by the time he had made his all-too-abrupt departure, there had been something different about their reactions to each other.

Just don't think about it, she instructed herself resolutely, pressing her forehead against the cool glass of the windowpane. It's late, you're tired and everything seems a little blown out of proportion right now. Tonight Mason had worried about her exactly as he would have worried about his sister, Emily. It was Mason who was having trouble accepting her as an adult, Lou reminded herself. It was his problem if he couldn't see her as a grown-up woman who was perfectly capable of taking care of herself. His problem, she repeated firmly. Not hers.

But the pep talk helped little. Still, Lou felt the void deep within her widen, and still she wondered if she would ever find someone to fill it. Mason would be able to if he realized it, she thought sadly. But she made a decision then and there that she was going to stop looking to him to do so. It was pointless and ridiculous to go on pining this way for a man who refused to open his eyes to the obvious, she scolded herself. If Mason was going to be so obtuse and thickheaded, why did she want anything to do with him anyway? Tomorrow was a new day, a new chance, a new beginning. It was the perfect opportunity to stop behaving like a lovesick fool. Starting tomorrow, Lou decided as she exhaled a deep sigh, things between her and Mason were definitely going to change.

"What do you mean, 'Pack your bags'?" Mason asked his editor the following afternoon as the two men sat at opposite sides of the latter's desk, eating lunch.

"You're going on a little trip," Paul Kelly told his best reporter as he licked the last bit of cream from inside his Twinkie.

Mason narrowed his eyes suspiciously. "Where?"

"The Caribbean."

"Why?"

"News story."

"I'm Central America, Paul," Mason reminded him unnecessarily. "Charlie Atwater is the Caribbean, remember?"

"Charlie's been kind of, uh . . . taken out of commission for a little while," Paul told him evasively.

Mason didn't like the tone of this conversation one bit. He'd received a very hot tip from a reliable source about some unethical behavior on the part of a certain presidential persona in a highly visible Latin American country who may or may not be playing illegal footsie with a few equally visible guys on Capitol Hill, and he was just itching to get going on his investigation. This Caribbean business was coming at a time that was a mite inconvenient for him.

"In what specific way has Charlie been taken out of commission?" Mason asked cautiously.

"Prostate trouble again."

Mason grimaced and crossed his legs reflexively. "Oooh, again? Poor guy."

"Yeah," Paul muttered. "And poor us. From what I hear, some interesting stuff might be going on down in Sonora what with the change of command and upcoming elections and all. And I'm short the one guy who could cover it. So I'm pulling you for the story instead. I want you to leave by Wednesday if you can."

"I don't want to go to Sonora, Paul," Mason hedged. "I've got this great lead that Presidente Ramiriz has just made an offer to six senators on the Hill—"

Paul lifted a hand to stop the flow of words. "It'll have to wait, Mason. I'm sorry, but this takes precedence."

Cripes, what was it about Sonora? Mason wondered silently. Some dinky little island nation that was of no concern to anyone until a few months ago suddenly had every western nation worried about the possibility of communists moving in. Now it was every politician's pet project. Not to mention Lou's.

Aw, dammit, he'd almost made it through lunch without thinking about her. Inevitably, thoughts of Lou led to thoughts of Lou's legs, and that always got Mason's blood stirred up to the point where he couldn't think straight. He'd spent the past four hours taking serious pains to avoid her, a substantially difficult maneuver considering the fact that they worked on the same floor. He'd even taken the two flights of stairs necessary when he'd had to use the men's room because he hadn't wanted to go past 'The Social Scene' offices for the one on his floor. He couldn't believe he was behaving like such a coward. Running scared from a five-foot-three-inch, one-hundred-and-seven-pound female. Boy, was he a sorry excuse for a man.

"Listen, Paul, there must be someone else who can do this—"

"There is," his editor agreed with a quick nod. "In fact, both of you will be covering the story as a team."

"Well, if you've got someone else, then why do you need me?"

Paul lifted his diet soda to his lips to wash down the last bite of Twinkie before replying. "Because you're the best newsman I have, and the other reporter isn't nearly as seasoned."

Mason studied Paul with a clenched jaw, afraid to ask his next question. "Who is the other reporter?"

"Lou Lofton," Paul replied absently, dabbing at a cola stain on his tie. "She's made a good contact with a member of Papitou's entourage who's going to be returning to the island on Monday. The two of you know each other well, and I think you could teach her a lot about—"

"You have got to be kidding," Mason interrupted. "Did she put you up to this?"

Paul glanced up quickly at Mason's tone of voice, clearly puzzled by the other man's reaction. "No. I mean, yeah, she approached me this morning and told me about her relationship with Albert Michaud—"

"Lou does *not* have a *relationship* with Michaud," Mason insisted vehemently.

The editor's dark eyebrows arrowed down in surprised confusion. "Okay," he answered slowly. "She told me about, uh, about meeting Michaud, and asked if she might pursue a story along the lines of what the general mood might be down in Sonora." Paul shrugged, clearly unconcerned, before he listed the reasons for his selection of Lou. "She's a smart kid, Mason. Her reporting skills are up to par. We're short-handed around here, and she's already got a good rela— er, that is, she's already established a contact. I don't see what the problem is with sending the two of you down to Sonora to cover the events on the island during the upcoming election."

Mason angrily shoved the remainder of his uneaten lunch across the length of the desk and scraped his chair away impatiently. "You don't see what the problem is?" he asked with barely controlled fury. "I'll tell you what the problem is." Tangling his fingers in his blond hair in what was fast becoming a familiar gesture, Mason rose and began to pace like a caged animal. "The problem is that the political climate on Sonora right now is still pretty shaky. The problem is that Lou's already risked her life once, trying to rescue my sorry butt and put a bunch of hoods behind bars. She's just now starting to live a normal, safe, secure life, and I'm not about to see that screwed up."

"Mason—"

"The *problem* is," he went on relentlessly, not sure now if he was trying to convince himself or his editor, "that she's little more than a kid out of school. She doesn't have the experience or the grit it takes to cover a story like this."

"Mason—"

"The risks and dangers of this little venture could be enormous, Paul. Lou's too young, too naive, too—"

"Mason!" Paul finally thundered to get the other man's attention.

Mason spun back around, and he glared at his editor resentfully. "What?" he snapped.

"Lou is a twenty-five-year-old woman who was instrumental, if not completely responsible, for the FBI landing one of the biggest drug rings in North America," Paul pointed out angrily. "She saw more trouble with her baby-brown eyes before her twentieth birthday than most people see in their entire lifetimes. And she can be tough as nails when she puts her mind to it."

"That's just an act, Paul. She's a kid, she's—"

"Get it through that thick skull of yours, Mason. That *kid* isn't a kid anymore. Lou wants to be a newswoman, and I think she has everything it takes to make a superior one. Why is that so hard for you to see?"

Why indeed? Mason asked himself with some difficulty, turning his back on Paul again lest the other man see the turmoil he felt boiling up inside. When had Lou Lofton become such an overwhelming creature to be reckoned with? Why was he the only one who seemed to be able to look beyond the exterior walls she erected to glimpse the vulnerable, frightened kid he knew was still lurking in the shadows? How come everyone suddenly felt compelled to point out to him that Lou was all grown up? Hell, he knew how old she was; he realized she was a college grad and a working woman. But that didn't change the fact that she still needed watching over. Did it?

"Look, Paul, I just don't think she's ready for an assignment like this," Mason muttered without turning around.

"I think Lou ought to be the one to decide that."

Mason took a deep breath and held it for long moments before releasing it, remembering everything he could about Lou Lofton. He saw her as she was the first time she stumbled into the newsroom that fateful night so long ago, looking poor, ignorant and fearful. The ignorance, he soon came to discover, had been nothing more than a prejudicial judgment on his part. The poverty and fear, however, had been all too real, as he'd come to realize when he'd found himself held captive in Hack's Crossing. Still, there had always been a certain dignity about Lou. Despite her meager beginnings, she had learned to read and write articulately, had made herself look nice no matter what the situation. And there had been a few weeks there when she'd been the only person in the world who was able to keep him alive.

On the heels of that image came another, the vision of Lou Lofton addressing her senior class at the university. Her speech had been eloquent, forthright and sincere, and her topic had been chances. Chances offered by life, chances offered by people. Mason smiled sadly now to remember it. Lou had been presented with very few chances of either variety in her lifetime. But the one or two that had managed to come her way, she had grabbed on to with all her might. And boy, the changes she'd made with them. Who the hell did he think he was to deny her another chance now?

"Okay, Paul, you win," he said finally, shoving his hands deep into his pockets before facing him again. "I guess you've already discussed the arrangements with Lou."

Paul nodded, grinning like a proud papa. "She's very excited, you know."

Mason emitted a single humorless chuckle, raised his eyebrows in resignation and nodded. "Yeah, I don't doubt it for a minute."

"Remember your first international assignment?"

This time, it was Mason who grinned, shaking his head with quiet laughter. "How could I forget? Seventeen nights holed up in the hills of El Salvador with nothing but rain, dysentery and bunch of ticked-off guerrillas to keep me company. What a nightmare. I was only twenty-four years old. Jeez, that was twelve years ago."

"With me, it was the fall of Saigon," Paul rejoined dreamily, settling his elbow on the desk and cupping his chin in his hand. "It was purely a fluke that I happened to be there then. I was only twenty-one. Missed the draft because I was almost deaf in one ear, only to land right smack-dab in the middle of the madness. Talk about nightmares."

For long moments, the two men sat in thoughtful silence, each caught up in memories neither would fully understand. Finally, it was Paul who broke the silence again.

"Ever wonder when we'll be too old for this stuff?"

"It will never happen," Mason assured him definitely. "Never."

Paul nodded his total agreement. "Yeah, Lou Lofton has some pretty exciting times ahead of her."

Unbidden, the sight of Lou standing with her little red dress hiked up around her thighs blazed its impression in the very front of Mason's mind. Oh, man, he thought, as a strange sensation of something warm and dangerous began stirring around in his midsection. He closed his eyes in an effort to chase away the vision, but it just grew starker and more vivid instead. Exciting times, indeed, Mason speculated. But at the moment, he wasn't altogether sure he could convince himself that those experiences would be precisely journalistic in nature.

Maybe the real problem wasn't that he was going to be working with Lou in Sonora. Maybe the real problem, he thought as a cold wave of inexplicable fear rippled through him, was that he was going to be working with Lou up close.

Chapter Three

"So, how was your dinner with André Thursday night?"

Lou offered Mason a bland expression and corrected patiently, "Albert. His name isn't André, it's Albert."

"Whatever."

Scowling at him, she replied, "It was fine. We had a very nice time together."

Lou and Mason were enjoying the last of their own Sunday dinner at Lou's tiny kitchen table—a consolation meal for Mason since he missed out on his usual Thursday repast—and Lou supposed she should be grateful for even this small, if sarcastic, communication from him. He was wearing the navy blue ski sweater she'd knitted for his Christmas present, a clear indication that he was trying to make amends for being such a jerk the other night. But he'd also been ominously quiet all afternoon, a very strange and surpris-

ingly unwelcomed development. Normally, Mason
Thorne ran off at the mouth more than any human being she'd ever met. Today, however, she couldn't remember him speaking more than two dozen words.

"Is Michaud aware of the fact that you work for one
of the most widely read and highly respected newspapers in the nation?" Mason glanced up to fix her with
his most intense gaze and pointed his fork at her as if
accusing her of a heinous crime or trying to draw her
attention to a stain on her gray sweatshirt.

"Of course he is," she told him, dropping her chin to
inspect the upside-down words, American University,
emblazoned across her chest just to be sure she hadn't
lost part of her supper there. "I've been very up front
about myself."

That was the understatement of the century, Lou
thought dryly. She and Albert had become instant
friends long before dinner Wednesday night. Almost
immediately after meeting, theirs had become a
strangely comfortable relationship, as if two friends had
come together after being apart for several years.
Whatever romantic implications either of them might
have initially expected or wanted at the embassy reception had vanished by that evening's end, and they had
ended up talking nonstop about everything from their
childhoods to where they hoped to retire. Both had left
with the realization that they simply enjoyed each other's company immensely and wanted to spend time together as new friends. Albert had even wound up telling
Lou all about his recent, nearly devastating divorce
from the only woman he'd ever loved, and Lou had in
turn found herself pouring her heart out to Albert with
all the details of her feelings for Mason.

Lou felt now that Mason might be a little bit off base in his assumption that the new regime on Sonora was going to be as repressive and secretive as the old one. Naturally, she wouldn't draw any conclusions until she'd seen and investigated for herself, but she had amazingly acute instincts where people and situations were concerned, and right now, her gut reaction told her that Albert Michaud was a very nice man who had only his country's best interests at heart. She couldn't believe someone like him would have anything to do with a man such as Marco Papitou unless the general's goals for Sonora were equally honorable and beneficial.

That was why she had approached Paul Kelly with the prospect of doing a story about all the changes taking place on Sonora. Opinions in the rest of the world seemed to be wary of the new government at best, and Lou had thought that a new point of view, a more cooperative, optimistic point of view, might yield a substantial news item. After a lengthy discussion with her, Albert had deemed it a wonderful idea, knowing his country could use all the positive press it could get right now. And when the news editor had found the idea equally appealing, Lou had been delightedly stunned. Mason had always assured her that Paul Kelly wasn't the kind of man to whom one could make suggestions and find them even considered. Nor was he, Mason had said, the kind of man who wanted to see a woman covering stories of international importance. To Lou's surprise, she had found Paul to be just the opposite. He seemed to be as excited about the prospect of having a contact within the general's entourage as she was. And as for her feminine gender, it had never once come up in the conversation as an issue.

Lou studied Mason suspiciously as he pushed his peas and carrots around on the plate, wondering if he might be up to something. Then shaking off her apprehension as silly, she focused her attention back on her own meal. Mason would never purposely try to prevent her from rising to the top of her profession. Would he? No, of course not. He only wanted her to be happy, he'd said so a million times. Still, the uneasiness lingered in the back of Lou's mind, not quite willing to be put to rest.

"Are you all packed and ready to go to Sonora?" Mason asked offhandedly as they cleared away the remnants of their meal.

"I pretty much know what I'm going to take, but I haven't started the actual packing yet. Why?"

He shrugged innocently as he reached for a dish towel. "No reason. Just curious."

Lou stared at him pointedly until he looked up to face her. "Mason, if you're thinking you might be able to keep me from going down to Sonora, then you've got another think coming."

Mason gazed back at her mildly. "Lou, I don't know what you're talking about. You know, you're getting awfully paranoid these days."

"Just because I'm paranoid doesn't mean you're not out to get me."

He chuckled before assuring her, "No one's out to get you, Lou. Especially me. I just want to make sure you pack everything you're going to need."

Lou shrugged. "I've got notepads, pens and pencils, a tape recorder and tapes, camera and film, a few items of clothing appropriate for the tropical weather. What else could I possibly need?"

Sighing at her sad lack of experience, Mason supplied, "How about mosquito repellent? Something for stomach queasiness and dysentery? First-aid kit, bottled water, sunscreen, antiseptic, a Swiss army knife if you have one, and a couple of paperbacks for all the times you'll be waiting around for something to happen."

Gazing down into the soapy dishwater, Lou rubbed too vigorously at a gravy stain. "I would have remembered all those things, too," she said softly. "Probably."

"Yeah. Probably. Boy, I won't be able to let you out of my sight down there for a second. God knows what you'll wander into."

"I'll be just fine, Mason," Lou promised him evenly.

"You'll probably wind up sick in bed with Montezuma's revenge or a severe piña colada reaction the whole time anyway, and my job of baby-sitting you will be done for me. Then I can write the story and we can both get back to living our lives again."

All right, that does it, Lou thought angrily. Turning to him once more, she settled her hands on her hips in challenge and threw him a furious look. "Mason, your *job* down on Sonora will not be to act as my baby-sitter, and *I'm* going to be the one who writes this story. As far as I'm concerned, you can spend the whole time sightseeing with bimbo tourists. Albert says there are some beautiful beaches and great casinos on Sonora, and I know how much you like to entertain big, blond floozies."

"Now, just hold on there," Mason argued, stopping her abruptly. "They don't necessarily have to be big. Or blond, either."

Lou ignored him. "It wasn't my idea to bring you into this, it was Paul's. He thought that since I'm kind of inexperienced at this, another reporter might be helpful. *He* was the one who picked you, not me. If I'd had a choice, I would have asked for Charlie Atwater."

"Wait a minute. You think Charlie Atwater is a no-talent bore who can't write worth a damn."

Jutting her chin aggressively, Lou assured him venomously, "I'd rather spend my time down there with a no-talent bore than with an egocentric Romeo who can't get it out of his thick head that he's not my brother and he's *not...my...keeper!*"

For a long time, neither of them spoke, just glared at each other as if words would be useless. Suddenly and decisively, Mason wadded up the towel in his hand and threw it onto the countertop, then straightened to his full six-foot-two height, flexing and hardening every muscle in his arsenal as he did so. Lou's cheeks flamed with color, though whether it was a result of her anger or her fascination with Mason's masculine form, she wasn't sure. Yet she refused to back off. They'd been building up to this showdown for a long, long time, and high noon had finally arrived.

"What are you trying to imply?" Mason asked her quietly. Too quietly, she thought.

After taking a deep breath for fortification, Lou replied softly, "I'm not implying anything. I meant exactly what I said."

Several more moments dragged by before he spoke further, but when he did, it was only to ask, "Do you really think of me as an egocentric Romeo?"

The breath Lou had been holding left her lungs in a quick *whoosh.* That's all he could say? He wasn't even going to mention her second point, the point she'd meant to be the most important? Everyone who knew Mason considered him an egocentric Romeo, she wanted to point out, himself included. So why did he look hurt and resentful at such a description? And why was he ignoring her other fiercely emphasized accusation that she considered it so crucial they address? Mason Thorne was without question the most exasperating man she'd ever had the misfortune to meet.

It would be pointless to argue with him in his current temper, Lou thought defeatedly, assuring herself that she was not retreating from the confrontation she knew they would have to face eventually. Mason was just one of those people who had a one-track mind, and if he focused it on something specific, like her opinion of him as an egocentric Romeo, then nothing was going to distract his attention elsewhere.

"Oh, just forget it," she muttered under her breath as she went back to doing the dishes. "Everything will be fine on Sonora. You won't have to worry about me."

Mason watched Lou's withdrawal with mixed emotions. First and foremost, he was relieved that their conversation hadn't escalated to yet another one of Lou's litanies that she could take care of herself without any help from him. But there was something else combined with his relief this time, some weird response that he hadn't experienced before. Concentrating very hard on what she had just said and how he had just reacted, Mason realized with a start that it was *confusion* he was feeling. How very odd. Why should he be confused when what had just occurred was little more than a daily event lately—the phenomenon wherein he had to take Lou aside and explain the facts of life to her? Not the figurative facts of life, of course. Certainly she must already know all about those, mustn't she? It was

the literal facts of life he kept having to force her to see.
Lou was still lost in some kind of teenage fantasy that
she was perfectly capable of watching out for herself.
And such was simply not the case. Mason knew that
without question.

So why, then, did he feel confused? Studying the
slightly built woman standing beside him in her jeans
and sweatshirt, Mason saw that Lou was now as she had
always been; young, innocent and in need of supervision. Her outburst of a few moments ago only proved
that perfectly. If she were indeed the mature, capable
adult she kept claiming to be, such emotional erup-
tions wouldn't occur. Certainly *he* never overreacted
that way. He really was going to have to keep an eye on
her once they arrived on Sonora. There was no telling
what might happen to her down there.

As the plane banked sharply to the left, Lou got her
very first glimpse of Sonora. To say she was excited
would be a gross underestimation of her feelings right
now. Because not only was it her first sighting of the island nation whose land mass was slightly smaller than
Puerto Rico to the northeast, and whose population
hovered at just over three and a half million, but it was
her first time in an airplane, her first excursion out of
her native country and her first opportunity to be alone
with a man for more than a few hours. And not just any
man, either. For the next nine days, she and Mason
would be together by themselves on what was reported
to be one of the most beautiful tropical utopias in the
world.

Despite the political troubles and social problems that
had plagued the small country for more than half a
century, Sonora was reputed to be a topographical par-

adise. Endless stretches of sparkling white beaches surrounded the island, lined with palm trees and quaint, pastel-hued houses. Even the capital city of Madriga was described as a progressive center of commerce, offering an abundant variety of hotels, restaurants, nightclubs and places to shop. The average annual rainfall was less than twenty-five inches. The median high temperature a delightful seventy-six degrees. Culturally, Sonora claimed its historical roots in both the French and Spanish settlers who originally established colonies there, and the local language was a lively mix of both that resulted in a fast-paced patois that Albert had assured her neither she nor Mason would understand. However, Spanish and French, as well as English, were spoken by nearly everyone, and because Lou had taken four years of French in college, she was quite certain she would do very well. For additional preparation, she had read up on the history and geography of the island and hadn't been able to resist picking up a few brochures at the travel agency as well. She knew without doubt that she was going to have a wonderful time.

Looking over at her companion, she discovered that Mason was still fast asleep. She wondered how he could manage to be so relaxed. Of course, he'd been seeing and doing things like this for a long time, Lou remembered. It was something he took great pride in pointing out to her over and over again whenever she tried to prove her abilities to him as a reporter and an adult woman. He always referred to it right after reminding her that he was eleven years her senior and, biologically speaking anyway, old enough to be her father. And when Lou tactfully asserted that eleven years old was not generally considered the standard age that males became potentially parental, Mason simply lifted his head proudly and announced that it was for all the Thorne men.

How had she managed to fall for someone like him? Too old for her indeed! Who did he think he was kidding? There were times when she felt like *his* parent. She'd experienced a good deal more than most women her age. Her trip through the school of hard knocks had come long before she'd left Hack's Crossing, before she'd even known of Mason Thorne's existence. Life in the mountains had often been hard and brutal. Before Steven Destri had pulled them all into the smuggling operation, she'd never considered that there might be an entire world thriving outside her hometown. A world where houses boasted more than four rooms and claimed such wonders as electricity and running water. In Hack's Crossing, Lou's day had begun before sunup with back-breaking labor, and she had fallen into bed exhausted when people like Mason were just getting ready to party. Times had been hard for the people in her community. But somehow, they had been strong enough to make it through one more day.

Lou had spent the past six years trying to convince Mason of that. But there was something in him that refused to believe she could survive such experiences without help from him. She knew that in his eyes, she was soft, fragile and naive, in danger of breaking under the slightest stress. She just couldn't make him understand that she had not been such a person when he'd found her, and she was nothing like that description now. He just wouldn't listen.

If she were honest with herself, Lou had to admit that it was kind of nice to have someone like Mason to lean on after all these years. Her mother had died when she was six years old, leaving her to cook and clean for a bear of a man and five monstrous brothers, all older than she. When her father had been killed in a mining accident just after her twelfth birthday, his brother, Lou's Uncle Fairmont, had stepped in as her guardian, but little else had changed. Along with Steven Destri, who'd been no more than a gangster in snake's clothing, the examples of men provided for Lou up to that point in her life had nurtured a strong desire to keep a good bit of distance away from them whenever possible. And it had scared her senseless to accept the knowledge that as long as she lived in Hack's Crossing, she would be utterly dependent on such beings for her very survival.

Then she'd gone into D.C. one day with her cousin under the pretense that she just wanted to see what the big city was like, and had seized the opportunity to escape for a few hours and seek out help from someone who could put a stop to the terrible things going on in Hack's Crossing. That had led her to Mason's desk at the newspaper, and everything else had just fallen like dominos into place. It was strange how one thing led to another that way. What could have been the worst thing to ever happen to her—Destri's arrival in Hack's Crossing—had ended up bringing her the best life had to offer instead.

Lou felt a soft nudge at her elbow, then Mason mumbled something quietly in his sleep and wrapped both hands possessively around her upper arm. He was dreaming, she told herself as her heart began to hum in a warm, irregular way at the feel of his fingers gently stroking the downy hair on her arm. Dreaming of someone other than herself. She continued to observe him as the airplane began to make a more rapid descent, marveling at the thickness and length of his dark blond eyelashes, waiting for the moment when they would lift to reveal the eyes as clear and pale blue as the shallow depths of the ocean below. Gradually, Mason began to stir, turning his face more fully against her arm, then he pressed his lips to her heated, sensitized skin exposed above his fingers.

Something grabbed hold of Lou's heart and set it on fire at the sensation of such an exquisitely tantalizing caress. Wishing it could go on forever, but knowing that was an impossible desire, Lou gently covered his hand with hers and whispered, "Mason."

Slowly his eyes began to flutter open, but not before he murmured something frankly erotic against her arm. Lou felt heated color seep up from her breasts into her face at the explicit, if very intriguing, suggestion. Then suddenly, Mason seemed to realize exactly to whom he had just uttered his offer and he snapped to attention in his seat, quickly releasing her arm and settling her hand back into her lap beside the other one. He took a deep, hasty breath and released it, ran his hands hurriedly through his hair to straighten it and proceeded to pretend she wasn't there.

Lou allowed him the luxury of ignoring her for all of fifteen seconds before she remarked, "We'll be landing any minute."

"Good," Mason ground out hoarsely. Then clearing his throat roughly, he added, "Seat belt fastened?"

"Yes."

"Cigarettes extinguished?"

She bit her lip to keep from grinning. He knew full well she didn't smoke. "Yes."

"Seat in an upright position?"

"Yes."

"All carry-on luggage stowed safely below your seat or in the overhead compartment?"

Now she couldn't help but chuckle. "Yes."

Finally, Mason turned to gaze at her, his eyes bright with some unknown fire, his smile warm and playful, as if he were letting her in on a big secret. "Ready for adventure?"

Lou nodded and smiled back. "Yes."

"Then let's get this show on the road."

The Hotel San Sebastian was about as five star as an establishment could get, Lou decided as she gazed around her suite on the fourth, and highest, floor. Not that she had spent any great length of time in luxurious surroundings with which to make comparisons, of course, but one didn't need an excessive amount of touring experience to realize that the cream silk bedspread and canopy, the blue damask wing chairs and the marble Jacuzzi in the bathroom weren't exactly basic travel lodge accessories. There were fresh flowers on the walnut dresser and an enormous basket of fruit on the table beside French doors that led out to a balcony overlooking the sea. Albert had been more than generous in making the arrangements for her and Mason.

After changing from her travel clothes into a short, sleeveless sundress of yellow gauze, Lou stood at the open French doors and stared out at the Caribbean that spilled like a bright blue sheet of glass toward the horizon. To her left was Mason's balcony, and to her right was sprawled the city of Madriga, its pastel stucco and stone buildings glittering in the afternoon sun like a string of softly colored beads. The Hotel San Sebastian must be considered a skyscraper, she mused, because she'd read that construction of the buildings here was kept below five stories by law to lessen the damage threatened by the summer hurricane season. To Lou it just made the city that much more appealing. For the next nine days, she promised herself, whenever she got a break from her assignment for the paper, she was going to do everything the guide books recommended.

A knock on the door connecting her room to Mason's interrupted her planning, and she pulled herself away from the sunny vista with some reluctance to allow him entry into her suite. He, too, had shed his earlier outfit for one more suiting the tropical climate. Now he wore loose khaki trousers and a white, short-sleeved safari shirt of lightweight cotton. He didn't look pleased as he pushed past her into the room, taking in her attire as he did so, and Lou closed the door behind him without comment.

"You can't possibly run around dressed like that while we're here," Mason said pointedly, waving his hand toward her general vicinity. "It's completely inappropriate."

Puzzled, Lou glanced down at her dress before asking, "Why not? I've been watching people out in the street pass by for the last twenty minutes. This is perfectly acceptable and very similar to what other women in Madriga are wearing."

"The women out there aren't journalists, Lou," Mason told her in a tone of voice that indicated she should know better than to assess herself in such a way. "They're tourists. You're in the press corps, baby. And newspeople like us wear the standard-issue and internationally recognized uniform of *this*." He grabbed a handful of fabric from his pants. "Khaki. It's spoken everywhere."

So *that's* why she always felt so overdressed at newspaper and communication functions, Lou thought with wonder. What a revelation. They really should provide a class in journalistic fashion trends as a requirement toward the degree.

"I didn't bring anything khaki, Mason." She shrugged, unconcerned. "I guess I'll just have to do the best I can with my other things."

Mason offered her a hopelessly disappointed expression. "Maybe we'll be able to find something for you in town. Come on. Let's have a look around."

For the remainder of the afternoon, Lou and Mason explored Madriga, whose city limits consisted of less than fifteen square miles. Within that area, though, Lou found more to stimulate her senses than she could remember feeling since the first time she'd gone into D.C. She practiced some of her French and was delighted to discover that she could understand and be understood, and saw that, by and large, most of the citizens in town were very happy that Marco Papitou had assumed the highest government position. Everywhere she went, Lou noted examples of a daily life seemingly uninterrupted by political unrest. Still, she knew better than to think everything was perfectly safe and normal here. Just yesterday, she'd been told, there had been an outburst of fighting between loyalists and rebels in the hills outside of town. But all in all, an orderly pace had apparently been established on Sonora, and the population seemed, for the most part, content.

As the dinner hour approached, Lou and Mason found a small restaurant near a marina serving up local delicacies and fresh seafood for a very modest price. As they nibbled on appetizers of conch fritters and artichokes stuffed with crabmeat, Lou mentioned her observations to Mason and suggested that maybe things on Sonora weren't as bad as the outside world seemed to think.

"Don't you believe it," he cautioned her. "Remember that we're here at the behest of General Papitou, and the government officials are only going to show us what they want us to see. I mean, look at the hotel Michaud set us up in, for example."

"Oh, Mason, I think the reason we're staying in the Hotel San Sebastian is because the government wants to show us it can be a very good host, not to bribe us into writing a favorable story."

Mason made a rude sound of disbelief and dipped another fritter into the hot-mustard sauce. "Yeah, right. Just you wait. Starting tomorrow, they'll chauffeur us around to their immaculate, up-to-date hospitals, their fabulous schools, the newly renovated power plant, the modern water-treatment facility, the clean, safe prisons..." His voice trailed off as he popped the fritter into his mouth and enjoyed it like a man who'd gone months without food.

"And why is that so terrible?" Lou wanted to know.

"Because they'll be showing us the facilities that provide services for the wealthy citizens and the military. Of course, they'll neglect to point that out to us. And what they'll also neglect to mention is that the poverty-stricken areas that make up ninety percent of Sonora's population are completely without water, hospitals, schools and electricity. And what they won't show us are the special rooms below the fine prisons that house instruments of unspeakable torture that still see plenty of use today."

Lou shuddered visibly at Mason's grim analysis of the situation and felt her stomach recoil as she considered the possibility that beyond the beauty of Madriga and the palm-lined beaches, stark poverty and disease might be the way of life here. Mason must have noticed her reaction, because he stopped wolfing down his food and reached across the table to curl his fingers lightly over hers.

"I told you it wouldn't be what you think, Lou," he said gently. "I tried to warn you about what you might see here, what you might encounter. It isn't pretty sometimes—the truth. But there you have it just the same."

Lou gazed back at him evenly, trying to keep her voice steady as she replied. "I didn't shudder because I was facing the ugliness of the truth, Mason. I shuddered because Sonora unfortunately sounds a lot like my hometown."

His blue eyes hardened like chips of ice at her assertion, and she knew he was going to object. But she wanted him to realize once and for all that she wasn't the soft, fragile flower he insisted on thinking she was, so she quickly plunged on.

"When you were there, all you saw was the inside of a freight car at the railyard. I don't think you realized just how isolated you actually were, though. Hack's Crossing is way up in the mountains of West Virginia. *Way* up. Up where it's so beautiful and peaceful and quiet, you think God must have made it that way because it was so close to Him. But it's far, far away from civilization. There are no utilities, hospitals or schools, no amenities at all. You can't farm or tame the land. The only jobs to be had are the ones in the coal mines that will wind up killing you anyway, and those are getting scarcer all the time. The people there are poor and hard and hungry, and in the winter, it gets so cold and lonely, you sometimes wonder why you don't just crawl up inside yourself and die."

Feeling Mason's hand clench her fingers convulsively, Lou paused, surprised to realize her voice had grown in volume and vehemence as she talked about her past. "Look," she finally concluded softly, "all I'm saying is that the most beautiful places on earth can also be the ugliest sometimes. And there's different kinds of poverty. Some people do without money and food, some do without family and friends, some do without any love at all. We just have to do the best we can with what we've got, and we have to see through the bad things to find what's good. Because there's always something good at the bottom of it, Mason. I don't care what anybody says. Maybe Sonora has its secrets and ugly truths, but there are a lot of things about this island worth praising. And when I file my stories for the paper, they're going to include *everything* I do and see down here."

Mason looked at her for a long time without speaking. Just when Lou was sure he might never talk again, his lips curled into the slightest hint of a smile and his fingers began to massage hers gently once again. Very quietly he asked, "Tired of yellow journalism, are you?"

Lou grinned back. "The media always promotes the worst possible scenario, you know. It's common knowledge."

He chuckled softly. "Is that a fact?"

Nodding slowly, Lou interwove her fingers with Mason's and assured him, "Things are never as bad as they seem."

This time Mason took her hand completely in his and squeezed it hard. "You think so, Lou Lofton? Well, we'll just see about that."

Chapter Four

The following morning, Lou awoke feeling more rested than she had in years. She knew it was very early because when she sat up in bed and gazed past the French doors leading to the balcony that she'd left open to allow in the evening breeze, she could see that the sky above the dark blue Caribbean was still a soft lavender streaked with pink and orange in preparation for the sun's appearance. Stretching her arms high above her head, Lou sighed contentedly and inhaled the fresh, salty fragrance of the sea, wishing she could stay on Sonora forever.

After dinner last night, she and Mason returned to their respective rooms, she to organize the notes she had taken that day, and he to outline their agenda for the upcoming week. Lou hadn't bothered to tell him that she'd already decided what she was going to do and where she would be going to research her story because she knew she'd only be met with Mason's flat refusal to pursue the investigation her way. He was insistent that the new regime on Sonora was no better than the old one and that General Marco Papitou would only trade one kind of tyranny for another. Lou, however, still wasn't convinced. She planned to interview a number of government officials, as well as average members of the working-class community. She had even arranged for herself and Mason to go inland to visit some of the peasant villages so that she could gain a fuller view of the different types of people who called the island home. The only task facing her now was in convincing Mason to let her do her job unobstructed.

A small, muffled sound from the next room caused Lou to look in that direction, and she cocked her head curiously, waiting to see if she would hear it again. A moment later she did, only this time it was louder and more insistent. Drawing her eyebrows together in puzzlement, she realized what she was hearing was the sound of someone moaning, as if in pain. Quickly, she scrambled out of bed and threw a short ivory silk kimono on over the matching teddy, belting the sash hastily as she reached for the connecting door. When she entered Mason's room, it was to find him curled up on his bed, clutching his stomach and groaning as if he stood at death's door.

She hurried to the side of his bed and placed her palm gently over his forehead, alarmed to discover he was burning up with fever. "Mason?" she asked anxiously. "What's wrong?"

His reply was another groan, followed by a murmured complaint she couldn't understand.

"What? I didn't hear what you said."

"I think it was the conch fritters," he repeated roughly. "I've been sick all night."

"I'm calling the hotel doctor," Lou announced, reaching for the phone.

"No, don't," he told her, rolling over to circle her wrist with a grip that was surprisingly firm, considering the fact that he seemed to be in so much pain. "Just get me some more water and another antacid from my kit in the bathroom."

"Mason—"

"Lou, do as I say."

She frowned at him, but even in his debilitation, Mason made it clear he was still a force to be reckoned with and would brook no argument. Obediently, Lou did as he instructed, then sat on the edge of the bed with her fingers woven nervously together, watching him anxiously as he swallowed the medication.

"There," he muttered with a grimace when he'd drained the glass of water. "I'll be good as new in no time." However, he punctuated his assurance by grimacing and clutching his abdomen once again in pain.

Lou said nothing, but continued to watch him closely, worried about his lack of color and the fact that he was perspiring when the morning air was decidedly cool. Unable to prevent herself, she lifted her hand once more and placed her palm gently on his forehead before sliding it down to cup his cheek.

"You're still too warm," she said softly, feeling her heart jump about erratically behind her rib cage as the pads of her fingertips traced over his rough morning beard. "You have a fever. I don't think you should get out of bed for a while."

As the waves of nausea he'd suffered all night began to subside a little, Mason took a long moment to study

Lou and felt his temperature rise even more. My God, when had she become so beautiful? he wondered wildly. In the dim morning light, her ivory skin seemed like the most perfect porcelain, setting off her brown eyes and making them look huge and full of emotion. As his gaze traveled farther down, he noticed that her lips were parted slightly, full and inviting, reddened from sleep and just begging to be kissed. The sash of her robe had come undone, and the garment now hung open to reveal sleepwear unlike anything he'd ever known Lou to own—a pale, lacy creation of some soft, clingy fabric that draped her lush body only enough to cover what a man shouldn't be allowed to see anyway. Mason's heart slammed against his chest at the feel of her warm hand on his cheek, and his body leapt into response, demanding that he take what was rightfully his. And for the briefest of moments, all he wanted to do was lean forward to touch Lou in the most intimate of ways, then press her fully back on the mattress and do as his body insisted.

Oh, man, what am I thinking? he asked himself crazily. He *must* be delirious with fever if he was considering making love to Lou. She was just a kid, for God's sake, he reminded himself, barely out of school. And he had just spent the entire night in the bathroom being about as sick as a man can be. Even if he honestly believed that he actually *wanted* carnal knowledge of Lou—which, of course, was ridiculous and certainly must result from his current malady—he would be far too weak to perform. Yet even as the thought occurred, his body reacted in such a way as to let him know that it was indeed ready, willing and more than able to enjoy a mighty tumble with Lou.

Tamping down the realization with every last scrap of energy he possessed, Mason cupped his hand over the one Lou still laid against his cheek and moved it gently away to place it in her lap. Then after a moment, when he noticed he had allowed his hand to linger too long on the warm, bare flesh of her thigh, he snatched it quickly away again and wove his fingers savagely through his hair.

''Where did you get that?'' he demanded with sudden vehemence.

Lou looked puzzled. ''Where did I get what?''

Mason gestured nervously toward her abdomen. ''That...that thing you have on. Where did it come from? What happened to those pajamas you used to have? The flannel ones with the cowboys and horses on them? I kind of liked those.''

Lou shook her head hopelessly. ''Those were hand-me-downs from my brother Delbert. I had them when I first came to Washington. Good grief, Mason, I threw them in the garbage as soon as I started college. I couldn't stand to look at them anymore. I bought this...'' Lou hesitated. She had, in fact, bought the teddy and robe just before taking this trip to Sonora, because, she had to admit, she had rather hoped Mason might see her in it. However, she hadn't planned on the situation being quite like this. ''I bought this a while ago,'' she said evasively, ''because I like the color, and...and it was on sale.''

Mason eyed her warily, wondering if she'd bought it to impress someone of the male persuasion. Michaud maybe? He was going to have to keep his eye on that guy. He didn't trust him for a minute. Especially where Lou was concerned. A sudden wave of nausea washed over Mason then, and as much as he wished it was the thought of Albert Michaud that brought it on, he knew instead that the illness plaguing him all through the night had no doubt been brought on by the local delicacies he had so hastily consumed for dinner the evening before. Great, he thought. This was just great.

"Mason, are you all right?"

He heard Lou's quietly uttered question and turned to look at her again, wishing she would close her robe and get the hell out of his room so he would be left alone to have a little chat with his mutinous libido. Instead, he only muttered, "I'm fine. I just need to eat a little something. If you could call room service and have them send up some breakfast—"

"Dry toast and tea," Lou told him.

"What?"

"Dry toast and tea. It will help your stomach. My grandmother Hattie Lofton always used to say that—"

"Can the mountain remedies, Lou. What I need is Eggs Benedict, some hash-browned potatoes, maybe a little slice of cantaloupe on the side and a pot of black coffee."

Lou drew her lips together in a thin line, but she picked up the phone and ordered what he'd requested. She also asked the kitchen to send up some dry toast and tea, ignoring Mason when he shook his head and called her crazy. However, after room service arrived, and Lou presented Mason's Eggs Benedict with an exaggerated flourish, he took one whiff of the fragrant food and turned green. As he retreated to the bathroom, Lou ate his breakfast for him, and when he returned, he grudgingly consumed his toast and tea.

"It will make you feel better," Lou assured him without a trace of censure.

Mason mumbled something she was certain she didn't want repeated, and she hid a smile as she rose to leave.

"Where are you going?" he asked when he realized her intention.

Lou turned around, but kept walking backward toward the door. "To take a shower and get dressed. I have a big day ahead of me. Albert has arranged for me to interview the acting mayor and first lady of Madriga, some local businessmen and some higher ranking officials of the military. He's going to try to get me in to see Marco Papitou before the week is over, if the general has time." She had her hand on the doorknob when she made her final announcement. If she could just get it open and hurry through before her words sunk in to Mason's feverish brain, she would be home free.

"Whoa, whoa, whoa," Mason said adamantly, rising from the table, but gripping it soundly with both hands. "Hold on there, little buckaroo. You're not going anywhere without me there to keep an eye on you."

"Mason, I'm perfectly capable of taking care of myself," Lou insisted. "You're way too sick to be up and working. And Albert went to a lot of trouble to make these appointments. I'm not about to miss them."

"You're not going alone," he told her.

"I am so," she persisted.

"You are not."

"I am so."

"Are not."

"Am so."

"Lou—"

"Mason—"

Why did it always degenerate into such a childish argument when they disagreed? Lou wondered. Probably because Mason kept treating her as though she were twelve years old, and probably because he refused to grow up himself. Without a word, Lou turned the knob of the connecting door and began to duck back into her room. Mason took a step toward her with masculine intent and for a moment, she was quite certain he would come after her and lock her in her room like some medieval lord. But after taking two more steps, he paused, settling his hand gingerly on his stomach, then turned to hurry off to the bathroom. Lou's heart went out to him. Truly it did. But Mason was a grown man who could take care of himself. And she was a grown woman who had a job to do.

She rushed through the door and locked it behind her, then quickly headed for the shower. As she dressed hastily in a belted, chocolate brown sleeveless sheath— something she hoped would be cool as well as professional looking—she thought about how being left on her own today might provide her with her only chance to prove to Mason once and for all that she was an adult woman and a very good reporter. With any luck at all, by the time they left Sonora, he'd be thoroughly convinced of both.

The interviews went even better than Lou could have hoped, and by late afternoon she had nearly filled a stenographer's notebook with her scrawling handwriting. Now she sat at a corner table in the sunny, formal dining room off the lobby of the Hotel San Sebastian, sipping a cool lime soda, oblivious to the fact that she was the sole occupant of the cavernous room. She was too busy reevaluating everything she had seen and heard that day.

She was more than optimistic that Marco Papitou was the best thing that had ever happened to Sonora. Everyone with whom she had spoken that day had nothing but respect and reverence for the man, and she herself had seen the unquestionable results of his short time in office. Schools and hospitals were being renovated and built all over Madriga, and homes that had been without plumbing and electricity for generations were now being supplied with amenities for free. The citizens were happy and insisted that what few rebels and guerrillas remained in the hills outside of town were nothing more than thugs and bullies who had been given guns by the previous government and were simply too mean and vicious to give them up.

Lou jotted down more notes, her mind working frantically to recall every moment of the day that had passed. What an exhilarating experience! To have been left to her own devices in a completely different culture, exploring all the facets of life that she wanted to investigate without being challenged every step of the way. Lou realized with a start that she'd never been allowed such an adventure before. Mason had always hovered around her like a mother hen whenever she'd tried to spread her wings, looking over her shoulder to prevent any mishaps before they could be made.

Freedom, that's what she was feeling, she thought. She'd never experienced it before. In Hack's Crossing, she'd grown up with the responsibilities that went with cooking and cleaning for her father, uncle and brothers, household chores that had used up ninety-nine percent of her day. On the few occasions when she had found a moment or two to herself, she had never even considered doing something to gain personal satisfaction and had instead used the time to get ahead with the laundry or sewing. Moving to Washington hadn't changed that at all, but had only given her different responsibilities. First, there had been college, then working at the paper on assignments she'd had no desire to pursue. And instead of cowering in the shadow of her family because she was afraid she wouldn't please them, she hovered in the shadow of Mason Thorne—because she was afraid she didn't please him.

It was as if a little light went on in the very back of Lou's brain at the realization, and she glanced up to stare at her surroundings blindly. Suddenly everything made sense to her. The reason Mason continued to treat her like a child was because she continued to act like one. She had always depended on someone else, some kind of father figure, be it good or bad, for her survival. Always. First it had been her father, then her uncle, then after leaving Hack's Crossing, Mason Thorne. Here she was, a twenty-five-year-old woman with a college degree and a home of her own, and she had never been offered the opportunity to grow up.

No, that wasn't true, she amended. She'd had the opportunity to do so as soon as she'd come to Washington. She just hadn't taken it, had instead fallen right back into the trap she'd been caught in while living in West Virginia. It had been easier and less scary to rely on Mason to get things done for her, and knowing he was always there had kept her from feeling totally alone. Obviously he'd picked up on her need for guidance and nurturing, and when his sister had married, he had seen in Lou the perfect opportunity to keep providing the care for another he had become so accustomed to giving. And that's how things had remained all these years. Yes, Lou's affection for Mason had long outgrown the puppy-love infatuation it had once been, but his feelings for her were obviously unchanged from the brotherly fondness he had always felt. Why should that surprise her when she kept turning to him whenever things went awry in her life?

Because that's what she invariably did, Lou reminded herself. When she'd needed to get out of Hack's Crossing, whom had she run to? When she'd wanted to go to college, whom had she asked for help? When she'd desired a job at the newspaper, whom had she petitioned? And when that job turned out to be working on columns that hadn't satisfied her, whom had she asked to pull strings to get her reassigned? Lou shook her head hopelessly, chastising herself for her behavior. How could she possibly expect Mason to see her as an adult woman who could stand on her own when every time she needed or wanted something, she looked to him instead of herself?

Boy, nothing like a little soul-searching and self-enlightenment to top the day off right, Lou thought sardonically as she took another sip of her soda. Still, she suddenly felt as if the weight of the world had been lifted from her shoulders and presented to her for her inspection. It occurred to her then that she'd been offered another chance to grow up and prove herself in the guise of this story on Sonora. There was more at stake here than simply her journalistic abilities. And this time, Lou told herself, she wasn't going to blow it.

Settling more comfortably into her chair, she flipped another page of her notebook and went studiously back to work. So caught up in her writing did she become, in fact, that she scarcely noticed when the sun began to sink in a slow blaze of pink and gold below the ocean outside the panorama of windows beside her. Nor did she pay much attention when uniformed waiters began to set the tables all around her, absently declining when asked by one of them if she wanted to order dinner. She only became aware of how late the hour had grown when she finally glanced up from her work to find that the dining room was nearly full. People on Sonora ate dinner very late, she remembered. Usually not before eight-thirty or nine o'clock. Risking a quick peek at the thin gold watch circling her wrist, Lou was shocked to discover it was precisely 9:10. She had been sitting in the dining room for four hours, working on her story. Mason was going to be frantic.

She hastily began to gather up her things, stuffing her notes, pens and steno pads into her canvas portfolio, unconcerned about whether they remained in order. A guilty little voice in the back of her head reminded her that today was the day she started living life for herself and stopped worrying about what Mason thought. Lou shouted angrily back at the voice that she would think about that tomorrow. When she had scooped everything up off the table, she turned to hurry out, but halted dead in her tracks when she saw Mason barreling through the dining room toward her, looking like a man possessed. Oh, boy, was she in trouble.

Her heart thumped an erratic tattoo that grew louder and more ominous with every step he took, and for a moment, Lou actually forgot to breathe. He may have appeared pale and haggard when she had left him this morning, but he had recovered magnificently. Wearing his journalist's uniform of white safari shirt and khaki trousers, he had recently showered and shaved, and even seemed to be a little more tanned than he'd been before. He stopped only inches before he would have run her over, towering above her and looking for all the world as though he wanted to throttle her into unconsciousness. She should have remembered he had a strong constitution.

"Where the hell have you been?" he growled in lieu of a greeting.

Lou took a deep breath and told herself to remain calm. Mason wasn't her father. He wasn't her keeper. She didn't have to answer to him or anyone. "I've been working on my story," she replied levelly, pleased that her voice belied none of the nervousness she felt.

"I called Michaud," Mason announced roughly, as if the very mention of the other man left a bad taste in his mouth. "He said your last interview was scheduled for two o'clock this afternoon and that you left the mayor's house a little after three." She could tell Mason was barely containing his anger as he concluded, "I repeat, Lou. Where the hell have you been?"

"Here, dammit," she snapped at him, unmindful of the curious gazes they were earning from the other diners. "In the dining room. I've been organizing my notes and working on my story since five."

"That leaves two hours unaccounted for," Mason pointed out, clearly indicating he demanded a more thorough report of the day's activities.

That did it, Lou thought. She'd had enough. "Two hours, huh? You want to know what happened in that two hours? Okay, fine. First I was kidnapped by a white slavery ring and taken to an opium den where I was forced to perform unspeakable sexual acts with paying customers from OPEC and the EEC. Then they crated me up and shipped me to South America, where I was taken to an ancient city and sold to a Mayan king. After he used and abused me sexually, he put me to work in his mines, where I uncovered an emerald the size of Rhode Island and used it to buy back my freedom.

Then I swam across the Caribbean, fighting off pirates and sharks, until I got back to Madriga. After that, I had a bite of lunch and did a little shopping, then I came back to the hotel. Okay?''

Her West Virginia accent had returned in full force, Mason realized. That meant she was pretty mad. All right, so maybe he was overreacting a little. But he'd been worried sick about her all day, his anxiety over her welfare making him twice as nauseous as a bout with conch-fritteritis. When she hadn't come back to her room by late afternoon, he'd felt he had no other recourse but to go out looking for her. He'd checked here in the dining room first, thinking she might be having a bite of lunch, but either he'd missed her or she'd been sitting faced away from the entry in one of the high-backed chairs. This trip was her first time outside the States, her first time experiencing another culture. There were things Lou didn't understand about foreign countries, things that could get her into trouble. He just wanted to keep an eye out for her, that's all. He just wanted to make sure she stayed safe. Why couldn't she understand that? Why did she always have to get so mad at him?

As he watched her watching him, Mason felt all the fear and anxiety leave him in a rush. Now that he knew she was fine, he could relax. With just the hint of a smile, he pointed out quietly, ''There aren't any opium dens on Sonora.''

When he smiled at her like that, it was impossible for Lou to remain angry with him. Meeting his gaze steadily, she replied, ''The way you reacted, you'd think there was one on every corner. And incidentally, at the moment, the company I'd find there would probably be preferable to what's offered here. At least there—'' Lou stopped herself abruptly before she could tell Mason that at least there she would be treated like a desirable woman, able to enjoy the activities she knew so little about. Even though she had a new outlook on her relationship with Mason, it still felt strange discussing sex with him, even in jest.

"At least there what?" he prodded.

"Nothing," she mumbled quickly, feeling heat seep into her cheeks.

"You were going to say something about those unspeakable sexual acts, weren't you?"

"No. . . ." She felt her cheeks burn more.

Mason laughed, a dark, rich sound that emanated from deep within his soul. "Come on, I'll buy you some dinner on the *Standard*'s expense account. You've already got the best table in the house. I'm surprised the maître d' didn't throw you out on your can for sitting there for four hours without ordering anything."

He put his hands on her shoulders to spin her around, and Lou felt warmth permeate her entire body. "He's too polite to do that," she said. "I think he kind of has a crush on me. Besides, there's still one or two tables left unoccupied."

But the waiter who approached them when they were seated seemed to be very relieved they intended to order nonetheless. As if to make up for her severe breach of restaurant etiquette, Lou found herself asking for a little bit of everything on the menu, starting with a cocktail, then soup, then salad, wine with her entrée and coffee with dessert. In between came a number of courses that seemed to be exclusive to the island of Sonora. Every time the waiter removed one plate from before them, he replaced it with a tiny serving of citrus sorbet. Mason told Lou it was to cleanse her palate before the next course, but she preferred to see it as extra helpings of dessert instead. It was nice being pampered this way for a while, she thought as she nibbled at her lobster and tasted her wine. But she didn't think it was something she'd want to do forever. She discovered, much to her delight, that she honestly couldn't wait to get back to Washington and start taking care of herself. Then in a fit of philosophizing, she thought, Why wait until then?

When they were finally able to push themselves away from the table, Lou and Mason did so with some reluctance. As he signed the check and added a generous tip, she picked up her portfolio and pulled the strap up over her shoulder. It seemed heavier, thanks to the lethargy that followed such a sumptuous meal, and she sighed deeply as if such an act might bring her strength. It didn't. All she could think about now was going back to her room and stretching out across the bed. However, Mason apparently had other ideas.

"Let's walk off our dinner on the beach," he said as he took the weight of her portfolio from her shoulder and transferred it to his own.

"Mason, I feel barely able to crawl to the elevators right now, let alone plod through sand."

"Oh, come on," he cajoled with a mischievous smile. "How often do you get the chance to walk along the beach in the moonlight?"

She lifted her eyebrows at his curiously romantic statement. "In Washington?" she asked. "Every weekend. The Maryland coast is only a couple of hours away, remember? Unless you've forgotten that your sister and brother-in-law have a house in Cannonfire that sits right on Chesapeake Bay."

"No, I haven't forgotten," he replied blandly, shaking his head at her in disappointment. "It's a damned nice house, now that they've fixed it up. Let me rephrase my question. How often do you get the chance to stroll quietly and languidly along the pearly white, powder-soft beaches of the blue, blue Caribbean Sea while the silver mask of night hangs high in the sky above you?"

Lou stared at him as if his brain had just blown a gasket. What on earth had come over him? "That doesn't sound like rephrasing to me," she said, stalling. "That sounds like embellishing. Excessive embellishing at that. You know, if you had written something like that for my technical writing professor at American University, he would have told you to—"

"Lou."

"What?"

"We need the exercise."

"Oh. Well, since you put it that way..."

They stopped off at the concierge's desk long enough to check Lou's portfolio, then headed through the plush, palm-lined lobby of the Hotel San Sebastian until they came to the doors that led to the pool and, beyond it, the beach. The night was warm and balmy and quiet, the sounds of Madriga only faintly detectable thanks to the buffer of the hotel and the lapping whisper of the surf only yards away. A handful of tourists were gathered by the pool, the men wearing pastel-colored *guayabera* shirts, and the women dressed in brightly flowered sarongs. They greeted Lou and Mason like old friends as they passed, lifting elaborate concoctions from the bar decorated with parasols and pineapples in salute. When the two of them finally reached the beach, Lou removed her flat sandals and dangled them from her hands, and Mason followed her example by tossing his own shoes onto the steps that led to the pool. Lou, suddenly feeling inordinately carefree, decided to do likewise.

It was a beautiful night. Somewhere off in the distance, perhaps at another one of the hotels that lined the beach, strains of salsa music punctuated the darkness. A woman laughed, a sea gull cried out in delight and the night breeze sifted through the palm trees like a lover's breath. For a moment, Lou closed her eyes and listened to the sounds of the surf surrounding her, sounds that seemed different somehow from those that normally accompanied her trips to visit Emily and Mick Dante on Chesapeake Bay. The cadence and fragrance of the ocean, too, seemed different here than it did in Cannonfire, but was every bit as bewitching. Running her tongue slowly across her upper lip, Lou tasted salt and smiled sadly. Sometimes things could seem different without being so at all, she thought. No matter where she went in the world, no matter how the ocean's moods might change, its water would always be salty. And no matter how much she might try to assure herself otherwise, Lou would always, always need Mason Thorne.

When she looked over at Mason, it was to find him gazing at her with undisguised curiosity.

"You look so sad all of a sudden," he said quietly. "What are you thinking about?"

Lou wasn't sure what made her reply to his question the way she did. Maybe it was because of the wine she'd consumed with dinner, or maybe because of the romantic aspects of their surroundings. Or maybe it was just because she was growing tired of hiding her feelings for Mason. Slowly, silently, she covered the short distance that lay between them, put her hands gingerly on his broad shoulders and then stood up on tiptoe so that she could touch his lips softly with her own. No other parts of their bodies touched, and Lou drew no closer to him than was absolutely necessary. The kiss lasted only for a moment, was only a brief, gentle caress that barely constituted a whisper. But for Lou, it was enough. For now.

When she stepped back again, her heart was pounding, her breathing ragged, as if her simple gesture had been a sexual consummation of the most explosive intensity. She studied Mason cautiously, amazed to discover that he had closed his eyes during her kiss, and when he opened them again, she was shocked to see a heated passion to rival her own burning in their pale blue depths. Then as quickly as she thought she detected it, the fire was gone, replaced by the cool calmness he normally assumed.

"Why—why did you do that?" he stammered, and if she hadn't known better, she would have thought he sounded almost breathless.

Lou met his gaze levelly as she replied in a quiet voice, "You asked me what I was thinking about."

"You were thinking about kissing me?"

She nodded silently.

"And that made you sad?"

Lou hesitated a moment, then nodded again.

Mason shook his head slowly in confusion. "I don't understand."

For a long time, Lou said nothing, only stared at him with a deep longing, wishing things could be different. Finally, she mumbled quickly, "Neither do I, Mason."

With that, she abruptly pivoted and ran back toward the hotel. As Mason stood watching the tiny sprays of sand kicked up by her feet, he heard her quiet voice fill with anguish and echo across the darkness again, "Neither do I."

Chapter Five

On Friday, Albert had arranged for Lou and Mason to travel into the hills outside Madriga so that they could see how some of the smaller communities on Sonora operated and discern the opinions of those citizens concerning the changes taking place on the island. However, in light of the events of the evening before, Lou awoke in no mood to see Mason until she could straighten out her own feelings and reevaluate all that had transpired on the beach in the moonlight only a matter of hours before. What on earth had come over her? she wondered now, amazed at her behavior. It was as if another person had stepped into her skin and taken control. Still, she couldn't deny that it had been a very nice kiss, however chaste, and one she would welcome again. Only next time, she thought morosely, it might be nice if Mason were the one who instigated it.

Throwing back the sheet, Lou rose from bed and began to pace the length of her suite. What was she going to do? As she saw it, there were two ways she could handle the situation when she encountered Mason this morning. Either she could act flustered and embarrassed, which was her instinctive response—and, she was sure, the one Mason would be expecting—or she could be cool and calm, pretending nothing out of the ordinary had happened, which would be how Mason himself would react. Reminding herself that yesterday she had made some promises to finally take charge of her life, Lou squared her shoulders, set her jaw resolutely and chose to take the latter course. She was a big girl now, and it was time to start acting like one. Any other woman in her position would be matter-of-fact about the entire incident. She wasn't on Sonora to pursue a romantic liaison with Mason anyway. Well, at least not primarily. She was here to investigate a news story. And first and foremost, Lou told herself, she was a newswoman. Therefore, her job had to come first.

That settled, she went about her morning rituals and called room service for breakfast. There was a knock on her door just as she finished tucking her sleeveless, dark olive cotton blouse into pants of the same fabric and color. Lou opened it absently, assuming her caller would be a waiter in the standard blue Hotel San Sebastian uniform, delivering her coffee and pastries. Instead, she saw Mason holding her order, looking scrubbed and handsome in a different white safari shirt from the day before and a different pair of baggy khaki trousers.

"Didn't you pack anything to wear that has a little color to it?" she asked impulsively by way of a greeting, trying to slow the rapid fire of her heartbeat the sight of him always inspired.

Seeming nonplussed, Mason replied, "I told you—"

"I know, I know. Khaki is the internationally recognized uniform of the press corps, spoken everywhere, et cetera, et cetera, et cetera. But you look so nice in blue, Mason."

He didn't respond, but kept looking at her as if she were someone he'd never seen before in his life. Fearing he was about to make some reference to the night before and get their conversation off to a bad start, Lou indicated the coffeepot and covered tray he held in his hands.

"Are you moonlighting for the hotel, or did you mug the waiter who was bringing my breakfast to me?"

Mason looked down at his burden, seeming surprised that he held it, as if he'd forgotten it was there. "The waiter was about to knock as I was coming out of my room to go downstairs to the dining room. I told him I'd deliver your breakfast to you." After a moment's thought, he gazed at her intently and added, "Why did you only order something for yourself? Didn't you want to have breakfast with me?"

Lou paused for the same amount of time as he had before answering, meeting his gaze just as pointedly as it was offered. "Why were you going downstairs to the dining room alone? Didn't *you* want to have breakfast with *me?*"

He stepped past her into the room and said, "Point taken."

Lou closed the door behind him, searching her brain frantically for something, anything, to say that would circumvent a discussion of their kiss on the beach last night. Lifting the lid on the tray, she found her opportunity.

"There's more than enough here for both of us. They even sent up two coffee mugs." She took the tray from him, set it on the table near the doors leading to the balcony and poured them each a cup of coffee, all the while waiting for Mason to say something.

"I guess the guys down in room service automatically think of us as a couple," he replied.

Lou faltered only a little at his statement, losing her grip on the croissant she had begun to tear apart, missing the piece that tumbled from her fingers when she tried to retrieve it. Mason deftly caught it in his palm, then waited until she looked up to meet his gaze before he gave it back to her. When he did, however, it wasn't to place the bite-size morsel back into her hand. First, he took the butter knife and slowly spread a generous helping of pale yellow across the bread. Then, his eyes never leaving hers, he lifted it to Lou's lips, silently encouraging her to part them. She was helpless not to obey, and when she did so, slowly and uncertainly, Mason tucked the bit of croissant into her mouth, his fingers lingering as she closed her lips again, his thumb rubbing very gently across her lower one before his hand dropped back to his side. The entire action lasted only a matter of seconds, but Lou suddenly felt as if a hundred years had gone by. Mason was making it very difficult for her to remain indifferent about their kiss of the night before.

The only way she could think to respond to his gesture was to mumble her thanks, then she quickly snatched a napkin from the tray and wiped her mouth in an effort to dispel the sensation of Mason's gentle caress. It didn't work. She doubted she would ever quite be able to forget the way his fingers had felt rubbing softly against her lips.

"Lou—"

"Mason," she interrupted before he could say anything of a personal nature. "Albert has given us the use of a Jeep today so that we can drive into the interior of the island. I have a map of Sonora, and I've marked all the villages I'd like to visit. We can make the rounds in less than a day. It won't take long."

Mason's expression indicated he was anything but pleased with the new turn of events. "How many times do I have to tell you that anything Michaud and the government officials arrange for us will be colored by their own pen? Don't you see how—"

"This is something *I* arranged, Mason. Not Albert. Me."

"And just how did you arrange it?"

"I told Albert I wanted to talk to people besides the residents of Madriga, and he said he'd have a Jeep here by eight o'clock for our use, however we needed it."

"Lou—"

"I never told him which villages we'd be visiting, and he never asked."

"Lou—"

"Don't *you* see that the Sonoran government honestly wants to show the rest of the world once and for all that their intentions are genuinely honorable?"

"Lou!"

"What?"

Mason gazed at her for a long time, exasperation darkening his blue eyes. He pressed a palm hard against his forehead, shook his head and glared at her. "When do we leave?" he finally asked.

Lou smiled triumphantly. "Right now. Just let me get my things."

When they went down to the lobby and inquired at the desk, they discovered that Albert had indeed made good on his promise and that there was a Jeep awaiting them, all gassed up and apparently brand-new. Mason was sure it was yet another example of how Papitou's people were trying to butter them up, but Lou was less suspicious. As she made to climb into the driver's seat, Mason began to chuckle lightly and she paused.

"What's so funny?" she wanted to know.

"You actually think for one minute that I'm going to let you drive?" Mason asked her incredulously.

"I'm the one who's been studying the map," she pointed out. "I'm the one who knows where we're going."

"Yeah, well, scoot over," he instructed. "I've driven on Sonora before. Years ago when another group tried to overthrow Senegal's regime. The island topography is tricky at best, and it's very easy to get lost in those hills. With you at the wheel, we might spend the rest of our days wandering around the mountains with no one ever finding us. I'll drive."

Lou's lips thinned in irritation at being so easily dismissed once again, but she conceded to Mason's wishes to avoid further delay. "All right. I'll be navigator."

Although she thought she heard him mumble something to the effect of, "Like hell you will," Lou remained stoically silent. When she slid over into the passenger seat, Mason climbed up to assume her former position, picking up the map to glance at it surreptitiously before announcing, "No problem. I know exactly where we're going. Next stop, Palmyra."

"No, wait," Lou said, placing her hand over his when he went to shift gears, only to yank it back quickly when she felt as if an electrical charge ran through her body from head to toe. "I, uh ... I wanted to go to Palmyra last," she told him a little breathlessly. "Dorano is the village I'd like to visit first."

"What difference does it make?"

"Dorano is the smallest," Lou explained. "Palmyra is the largest. I was hoping to see if some kind of pattern in opinion emerged as a result of the population size in each community."

"Why?"

His question threw her. "It ... It just seemed like it might help me keep my research straight."

Mason nodded, but didn't seem to think her hypothesis was in any way significant. "Okay, fine. Dorano first, Palmyra last. Any other instructions?"

Lou shook her head mutely.

Mason shifted into gear and the Jeep lurched forward. "Keep an eye out for rebels," he said evenly as they pulled away from the hotel, his expression indicating he was dead serious.

Lou took a deep breath. The only rebel she was worried about right now was the one inside herself that kept behaving like a stranger. If she and Mason could just make it through the day without voicing any reference to what had happened on the beach the night before, maybe everything would return to normal. Then with a sinking realization, Lou decided that was the last thing she wanted to have happen. They only had a week left on Sonora, and there were two things she wanted to accomplish before they left. One was writing and filing the best news stories she could get on paper. The other was settling things between Mason and herself once and for all. Whether that meant taking their relationship down a more intimate avenue or facing the fact that it would never go beyond the stalemate it had become, Lou wasn't yet willing to consider. She only knew that some kind of resolution would have to be made. She didn't want to face living with the knowledge that she hadn't even tried. Before their trip was over, some changes would indeed be made.

"It's got to be around here somewhere." Mason turned the map again and looked toward the setting sun. "We're facing due west, right? That mountain to our left is Grand Frère, and the one to our right is Albignon." He looked up again, scrutinizing their surroundings with a practiced eye. "Or is the one to our left Albignon and the one to our right Grand Frère?"

Lou couldn't believe this was happening. They had made it to all the villages she had wanted to visit except Palmyra, and they had been on their way to that one with time to spare when Mason had somehow managed to get them hopelessly lost. Now the sun was falling fast toward the horizon, and she remembered anxiously that nights in the Caribbean came all too quickly. Once it got dark, they'd never be able to figure out where they were, and then they'd have to wait until morning to find their way back to Madriga. She didn't relish the thought of having no shelter, no protection, no light and no food. Fortunately, they still had three bottles of water in the back seat that they had brought with them, and if they were lucky, they might stumble upon a banana or papaya tree. Lou had a few very basic toiletries in the big straw bag that she had purchased in Madriga her first day there, but certainly nothing that prepared her for a night in the wilderness.

As Mason studied the map, Lou watched the sun continue its speedy descent, and all too soon, the two of them were plunged into a purple twilight.

"We better find someplace to camp before it becomes pitch black," she said quietly, hoping her voice reflected none of the apprehension she felt when she considered the night that lay before them. Not only would she be camping out without supplies, but she would be alone with Mason for the duration of the evening. Lou wasn't sure which idea frightened her more.

Mason glanced up, surprised to discover that the sun had gone down to be replaced by semidarkness. He folded the map resolutely, grumbled something about how Lou should have let him go to Palmyra first, the way he had wanted to originally, and shifted the Jeep back into gear. Less than a mile ahead, they came upon a clearing well back from the road, and Mason deemed it an acceptable campground. Driving the Jeep up off the road, he crossed the field to where it ended just before a dense thicket of foliage and parked.

"We're back far enough from the road that no one passing by will be able to see us," he told Lou. "There's little chance anyone will stumble upon us. My only concern would be that they might want to take the Jeep." Among other things, he added to himself as he glanced over at Lou, amazed that she still looked fresh and lovely after having spent an entire day in the hot sun.

He was as apprehensive as she was about having to spend the night away from Madriga. There were any number of things that could go wrong out here, the least of which could be potentially life threatening. There were poisonous snakes, insects the size of some household pets, exotic plants that could easily produce allergic or even physically debilitating reactions. And those were the smallest of his worries. It was unlikely that they would come across any rebels—there were only a few stragglers left, and they were probably anxious to remain hidden—but if they did manage to bump into any...

Mason refused to think about what the consequences might be. He wanted to kick himself silly for having gotten them lost. His navigational abilities were phenomenal, his sense of direction flawless. It had only happened because Lou had been sitting so close to him in the Jeep, distracting him all day by wearing an outfit that revealed every last luscious curve and valley she possessed. He'd almost driven them over a cliff at one point because the wind had blown her shirt open at the collar to reveal a pink, lacy bra beneath. Mason groaned inwardly. During the six years he had known Lou, it had never once occurred to him that she might wear the same kind of underthings that other women wore to drive men into a sexual frenzy. Between that realization and the memories of her sexy sleepwear the previous morning and her chaste kiss the night before, his thoughts had become completely centered on getting to know Lou and her lingerie a little more... intimately.

Because of that, he hadn't been able to concentrate on getting them where they needed to go, and as a result, had landed them in their current predicament. Mason supposed that if he were the kind of man to lay blame on others, he could say this whole situation was all Lou's fault for having become such a damned desirable woman. Unfortunately, he knew he had only himself to blame for being so utterly susceptible to her.

With their ascent into the mountains and the setting of the sun, the air around them had become significantly cooler. He didn't really want to draw attention to them by building a fire, but when he saw Lou hug herself and rub her bare arms as if trying to warm them, he decided there was probably no harm in making a small one.

"Come on," he encouraged her after a moment. "Help me find some dry wood and we can build a little campfire."

Lou smiled at him gratefully. "Okay," she agreed, her voice indicating she was less than comfortable in their current surroundings.

"You realize of course that this is going to be a wonderful adventure," Mason told her.

She looked at him curiously. "What do you mean?"

Feigning offense, he clarified, "When you go to your ten-year reunion at AU, how many of your classmates are going to be able to say they spent the night in a Caribbean jungle with a Pulitzer Prize-winning journalist?"

Lou smiled, loving him all the more for making this effort to take her mind off of her fears. "You know, you never did tell me what you won that Pulitzer for," she told him.

"You never asked," he pointed out with a shrug.

"I'm asking now. When did you get it and what for?"

"About eight years ago," he replied. "It was for a story I did on the plight of orphaned children in San Salvador, El Salvador, who were forced to commit crimes in order to survive."

"I never knew you'd pursued any stories like that," Lou said. "Human stories, I mean. I thought everything you did centered on political issues."

Mason nodded. "Lately I have focused on politics, but when I first started out as a reporter, I was more interested in the people and culture of the countries I visited." He looked at her thoughtfully for a moment before adding, "Like you."

Lou started to say something in response, then paused when she forgot what it was. Mason was looking at her as if considering something that had never occurred to him before, and she wasn't sure she wanted to interrupt his thoughts. Instead, she turned and went to look for wood as he had asked, returning several minutes later with a small armful.

"Will this be enough?" she asked as she handed it to him.

"Plenty. I won't build a big fire, but it will be enough to keep us warm for a while." He stooped to arrange the wood into a circle of rocks he had made in her absence. "I think there's a blanket in the back of the Jeep if you want to wrap up in it while I'm getting this started."

Lou nodded and went to retrieve the blanket, returning with her straw bag and a bottle of water. Mason was in the same position as before, trying to nurture a tiny flicker of light into a substantial flame. She watched, fascinated as the light began to grow brighter, warming Mason's features and enhancing every hard line in his face. He really was the most handsome man she had ever met, Lou thought. And so much different from any of the men she had known while growing up in Hack's Crossing. Despite his tendency to swagger around sometimes, she'd discovered long ago that much of what he did and said was only for show. Mason Thorne was a rarity these days, a member of a vanishing breed—he was a decent guy. No matter how often he tried to flex his muscles, whether literally or figuratively, she knew deep down that he was as gentle as a lamb.

"I have a chocolate bar if you want to split it for dinner," she offered as she took her seat on the grass near the steadily building fire.

Mason smiled at her mischievously. "I have something better." He reached into the darkness just beyond the perimeter of light afforded by the fire and came back holding a small bunch of a half-dozen bananas.

Lou grinned back at him, delighted. "Where did you find those?"

"There are two trees full of them less than ten yards from the Jeep. And as we both know, nothing goes better with chocolate than bananas."

"Except for peanut butter."

"Well, that goes without saying."

By the time they'd finished their dinner, the darkness enveloping them had become a blackness so thick that they couldn't see more than three feet past the fire flickering halfheartedly before them. The air turned cooler than ever, and the thin summer blanket Lou had wrapped around herself offered little protection against the elements. Gradually, she found herself scooting as close to Mason as she dared in the hopes of drawing additional heat from his big body. When he draped an arm across her shoulders to pull her nearer, her desire to be close to him outweighed her fear of her reaction, and she snuggled into the familiar embrace. His body was warm and hard, and Lou sighed silently in contentment at the knowledge that she was so well protected.

"So, how are you enjoying your first overseas assignment?"

Lou could hear the smile in Mason's voice, but took no offense. Things hadn't exactly turned out the way she had planned, but all in all, she was doing what she wanted to do, pursuing a news story and getting closer to the man she loved.

"Actually, I'm enjoying it a lot," she responded truthfully.

Mason looked down at her doubtfully, but she returned his gaze with assurance. "I am," she insisted. "This is like nothing I've ever done before in my life. It's...exhilarating."

"Exhilarating," Mason repeated dryly, staring out at the dark jungle beyond the firelight. "Do you mean to tell me you never camped out in the mountains of West Virginia when you were a kid?"

"Oh, I did that often enough," she agreed. "I had lots of cousins up in Hack's Crossing, and one of us was always having a sleep over or something. But that's just it. I was always with my family, always in familiar surroundings doing the usual stuff. This is so exciting. I mean, this is my job now, Mason. You've probably been in situations like this a million times. But to me..."

Lou let her voice trail off, uncertain whether or not she wanted to continue.

"But what?" Mason encouraged.

She shrugged as she looked up at him, loving the way the firelight enhanced the ruggedness of his features and made his blond hair sparkle with gold and copper. "I just never thought anything like this would ever happen to me, that's all. I'm still not used to the fact that I have a future ahead of me that doesn't end at marrying a storekeeper's son and having six or seven children.''

"You don't want to get married?'' he asked, sounding to Lou as if he were a little distracted. "Have kids?''

She was unwilling to let him know how fiercely she did want those things eventually. Just not quite yet. Not the children anyway. So she only shrugged and said, ''I don't know. Maybe. Someday. But there are a lot of other things I want . . . need . . . to do first.''

Mason nodded. When he was her age, he'd said the same thing. But that was eleven years ago. He was thirty-six now. Most of his friends had been married for more than a decade. Some of them even had kids in high school. Would the day ever come that found him seated in the front row of a school auditorium as he watched his son or daughter pick up a diploma? It was something he seldom thought about, but now that he did, the contemplation brought with it some unsettling, almost melancholy feelings.

Just the thought of becoming an uncle in the near future made Mason's heart hum a little more happily, made his blood trip through his veins at an increased rate. When Emily and Mick had first revealed that they were expecting a baby, Mason's initial reaction had been one of incredulity. His kid sister was about to become a mother? It was too bizarre to consider. The more he'd thought about it, though, the more sense it made. If anyone would be a wonderful mother, it would be Emily. And Mick, despite his hulking size and hard-as-nails appearance, would no doubt be the softest touch in the world where his child was concerned. Mason smiled. What would it be like to hold a tiny little baby in your arms and know that it was part of you? Involuntarily, his eyes wandered to the woman who felt so perfect all snuggled up beside him. Lou would make a terrific mother, too, someday. He only hoped the man she married would appreciate her for everything else she had to offer as well.

When he thought of Lou marrying someone else, Mason frowned. Then he realized how he had phrased his thought, and his frown deepened. Lou married to someone *else*? Someone besides himself? Why would he think of it like that? Why would he for a single moment entertain the notion that Lou would be married to him? Hell, he didn't want to get married to anyone. At least, he didn't think he did. But if that was the case, then what was with all his soul-searching tonight? If he was so adamantly opposed to getting married and having children, then why was that precisely what was on his mind?

Mason lifted his free hand to his forehead and rubbed vigorously at a headache that had sprung up out of nowhere. Lou noticed the action and stirred.

"What's wrong?" she asked.

"What?" he replied absently.

"Are you all right? You don't look like you feel too well."

Mason dropped his hand back to his lap and stared at Lou for a long time. His expression indicated he was puzzled, almost angry, and she couldn't for the life of her think what she might have done or said to make him feel that way.

"What is it?" she insisted.

Mason shook his head. "Nothing. Just some crazy thoughts, that's all."

"What kind of crazy thoughts?"

"Forget it."

His tone of voice indicated that the matter was closed, and whatever Lou wanted to say next she kept to herself. The dark night enveloped them, punctuated by the chirping of crickets, the chattering of birds, and a few sounds Lou was hard-pressed to identify. An involuntary shiver passed through her body and she pulled the blanket more tightly around her shoulders.

"Are you cold?" Mason asked, curling his arm more securely around her.

Actually, Lou thought, when she was this close to Mason her body was virtually on fire. But there was no way she was going to tell him that. "A little," she said softly.

"Why don't you try to get some sleep? You could put one of the seats in the Jeep back and stretch out."

She shook her head vehemently. "I want to stay here with you."

"I won't be far, I promise."

Again, Lou shook her head. "I'm fine. I feel wide awake." As if to betray her, however, her mouth opened in an impressive yawn, and she blinked several times, feeling a little disoriented.

Mason chuckled at her unsuccessful attempt at deception. "Then just stretch out here and put your head in my lap. I'll wake you up if any rebels or monsters come along."

Lou made a face at him, but the invitation was too good to turn down. If she were honest with herself, she would admit that she was exhausted. She'd gotten very little sleep last night, thanks to her feverish preoccupation with thoughts of kissing Mason, and the day had been a taxing one, both physically and mentally. Her notebook was bulging with informational tidbits about peasant life on Sonora that she couldn't wait to start organizing and analyzing. As she succumbed to the lethargy that threatened to overwhelm her, Lou stretched out on her side and placed her head on the hand she flattened against Mason's muscular thigh. His flesh was warm and hard beneath the soft khaki fabric, and she imagined she could feel the pulse of his life-blood humming below her ear.

"Mason?" she asked quietly, a mischievous smile curling her lips at the corners.

"Yes?"

"Will you tell me a story?"

She felt his laughter before she heard the rumbling sound of it, and she, too, began to chuckle. Her question was a reference to the nights that had passed when she'd first come to Washington, D.C., from Hack's Crossing. Until a dormitory room had been made available to her at the university, Lou had stayed with Mason in his Capitol Hill apartment, and for her first week there had been plagued by nightmares of all that had transpired since their initial meeting. Mason had taken to telling her some wildly altered bedtime story every night to distract her from her troubles, tales of fantastic characters who wound up in the most bizarre situations. Invariably, Lou's dreams following such stories had been like Alice's excursions in Wonderland and through the looking glass, and eventually her nightmares had all but vanished. Considering their current situation, the desire to hear one of Mason's fractured fables somehow seemed fitting.

"Okay," Mason replied when his laughter had subsided. "Which one do you want to hear? 'Little Red Riding Hoodlum'? 'The Three Barristers'? 'Handful and Grateful'? What?"

Lou began to laugh again at the memory of the stories he mentioned. "No, none of those." Finally, she said thoughtfully, "I want to hear about Rip Van Bullwinkle, the moose who slept for a hundred years."

Mason smiled down at her. "That always was your favorite, wasn't it?"

Lou nodded.

"Okay, okay. You lie still and close your eyes, and I'll tell you all about Rip Van Bullwinkle."

Lou did as he instructed, loving the soft, deep timbre of his voice as Mason began to tell the story that had always left her smiling. Gradually, his words seemed to become quieter and more distant, as if coming to her from the very back of her mind. As she slowly began to drift off, Lou thought she felt Mason's fingers at her temple, brushing back her bangs and smoothing gently over her hair. Then, just before sleep thoroughly claimed her, Lou wasn't sure, but she could have sworn that Mason leaned down and placed a warm, lingering kiss on her cheek.

Chapter Six

Mason wasn't sure what awakened him in the middle of the night. He only noticed as he struggled into consciousness that he was snuggled up against the warmest, curviest, most luscious female body he had ever encountered, and that his hand was curled just below a very tempting breast. Instinctively, he pulled the body closer, inhaling deeply the feminine scent of her that was mingled with the smoky fragrance of a campfire and the earthy aroma of the great outdoors. She responded by pushing herself even more intimately against his agitated midsection, and he sighed contentedly with satisfaction. Then slowly, as wakefulness gradually overcame him, Mason remembered vaguely that he hadn't gone out with a woman last night or done anything else that might lead to such a sensuous awakening. Instead, he had told a harmless bedtime story to Lou and had then fallen asleep on the ground a good two feet away from her. Between then and now, though, he recalled that there had been a number of erotic dreams in which Lou had played a feature role, and waking up to discover that those fantasies had become reality was, to say the least, disturbing.

Yet for some reason, Mason didn't leap away from her as his brain dictated he do. Clearly, Lou was still fast asleep, and when he considered the events that had forced them to spend the night in the wilds of Sonora, he told himself his reasons for remaining pressed so intimately against her resulted exclusively from his unwillingness to awaken her when she so desperately needed her sleep. Therefore, Mason lay quietly behind Lou, with one arm pillowing her head while the other was wound protectively over her rib cage, waiting for her to regain consciousness. And if it took hours for her to wake up, he contemplated as he stroked his thumb over the gentle pulse of her heartbeat, well, then he'd just have to be patient, wouldn't he?

He recalled once more how Lou had looked in the firelight some hours before with her head resting softly in his lap. Sleeping soundly thanks to their strenuous activities during the daylight hours, she had been completely oblivious to everything around her, including his close scrutiny. The amber-and-orange light from the flames had leapt and danced like sparklers in her pale brown hair, and the soft glow had made her face luminous, as if to enhance the inner warmth he knew was such an integral part of her. It had seemed the most natural response in the world to lean down and press his lips chastely against the soft skin of her cheek. There was just something about Lou Lofton that warmed anyone with whom she came into contact. It was why the stories she wrote for the paper were so utterly human and why they so successfully captured the essence of whomever or whatever she was investigating. She inspired trust in others, could ease through the walls of resistance people tended to erect before they even realized what she was trying to do. It was only one of the qualities that would make her a top-notch journalist. Along with her intelligence, intuition, instinct and ambition, Lou was going to go straight to the top of her profession.

He had seen it today in the way she had interviewed the residents of every tiny community they had visited. Lou never condescended to anyone, but treated each person she interviewed exactly as she expected others to treat her—with dignity and respect. He had also been impressed by the fact that her French was evidently flawless, something he had determined by speaking with the subjects of her interviews in his own perfect Spanish. And as he'd looked over her shoulder while she was taking notes, he'd realized that Lou was asking the very same questions he himself would have posed for the story. She had told him on more than one occasion that she was a newshound. Today, he had seen her in action. And she was indeed a force to be reckoned with on the journalistic scene.

With a silent sigh, Mason gave himself a good mental thrashing because he hadn't seen all that earlier. Why hadn't he been able before now to admit to himself that Lou had everything it took to be a success? More important than that, why hadn't he been able to admit it to Lou? What was it she had accused him of being just prior to their leaving for Sonora? Oh, yes. She had reminded him in a very loud voice that he wasn't her brother and he wasn't her keeper. Had that been what he was acting like all this time? he wondered. Her brother?

When he thought about it now, he supposed Lou might have a point. He'd always felt responsible for bringing her into the investigation of the smuggling going on in Hack's Crossing, even though it had been Lou who'd initially alerted him to the story. And he'd felt responsible for the fact that her family had been taken away from her, even though the Lofton clan had chosen the wrong path all by themselves. After the investigation had been completed and all the perpetrators convicted without hope of a future on the outside, he'd seen Lou standing all alone in that courtroom with no one on earth left to turn to, and his heart had just about broken in two. It had been an unsettling reaction. Mason's heart had never gone out to anyone before, except where his younger sister was concerned. Instinctively, he had taken Lou under his wing and provided for her because he'd felt it was the least he could do.

Now, however, she was making a genuine effort to stand on her own. But that didn't mean she no longer needed his help, Mason assured himself. It was still a jungle out there—literally as well as figuratively, he thought as he surveyed their surroundings once again—and she was still far too naive where many things were concerned. Just as Lou inspired trust in others, she offered her own trust all too readily. Her friendship with Albert Michaud and her conviction that Marco Papitou was a prince of a guy were perfect examples of that. There was no way Mason was going to turn her loose into the world just yet, not when there was still so much she had to learn. Naturally, he thought, he was just the guy to teach her what was what.

A rustle in the bushes beyond the Jeep caught his attention, and he perked up his ears to hear more. No sound followed it, however, and Mason decided it must be some harmless little animal like a toucan or a small monkey or something. Or perhaps a snake, he added anxiously. Or maybe one of those weird poisonous rodents one of the bellhops at the hotel had warned him about yesterday.

"Lou," he whispered softly in her ear, still trying to dispel the warm thoughts that had taken root in his mind while he was holding her close. "Wake up."

"Hmm," was all she murmured in reply.

"Lou," he said a little more loudly, giving her a gentle shake that only served to rub her body more intimately against his. He stifled a frustrated groan.

"Mason?" she asked on a long sigh, obviously still not fully awake.

Much to his dismay, she turned in her sleep to face him, but remained snuggled every bit as close as she had been when he'd first woken up. The feel of Lou's back pressed against him then had been too troubling for Mason to consider. The feel of Lou's front in the same position, however, was too tempting to ignore. As she pressed her face into the curve of his neck, she curled her hand softly over his shoulder. Before Mason realized what was happening, Lou was skimming her lips softly across the bare skin she encountered at the opening of his collar, and any thought he may have entertained about dislodging her evaporated in a warm mist. For long moments, he only closed his eyes and fought off the trembling that threatened to overtake him and nearly succeeded until Lou's other hand went exploring along the length of his rib cage.

"Mason," she said again, his name coming out as a half sigh.

"Lou," he repeated with a little more fortitude, surprised to discover that there was a significantly large part of him that was reluctant to wake her and end her exploration. "You have to wake up now, honey. We need to get into the Jeep."

At the sound of the odd endearment on Mason's lips, Lou slowly began to emerge from the dream she'd been having about the prelude to making love with him. She wasn't alarmed by the content or subject matter of the dream because such nightly visions of being entwined with Mason in the most passionate of embraces had become fairly frequent during her sleeping hours. It was only when she came fully awake to realize she wasn't dreaming at all that Lou began to panic. When she understood she was in fact gripping his muscular shoulder with one hand while running the other along the length of his leather belt, Lou stiffened and rolled instinctively onto her back. Unfortunately, though, she forgot to let go of Mason as she did so, and succeeded only in bringing him down on top of her. His solid chest pressed in on her like a heavy weight as his hard thigh landed between her own two and came into heated contact with the most intimate part of her. Lou bit back a hungry moan. Yet when she realized Mason was doing nothing to move away from her and only remained towering over her like the promise of salvation, his breathing as erratic and ragged as her own, Lou could only stare at him hungrily.

He looked magnificent. The last embers of the fire offered only the slightest light to see him, but in the reddish glow that permeated the darkness, his features were made stark. His expression was one she'd never seen before, as if he were almost totally consumed by some unknown desire. Despite the cool air of the night surrounding them, tiny beads of perspiration had formed on his forehead. His body on hers was hot and damp, his chest pressing hard against hers over and over again with each rasping breath he took. One silky strand of pale blond hair fell over his eye, and involuntarily, Lou reached up to smooth it back. When her fingers lingered in his hair to stroke his scalp, Mason closed his eyes in anguish as if her gesture were the most painful thing he had ever been forced to endure.

In fact, her gesture was the most exquisite thing Mason had ever felt. And along with the heated sensations that sent his nerve endings bursting into flame, it was also his undoing. When he opened his eyes again, it was to see Lou gazing at him with such unadorned hunger and desire that he couldn't have resisted her if he had wanted to. And deep down in the dark recesses of his soul, he knew resisting Lou was the last thing he wanted to do. Only a few inches separated their mouths. Bit by bit, that distance shrank, until only a breath of air prevented their lips from joining. For an instant Mason luxuriated in the feel of Lou's breasts flattened against his chest and the heat of her feminine core settled against his thigh. Unable to help himself, he brought his leg up more insistently, smiling ferally when Lou closed her eyes and moaned with longing. He crushed one hand against her hip and rubbed it urgently along her body until he reached her rib cage, then pressed his thumb roughly against the side of her breast, loving the way her breath caught in her throat when he did so. His other hand curved possessively over her upper thigh, jerking it more closely against him, bringing another gasp from deep inside her.

Only then did he kiss her, and only with the lightest, briefest, most teasing of kisses. When Lou sought to deepen it, lifting her head from the soft grass to bring him closer, Mason chuckled sensuously and pulled away. As her head dropped back, he took advantage of the new position by tasting the hot, salty skin of her throat, an action that made Lou go limp all over. Once again Mason lowered his head to hers, touching her lips softly with his own, laving the corners of her mouth with tiny flicks of his tongue, wanting to tease her into a state of delirium.

Lou was on fire. She felt the hand cupping her derriere squeeze her more urgently, bringing her once again into hard contact with Mason's lean thigh, coaxing her, cajoling her, to take a wild ride. The fingers making maddening circles along the side of her breast began to move inward until she felt them brush gently over the aroused peak, which Mason began to roll over and over again beneath his persistent thumb. All the while he rubbed his lips over hers in the softest of kisses, ignoring her when she silently begged him for more by arching her body upward. Finally, she felt the tip of his tongue trace the outline of her mouth and she quickly lifted her head to draw him deeper inside.

It was a sensation like none she could have ever anticipated. The reality of finally joining with Mason in such an intimate dance far exceeded any meager dreams Lou had ever enjoyed. He felt and tasted wonderful. She tangled her fingers more insistently in his hair, trying to pull him closer, senseless to the fact that they were already as close as two fully clothed people could be. As the kisses intensified, Lou let her hands wander along the length of his hard back, lovingly fingering every vertebra along his spinal cord as she went. As Mason deepened their kisses further, Lou's fingers grew bolder, dipping briefly inside the waistband of his trousers before finally cupping over his lean, muscular hips.

By now Mason was lying prone atop her, his manhood settled intimately and masterfully against the heart of her femininity. Acting purely on instinct, Lou hooked her legs over his at the knees and pulled with all her might to bring him more fully against her, rising up to meet the impulsive, thrusting response of his hips that her action caused. Over and over again, both their mouths and their bodies mimicked the act of lovemaking, despite the barrier of clothing that made actual consummation impossible. So caught up in the mindscrambling motions did Lou become that several moments passed before she began to realize that Mason had halted his assault on her senses. Slowly, she began to realize that it was she alone who still instigated the kisses and pulled his body close and that he had stopped offering himself fully. All too soon the silver haze in which she'd been enveloped for what seemed like hours began to lift and Lou was made starkly aware of all that had just transpired.

Where Mason had been looking at her as if she were the woman of his dreams, he now gazed at her with what appeared to be confused disappointment. His hands no longer wreaked hot, sensual havoc on her body, but instead, were placed quite firmly on the ground on either side of her head as he lifted his upper body away from hers. The only reason his lower body remained where it had been causing her such a sweet pain was because she still had her legs wound possessively around him. Feeling more and more ashamed and embarrassed by the minute, Lou sheepishly spread her legs—releasing him instead of enveloping him—and let him roll away from her once and for all.

Immediately, Mason stood up and took several hasty steps away from her, running his big hands furiously through his hair as he kept his back turned. Lou sat up quickly, pulling her knees to her chest, trying to ignore how terribly sensitive her breasts had become during the embrace. Her heart still rattled loudly and irregularly behind her rib cage and she inhaled deeply and repeatedly in an effort to steady it. For long moments, neither of them moved, neither of them spoke. Mason gazed off silently into the blackness, and Lou wordlessly watched him do it. The darkness around them filled with night noises—crickets chirping, birds crying out, the wind ruffling the leaves of the trees—but neither she nor Mason contributed a sound. Above them, the moon hung like a bright silver dollar, masked by wisps of gray clouds, as if it were trying in vain to hide. It was exactly how Lou felt, too. She didn't understand what had just happened. And as much as she had welcomed and enjoyed it, she would give anything if they could turn back the clock and go back to the way things were before. At least then Mason had spoken to her. At least then he had looked at her.

"Mason?" she finally called out plaintively, her voice sounding small and uncertain, even to her own ears.

He lifted a hand to prevent anything else she might want to say, but didn't turn around to reply.

Lou hugged her legs more tightly against her and shivered, telling herself it was a result of the cool night breeze and not because of the cold shoulder Mason had turned to her. Just when she thought he would never acknowledge her again, he slowly pivoted and began to retrace his steps toward the remnants of the fire, where he picked up a stick and stirred the embers, then added a few more branches of dry wood to bring the flames flickering back to life. Still he said nothing, though, and still he refused to look at Lou. However, when he saw the striped blanket lying on the ground beside her, he neared her to pick it up and place it over her shoulders. Finally he did glance down at her, but quickly, briefly, as if the sight of her repelled him in some way.

"That…that shouldn't have happened," he told her quietly.

"Mason—" she began.

"No, let me finish. We had kind of a rough day, and the fact that we were forced to spend the night in the wilderness this way, with no one but each other to rely on… It may have made tensions run a little high. We've barely gotten any sleep tonight, and with our fears and anxieties regarding our current situation… Well, they may have gotten a bit blown out of proportion." He looked up at her then, but again couldn't maintain eye contact and quickly glanced away. "It's understandable, really—though I'm not trying to justify it, mind you—that we turned to each other the way we did. It was a perfectly natural response under the circumstances. But that doesn't mean it meant anything, Lou," he added expressively, finally spearing her with an intent scrutiny. After a moment, he looked away once more and mumbled something that sounded to her like, "Just thank God it didn't go any further."

Lou stared at him for a long time without speaking, trying to understand what he was saying. Didn't mean anything? she repeated to herself. *Didn't mean anything?* Maybe to Mason what they had just shared was the result of some aberrant, instinctive, survivalistic response, but to Lou, it had been the near fulfillment of a dream. She loved Mason. She wanted Mason. She wished more than anything that things *had* gone further, as far as they could go. But evidently to him, whatever had just occurred could be explained as "one of those things," and filed away to be forgotten.

Lou didn't know what to say. She'd never been placed in a situation like this before. There was so much she wanted to reveal to Mason, so much she needed for him to understand. At the moment, however, he appeared to be anything but receptive to an avowal of love from her. His expression indicated that he was as unwilling to discuss this matter further as she was to bury it. But at the same time, she was hesitant to continue lest she hear him say the words she did not want to hear him utter. That he didn't want her. That he didn't love her.

In the long run, Lou decided it was best to say nothing at all. Instead, she stretched out on the ground again in the position she'd assumed before and tried to fall asleep. When Mason called softly out to her several minutes later, she pretended not to hear him, and when she felt him lift her into his arms to carry her toward the Jeep, it was only through a supreme effort that she managed not to stiffen and cry out an objection. However, as he settled her across the back seat with such exquisite care and gentleness, Lou couldn't prevent the helpless tremble that shimmied through her. His response to the action was to draw the blanket up to her chin and tuck it carefully in around her, then once more, Lou felt the brush of his lips across her cheek. This time when Mason moved away, she only prayed silently that he didn't see the tears she felt replacing his soft caress.

*   *   *

When Mason awoke again it was with a speed that resulted in instant awareness. The first thing he noticed was that a blazing sun had risen well above the trees to brighten the cloudless blue sky, bringing the temperature up with it to soak the front of his shirt with perspiration. The second thing he noticed was that the barrel of a rifle was nestled with cold, lethal assurance against the side of his throat. From the corner of his eye, he followed the long length of dark gray metal until it ended in a set of broad, blunt fingers that had quite clearly released the safety on the gun and now gripped the trigger with eager-intent. Beyond them was an arm covered by ragged, muddy, olive-drab cotton, which, upon further inspection, he discovered was attached to the body of a short, swarthy man who looked anything but happy.

Not one to be put off by seemingly unfriendly foreign customs, Mason smiled graciously and greeted the newcomer, "Ah, *buenos días. ¿Qué paso?*"

The man standing beside the Jeep did not smile back, nor did he vocally respond to Mason's jovial greeting. Instead, he shifted to press the gun barrel harder against Mason's Adam's apple, inhibiting Mason's breathing and indirectly restating his own unwillingness to be communicative.

"*Parlez-vous français?*" Mason tried again.

Still the man offered no reply. For long moments, Mason studied him, taking in the tangled mass of black hair on his head, the bushy mustache and beard, the dark complexion that was becoming sallow and the too-thin body that was obviously the result of an inadequate diet. But it was the other man's eyes that held Mason's attention longest. As menacing as his stance was, his eyes were fearful and desperate, reflecting an almost pleading expression that Mason didn't fully understand.

No doubt he was a member of one of the unnamed rebel forces that had tried unsuccessfully to overthrow Papitou as soon as the general had assumed power. Now such groups lived off of what they could find in the jungle instead of returning to their former ways of life, for fear that they might be arrested for treason. Mason had mixed feelings about most of these bands. On one hand, he didn't blame anyone for mistrusting Papitou's claims to effect numerous reforms on the island. And some of the rebel factions that had risen up during the civil war on Sonora had been honestly concerned about the welfare of their island and their people. However, Mason also knew that all too often the reason some of these groups formed in times of social unrest was simply because they enjoyed violence and had a thirst for blood. He only hoped the man who had stumbled upon them this morning was a member of the former philosophy.

As he frantically searched his brain for something else to say that might divert the man long enough to disarm him, the rebel was joined by three others who emerged from the jungle behind him looking every bit as unhealthy and underfed—but as well armed—as the first. Immediately, Mason thought about Lou sleeping in the back seat of the Jeep, and he prayed diligently to all the gods for some kind of divine intervention that would protect her from harm. Slowly, so as not to alarm the man who still held a rifle at his throat, Mason turned his head to look over his shoulder and peer into the back seat. Expecting to see her sleeping soundly, oblivious to all that was going on, he was surprised to discover that Lou was wide awake and sitting up straight, staring levelly at their visitors with an expression that showed no fear or concern.

Assured that she was all right for the moment, Mason turned slowly back toward the men again, afraid to see how their expressions might have changed upon realizing the gender of their additional prisoner. Maybe they wouldn't realize, he thought with sudden, uncharacteristic optimism. She had short hair and was wearing masculine-looking clothes. Maybe they'd think she was a man, too. Then Mason remembered exactly how well Lou filled out those clothes—and he frowned. Like hell they'd think she was a man. He was relieved to discover, however, that they seemed completely unfazed by, and even uninterested in, the fact that Lou was a woman. In fact, if there was any change at all in their posture, they appeared to relax somewhat. The gun barrel pressed against his throat was gradually lowered and Mason gulped in several eager breaths of air before swallowing nervously.

"Are you okay?" he asked Lou over his shoulder.

"Yes, I'm fine," she assured him quietly. "Who are they?"

"I don't know. Rebels. But I'm not sure which faction."

"What do you think they want?"

He lifted his shoulders in an almost imperceptible shrug, then took his chances and turned fully around to look at her. "I don't know. I've tried speaking Spanish and French both, but I can't get a response."

"Maybe if I tried," Lou offered.

"No," Mason told her vehemently. "Don't bring any more attention to yourself than you have to. I don't trust these guys for a minute. Just stay quiet and pretend you don't speak any of the indigenous languages.''

Lou narrowed her eyes at him thoughtfully, assuming an expression that Mason decided could have meant anything. Then she turned to look at the group of men who still observed them closely.

"Parlez-vous français?" she asked them.

"I already tried that," Mason ground out.

All four rebels exchanged nervous glances, then the first one who had found them replied.

"Oui, je parle français," he verified for her in a rusty voice. *"Qui êtes-vous?"*

"Nous sommes Americains," she said, identifying their nationality, having been told and having experienced for herself that Sonorans thought very highly of Americans. Then, thinking that their occupations might also help plead their case, Lou added, *"Nous sommes les journalistes. Pour un journal aux États-Unis qui s'appelle* the *Capitol Standard."* There, that should do it, she thought. Even down on Sonora, it was one of the most widely recognized newspapers. Surely it would impress a band of rebels who no doubt had a story they wanted the rest of the world to hear.

All four men lifted their eyebrows in surprise and immediately launched into an animated conversation among themselves, a rapid-fire exchange of the local language. Lou had picked up a handful of words while she was on the island, but as she had been warned, the rebels all spoke too quickly for her to understand what they were saying. She looked at Mason to see if he could offer any insight, but found him staring back at her with undisguised and unbridled fury.

"What's wrong?" she asked him innocently.

He intensified his glare as he ground out, "I thought I told you not to draw attention to yourself."

"You said they wouldn't talk to you," she reminded him. "I thought they might respond more readily to me. You tend to look a little menacing you know," she added parenthetically. "Sometimes you just intimidate people, Mason. If you'd just—"

"Lou, in case you didn't realize, I was *trying* to intimidate them. I don't want to interview them. I want them to go away and leave us to find our way back to Madriga. Silly me, I was of the opinion that you might want that, too."

"Are you kidding?" she countered. "Mason, this could be the journalistic opportunity of a lifetime. An exclusive interview with one of the factions still trying to oust Papitou. Look at them," she added, gesturing toward the group of men who still engaged in a heated discussion a few feet away. "Aren't you curious as to why they're so intent on carrying on this campaign when they're obviously in no condition to continue?"

Mason followed her gaze briefly, then turned to look back at her again. "No. I'm not. I know why they're doing it. Because they think Papitou is a crook. And he is."

"No, he isn't," she assured him.

"Yes, he is," Mason replied.

"He is not."

"He is, too."

"Is not."

"Is, too."

"Mason—"

"Lou—"

At the recognition of the abrupt silence that had descended around them, Lou and Mason looked over at the group of rebels to find them staring back with equal curiosity. Just when Lou was sure they were going to smile and wave them on their merry way, all four men lifted their rifles with unmistakable intent and gestured that they get out of the Jeep.

"Great," Mason muttered as he climbed down to the ground. "Now look what you've done."

As he helped her out of the back seat, Lou snapped, "Well, if you hadn't offended them to begin with by glowering at them the way you always do, none of this would be happening."

They continued to grumble at each other as the rebels instructed them to place their hands on the backs of their heads and move forward down a path that led into the jungle. Because two of the men preceded them and two brought up the rear, Lou knew there was little chance of escaping, as it would be foolish to tear off into the jungle and become hopelessly lost. Therefore, she and Mason simply continued with their disagreement as they hiked through the dense, green foliage, each assuring the other that he was completely right while the other was totally off his rocker.

By the time they came to a primitive camp set up amid a clearing cut out of a thick grove of palm trees, Lou estimated they had traveled more than two miles. She felt grittier and more uncomfortable than she'd ever been in her life, her clothes soaked through with perspiration and her exposed skin covered with sticky sap and jungle dirt, red and itching after feeding thousands of hungry mosquitoes. Glancing quickly behind her, she discerned that Mason had fared no better than she and that, from his expression, his disposition was every bit as unpleasant as her own.

The rebel who had spoken to Lou in French earlier now turned to her and instructed them to follow him. Along with his *compadres,* he led Mason and Lou to a tiny, camouflage-spattered tent squatting at the edge of the rebel encampment and ordered them to enter it. Inside, the air was heavy, hot and difficult to breathe, mingled with dust and hundreds of tiny gnats. When Lou finally dropped her arms to her sides, she nearly cried out at the pain that shot through them from having held them on her head for so long. She and Mason were told to sit on the floor and wait until someone came back for them. As Lou dropped down onto the canvas that covered the ground, something big and squishy beneath it crawled to the other side of the tent. She squealed and jumped up, then moved to another place on the canvas, sitting down hard and raising a small cloud of dust. When it cleared, she saw Mason hunkered down in the corner of the tent diagonally opposite her—clearly wanting to put as much distance between them as possible—shaking his head ruefully at what she was sure he considered her typically feminine reaction to something icky.

"It was a rat or something," she said lamely in her own defense. "A really big one."

His eyes met hers for a moment, and she saw that they were full of disappointment and anger. She watched silently while he stood up as straight as he could, forced to stoop because the tent hadn't been constructed to accommodate his six-foot-two-inch height. He took five long strides toward the tent opening and pushed aside the flap, only to be greeted by the all-too-familiar barrel of a rebel rifle. Putting up two hands in the internationally recognized and accepted gesture that meant, "Hey, no problem," Mason let the

flap fall back into place, then returned to his former
restless pose in the corner opposite her. It occurred to
Lou idly that they were positioned as two boxers would
be before coming to the center of the ring to beat the
hell out of each other. Finally, his eyes fastened on hers
in the dim, dirty light of the tent and he sighed.

"Well, Nellie Bly, now what?" he asked through
gritted teeth.

Lou settled her elbows on her knees, placed her head
in her hands, tangled her fingers in the short strands of
her hair and inhaled a long, deep breath. That did
nothing but fill her lungs with dust, and she began to
cough with irregular hacking until she feared her chest
would burst from the effort. Suddenly, she felt a hand
patting and rubbing her back reassuringly, comfort-
ingly, and she looked up to find that Mason was no
longer her adversary but her aide. She smiled at him
gratefully, expelled three more ragged coughs, then
shook her head vigorously and palmed away the tears
that had formed in her eyes as a result of the hacking fit.

"Thanks," she said hoarsely, lifting a hand to let him
know she could breathe on her own. "I'm fine now."

Mason frowned at her. "You sure?"

Lou nodded. "Yes."

Instead of going back to the opposite side of the tent,
Mason sat down beside her, drawing his knees up in
much the same position as she had assumed. For a long
time neither of them spoke, only stared blindly out at
the emptiness enclosed by the four canvas walls. All Lou
could think about was how nice it was going to be when
they got back to the hotel so she could enjoy a very long
soak in a bath full of bubbles. She'd make sure she used
an entire bottle of the spicy-smelling stuff the hotel
provided, and the water would be very cold, she thought

as she felt a trickle of sweat stream down her neck to settle between her breasts. After her bath, she would call room service and order prime rib, new potatoes, steamed asparagus and a basket of piping hot dinner rolls. For dessert, she wanted Häagen-Dazs key lime and cream. Yeah, that's it, she decided. A whole pint of it. Two pints even. Why not? Then she'd take another cool bath and—

"Lou?"

She was reluctant to let Mason interrupt the fantasy of supper and sanitation that had taken root in her mind, but the tone of his voice tugged at something deep inside her. When she looked over at him, it was to discover that the anger in his eyes had been replaced by some softer, more tolerant emotion she was afraid to identify. His pale blue gaze was fixed on her intently, as if he were thinking about the most serious topic in the world. It was all Lou could do to keep herself from reaching a hand out to him.

"What is it?" she asked softly.

"I ... That is ... About last night ..."

She put up a hand to stop the flow of words she knew she didn't want to hear. "Don't, Mason," she pleaded. "You offered a more than thorough explanation of our actions last night. Let's not dwell on it, okay? Let's just ..." She sighed quietly. "Let's just forget that last night ever happened, all right?"

A flicker of something stark and angry flashed in his eyes at her suggestion, but it was gone before Lou could identify what it might be. After a moment, he nodded once quickly, then seemed about to say something else. Unfortunately, whatever it might have been was abruptly cut off by the entry of one of the rebels into the tent, his greeting the usual pointing of his rifle at their chests.

"Levez-vous!" he ordered them.

Both Lou and Mason stood as instructed, then followed the man back outside, squinting against the bright light of the afternoon sun. Once more they were told to put their hands on their heads, and once more they were accompanied by the usual gang of four when led across the compound. At one point, the lead rebel's steps slowed, and the man turned to gaze back at the two of them curiously. For a moment he seemed to be weighing an important decision in his mind, then as if making it, he took a new course to the left that led back into the jungle. After walking about a hundred yards, he stopped before a huge mechanical device, a menacing and dangerous-looking construction of twisted metal and rusting parts.

Mason had seen some pretty scary things in his years as a journalist and had found himself in some pretty frightening situations. But never had he been threatened with physical pain beyond what came with reasonable expectation in the line of duty. In other words, he had never been tortured. At that moment, however, he was quite certain his luck in that department had finally run out. He'd never before seen anything like the machine looming above the small group, but there was no doubt in his mind that it was capable of creating the most unspeakably excruciating pain known to humankind. For the first time he could ever remember, Mason Thorne honestly wondered if he were about to die. But superseding that fear was one that preoccupied him even more. As much as he was worried for himself, it was nothing compared to the terror that raced through him at the thought of Lou being exposed to something so heinous and deadly.

As his heart leapt into his throat, Mason turned to speak to Lou for what he feared might possibly be the last time, but was shocked into silence by the expression on her face. Of all the responses he'd expected to see reflected there—fear, terror, regret, anguish, sorrow—none of them would have caused her to smile as broadly as she was smiling now.

"What is it?" he asked her anxiously.

Lou dropped her hands from the back of her head and began to chuckle. "I don't believe it."

"What is it?" he repeated urgently.

She stared at the huge contraption for a moment longer, then turned back to look at Mason as if she'd forgotten he was there. But still she said nothing, only continued to chuckle in earnest.

"Lou, dammit," Mason ground out. "What the hell is that thing?"

"Oh, Mason," she finally said through her giggles. "It's...it's a still."

Chapter Seven

"It's a *what?*" Mason asked incredulously.

Lou shrugged matter-of-factly, as if they'd just stumbled onto the most common piece of machinery in the world, trying unsuccessfully to hide her smile. "It's a still," she repeated simply. "You know, a home-grown version of a distillery."

"I know what a still is, Lou," he informed her haughtily. "I've just never seen one quite so...elaborate before."

Lou nodded and took a few steps closer, seemingly oblivious now to the rebels who still turned their rifles toward them. "It *is* a rather archaic design," she agreed. "But not a lot different from my great-grandfather Lofton's."

"Your great-grandfather was a moonshiner?" Mason asked, wondering why he was so surprised by the revelation. Certainly at this point, there was little he should expect from Lou that would surprise him. What was actually amazing was that he found himself forgetting more and more frequently that she had come from a tiny, backward mountain community where things like stills were nothing out of the ordinary.

"Oh, yes," Lou replied with what he was sure was extreme pride in her heritage. "Great-grandfather had one of the best recipes in the Appalachian and Blue Ridge mountains combined. People came from miles around to sample it." She turned back to Mason with an impish smile. "If I'd known this still was so close, I could have come back here and whipped us up a little nightcap last night. That is, of course, as long as you don't mind your liquor being aged twelve minutes instead of twelve years."

Mason shook his head in wonder. This was all becoming just a little bit too surreal. "So why have these guys brought us here?"

"Good question," Lou said before posing the same query to the rebel leader in French. After a lengthy discussion with the other man, she turned back to Mason and explained, "He says it's broken. They want to know if either of us knows how to fix it."

He couldn't believe what he was hearing. Lou had been right earlier when she'd described meeting up with the rebels as a journalistic opportunity of major proportions. However, this was ridiculous. Here they were lost in the jungle on an island plagued by political tension and warring guerrilla factions, and of all the rebels who could have kidnapped them and given them a sensational story, he and Lou had to be carried off at gunpoint by a band of party animals who wanted them to repair an outdated still in time for happy hour. He threw up his hands in surrender. "Don't look at me," he said tightly. "Stills aren't exactly at the top of my list of things to adjust with my Craftmaster tools."

Lou rattled off something else in French to the four rebels, and they lowered their rifles as she approached the metal monstrosity. She fiddled with some of the twisted copper coils, bending them first one way and then another, and adjusted several tubes that went from what looked like a cast-iron cooking pot to a huge wooden vat before finally emptying into a small aluminum washtub. At one point, she even scaled one of the big palm trees so that she could get an aerial view of the contraption. When she scrambled back down again, it was with a new sense of purpose, and she went back to one of the mangled copper coils.

"Here's your problem," she told the rebel, then realized she was speaking in English. She pulled the coil from its fastening and approached him with it. *"Voilà,"* she said simply, bending it for his closer inspection before gesturing back toward the still. *"Je sais le problème."*

Several moments of animated conversation followed, and to Mason's amazement, Lou and the rebel leader went to work fixing the still together. Mason spent the hour that followed seated on the spongy, damp ground beneath a palm tree, marveling at the sight before him—Lou and the four rebels hunched over the still as if conducting the most analytical and momentous of scientific experiments. They talked and laughed like old chums, and when the operation was complete, each of the men slapped Lou on the back as if she were one of them. Any minute now, Mason thought dizzily, one of them was going to say something about it being Miller Time, and then he was really going to lose it. Instead, they all turned to Mason with big smiles on their faces and said nothing.

Finally, Lou broke away from the group and came to sit beside Mason. There was a streak of dirt decorating her cheek, and her bangs were plastered to her forehead with sweat. Her olive shirt and pants were beginning to take on a gray tinge and, if he were perfectly honest, he had to admit that she was becoming nearly as gamey as he. Crazily, he realized she had never looked lovelier in her life. Her brown eyes were bright with the light that comes from having done a good job, and she had clearly enjoyed herself immensely since stumbling upon the still. No doubt she and the rebels were indeed old chums by now, and Mason couldn't help but feel a little sorry for the four men. They'd obviously become victims of Lou's easy charm and subtle beauty, and would probably be pining for her for a long time to come. Well, that was just too bad, he thought further, because Lou Lofton was his.

Oh, no, she wasn't, he immediately corrected himself. She wasn't his at all—not like that anyway. He didn't want her to be. Lou Lofton was his to watch out for and take care of, that was all. He wanted none of this romantic mine-yours business cluttering up their relationship.

"The operation was a success," Lou informed him, disturbing his daydream. "Manolo, Étienne, Francisco and Bruce are all very pleased with how it all turned out."

"Bruce?" he asked, still distracted by the thoughts that had been troubling him since awakening beside Lou the night before. "Manolo, Étienne, Francisco and *Bruce?*"

"His mother was born in New Jersey," Lou said conversationally, as if that should explain everything. "Are you ready to go?"

He blinked at her in confusion. "Go where?"

"Back to the Jeep."

His confusion deepened and he narrowed his eyes at her suspiciously. "Just like that?"

Lou nodded. "Just like that."

"They're letting us go?"

"Uh-huh."

"Why?"

"They like us," she told him. "They were grateful we helped them out, and now they're letting us go."

"We're free?" The concept still wasn't clear to him. He had actually begun to kind of enjoy their situation and had been making mental notes about the story he would write as a result.

"We're free," Lou confirmed. "Not only did I bargain our release from them, but I got a lot of information that's going to make a great news story."

The mention of a bargain brought Mason's attention back to the conversation with a start. "What kind of bargain? Just what did you promise them?"

"I gave them Great-grandfather's recipe for white lightning."

"You what?"

"But I had to make a few alterations because corn doesn't grow on Sonora. They have to use bananas or papayas or mangoes, and the texture and sugar content in those are completely wrong. I only hope the changes work out. All in all, it might be best to make our getaway before they get back from their fruit-picking expedition in the jungle, just in case something goes wrong."

Mason looked at her for a long time before her meaning permeated his foggy brain. "Point taken," he finally said, rising from his seat on the ground and extending a hand to help Lou up from her position.

She smiled gratefully as she settled her palm warmly in his, then allowed herself to be pulled forward. The force Mason exerted to aid her, however, exceeded what was actually necessary, and Lou wound up pressed against him in a position whose intimacy rivaled what they had shared the night before. She didn't move away from him, only gazed up at Mason from beneath long, wheat-colored lashes, as if both asking him what he wanted and offering him everything she had to give. For a moment, he allowed the close contact to continue, loving the way Lou felt pressed against him—almost as if she belonged there—and a little unwilling to let her go. But then he realized his state of hygienic collapse was in no way conducive to initiating a romantic liaison—which, of course, he told himself, he had no desire to promote with Lou anyway—and he took an awkward step back.

"We better get going," he said softly.

"Okay," she agreed with a quick nod.

After a few hasty calculations, Mason discovered the trail they had followed to reach the rebel compound, and he and Lou began to backtrack toward where they had made camp the night before. All the while he forced himself to focus his concentration on getting them safely back to the Jeep and then to Madriga, and he tried not to think about the woman who kept up the rigorous pace effortlessly behind him. Lou was a real trooper, Mason decided. Maybe Paul Kelly hadn't been so off target when he'd said she was tough as nails. Ever since coming to Sonora, she had remained levelheaded and calm, had behaved exactly as an intelligent, responsible news correspondent should. *He* was the one who had contracted the weird tropical malady, and *he* was the one who had managed to get them hopelessly lost in the hills. And when they had in fact met upon a band of rebels, it had been Lou, not he, who had managed to secure their release. Maybe, he thought, just maybe, he had been wrong about Lou.

Darting a quick glance behind him, he discovered she was keeping up with him quite competently. Before long, they were able to find their way back to the Jeep and hurriedly scrambled inside. Without wasting any more time, Mason briefly prayed that the rebels hadn't drained their gas tank, twisted the key, gunned the engine, smiled broadly and headed back toward the road while Lou studied the map. When she told him to head south, he did so immediately, refusing to consider the fact that it was the first time he'd ever followed instructions from Lou without hemming and hawing and questioning them first.

It wasn't until a full twenty-four hours later that Lou began to finally feel like herself again. As she soaked in a sandalwood-scented bath before meeting Mason for dinner—the third such bath she had enjoyed since they had arrived back at the hotel shortly before seven last night—she thought about everything that had happened since landing on Sonora five days ago, and she realized she was no closer to understanding what was going on now than she had been before. Rubbing her forehead gently in an attempt to ease the migraine she felt threatening, Lou sighed dramatically and sank farther down into the hot water.

What on earth had happened out in the jungle two nights ago? she wondered yet again. She was still at a loss to know. Mason had never, ever shown any kind of interest in her as a woman before, had never indicated that he felt any kind of physical attraction toward her. So just what had been going through his mind when he had reacted to her with a passion and desire that put her own to shame? Lou didn't try to deceive herself that she hadn't instigated the entire episode by entwining herself around Mason in her sleep. And of course pulling him over on top of her had done nothing but make the situation even more volatile. But he hadn't pulled away from her, she reminded herself. He hadn't even tried. And when she'd offered him a kiss, he had accepted it wholeheartedly. By the time the interlude had ended, they had both been breathless and hot. There was no way their embrace could have escalated to the point that it had unless both of them had been very willing, very active participants.

So what did that make her? Lou wondered. A seductress? She almost laughed out loud at the thought. Halouise Lofton of Hack's Crossing, West Virginia, seducing Mason Thorne, Washington, D.C.'s leading ladykiller? Oh, really, it was just too funny to even consider. The girls back home would have a screaming fit. But there had to be something about her that Mason found attractive, otherwise he would have pushed her away long before things had gotten out of control. Then again, she conceded, maybe what he'd said to explain away their actions did hold a ring of truth. Tensions had been running high between them all day, and their senses were heightened because of the anxieties that had come with their predicament. But two people didn't come on to each other as she and Mason had that

night, in a virtual explosion of sexual fireworks, just
because they were a little tense and anxious. That was
silly. There had to be more to it than that. There just
had to be. Mason must feel at least *some* attraction to
her. Mustn't he?

"I wish I knew," she mumbled aloud to no one in
particular.

Only when her bath water began to grow cool did Lou
put an end to her sojourn in the tub. She finally felt as
if the last of the grime had been erased from her body,
and her mood lightened considerably as a result. As she
toweled off and entered her bedroom to dress for dinner, she contemplated once again the possibility that
Mason might see something in her that sparked his interest in a more physical manner. If there was such a
quality within her and if she could figure out what
it was, then all she had to do in order to...
arouse... Mason's interest would be to play that feature up more fully. She thought about it for a long time
as she chose her outfit, identifying all of her best traits
and analyzing Mason's reaction to them over the years.

She knew it couldn't be her looks because they were
average at best and Mason had dated some of the most
breathtakingly beautiful women she had ever seen. Even
if most of them were bimbos. Maybe it was because she
was a fast thinker. Lou liked to believe she had a quick
wit, but Mason seldom responded to it positively. In
fact, they'd probably gotten into more arguments over
her tendency to shoot her mouth off than over anything else. She was intelligent, too, she knew, but Mason never even seemed to notice that fact, let alone
appreciate it. With every characteristic she named about
herself that she liked, she found an equally relevant

reason to be certain Mason would dismiss it. Staring at herself in the mirror, wearing the white shirt and khaki trousers she had purchased in town that afternoon, Lou decided she had absolutely no idea what it was about herself that Mason might have responded to in the jungle. With a defeated sigh, she began to think that maybe he'd been right all along, and the fact that she'd been a convenient woman at a time when he'd felt a little tense may have been the only reason he had turned to her in heated passion.

"Great," she mumbled, feeling disheartened. "Now on top of everything else I've become to Mason—little sister, fan club, student and sidekick—I can add 'convenient' to the list."

A knock at the connecting door alerted her to the fact that her mentor and idol had arrived. Fixing conservative gold hoop earrings into her ears, Lou opened the door to find Mason looking his usual handsome best in his usual journalistic attire, and she couldn't help but smile when she realized they resembled bookends. He blatantly scanned her clothing several times before his eyes settled on her face, and she could have sworn they were lit with affectionate laughter when they did so. But the flicker of amusement was gone before she could be sure she'd seen it, only to be replaced by the normal expression of detached interest he always seemed to assume in her presence.

"All set?" he asked.

"Yes, I'm starving," she replied with an eager nod.

"You know, we have less than a week left on the island," he mentioned offhandedly as they made their way across the lobby toward the dining room. "The elections will be held Wednesday. If you want, after the polls close, we could go the whole tourist route and take in some of the local attractions. I'd hate for you to miss out on the nightlife, especially since this is your first trip out of the States. No one at the paper said we couldn't enjoy ourselves while we're here.''

Lou's heart skipped a beat at the prospect of spending the evening with Mason on an honest-to-goodness date. Despite their weekly Tuesdays out in Washington, the two of them seldom did anything but eat dinner and then go back to one or the other's apartment to watch a rented movie. Occasionally they went to a show at the Kennedy Center or one of the universities, and sometimes in the summer, they attended the free musical performances offered on the Capitol grounds. But those things were generally spur-of-the-moment decisions or enjoyed along with other people from the newspaper. They never had the feel of a real date. Wednesday night would be her chance, Lou thought. And for more than just an evening out with Mason. Wednesday night would provide her with the opportunity to once and for all identify what it was that Mason saw in her and use it to attempt a—the word almost stuck in her throat, even only thinking it—seduction.

Could she do it? she wondered. Oh, certainly she could spend an evening with Mason doing the tourist thing and having a wonderful time. But could she really seduce him? Even if she decided she was physically capable of such an act, would she be able to go through with it emotionally? What if Mason rejected her before she even got started? Or worse, what if he went to bed with her only to cast her aside when he decided she was small potatoes compared with the banquets he normally enjoyed with other women? Then again, how was she ever going to know unless she tried?

"I'd like to," she said, hoping her voice didn't sound as shaky as she felt, not sure if she was answering Mason's question or her own. "I'd like to very much."

The remaining days seemed to pass in a blur of excitement and activity. Lou and Mason ran themselves ragged day and night doing what newspaper reporters do, documenting the political atmosphere of Sonora, recording the opinions of the population, investigating government documents made available to them, writing and filing stories about everything they saw and heard. Mason's stories were straightforward, factual accounts, while Lou's stories leaned toward human interest and a more intimate view of the island culture and customs. On Tuesday night, the eve of the elections, Lou was even granted an interview with General Marco Papitou himself. The Sonoran leader had been reluctant to talk to the international press because of his fear that he would be misquoted or misrepresented. He'd kept track of the articles about Sonora that were appearing in all the major international newspapers, however, and had been very impressed by some of the ones that he saw in the *Capitol Standard*. He had considered them the most accurate in their portrayal of his homeland and had appreciated the scope of human emotion that pervaded every piece. When he'd read the name Halouise Lofton in the byline and realized she was still on Sonora to cover the elections, he had arranged for the interview to take place.

When Lou was first contacted and invited to do the interview, she was dumbfounded. Providing household hints and covering social affairs in no way prepared her to take on a project of such magnitude, regardless of her recent experiences on Sonora and the

well-received articles she'd written as a result. But when
she arrived armed with her camera, tape recorder, pad
and pencil to conduct what would be her first interview
with a person of international political importance, she
found the general to be an expansive and very cooperative subject. He answered her questions thoughtfully
in an honest, forthright manner, was in no way conde-
scending and seemed not to take issue with her youth or
gender. When she left his office at the governor's pal-
ace, it was with the opinion that Marco Papitou was a
well-educated, caring man who claimed all the wisdom
and drive necessary to put his island homeland back
together again and turn it into the proud nation it had
never had the chance to be. When she called Paul Kelly
at the newspaper to file her story, he announced proudly
that her interview would be featured on the front page
of the "International Forum" section the following
Sunday, and would no doubt be picked up by a syndi-
cate to be printed all over the world. Lou was ecstatic.
This trip had exceeded even her wildest dreams.

Mason, on the other hand, became more sullen with
each passing day. Try as she might, Lou couldn't put her
finger on what might be causing his moodiness. His
withdrawal had begun when Paul called to tell them
about Lou's invitation to interview Marco Papitou.
Mason had been as aghast as she, then had proceeded
to be very vocal in his belief that Lou was in no way
prepared to take on such a task. An interview with the
general, he had said, was of major international concern and should not be conducted by a novice. He'd
offered to do it himself, certain she would ask all the
wrong questions and then misconstrue everything she
heard in reply. And when Lou had insisted she *was* go-

ing to do the interview herself, Mason had only become that much angrier.

By Wednesday night the polls were closed, the elections were over and the only thing left was to discern the winner when all the votes had been counted. The tallying wouldn't be officially completed until the following morning, but there was little doubt in anyone's mind that Marco Papitou would be elected Sonora's first president. And as far as Lou was concerned, there wasn't a better man for the job. During her stay on Sonora, she'd worked hard to provide well-documented, true accounts of all that was going on. And in the long run, she thought now as she readied herself for her night out with Mason, she had done a damned good job while she was here. Even Paul Kelly had told her that some of her stories might possibly command Pulitzer consideration. But Mason's comments had been reserved at best, and had more or less consisted of his opinion that Lou was nothing more than a pawn in the general's propaganda game.

"And you, Mason Thorne," she said to her own reflection in the mirror, "are simply too pigheaded to admit that you were wrong."

As if summoning him with her quiet statement, there was a quick, loud knock at the door to her hotel room. Lou rose and glanced at herself one final time in the mirror, tugging down the red dress she had worn on her date with Albert Michaud so many nights ago. Had she known then that her meeting with the Sonoran diplomat would lead to all that she had experienced since coming to the island, Lou might have seriously entertained thoughts of running blindly in the opposite direction. No, that wasn't true at all, she knew. Despite some less-than-satisfying experiences, Lou wouldn't have missed this trip for the world. Because as a result of coming to Sonora and interviewing Marco Papitou, Halouise Lofton was a newswoman of international significance who commanded attention in the press corps. Now if she could get Mason to admit that, her life would be complete.

She opened the door to find a version of him she seldom saw, Mason dressed for a tropical evening out, wearing creamy trousers and a shirt the color of the Caribbean, a silk tie splashed with the bright hues and patterns of jungle blossoms knotted at his throat. With his tan and sun-washed gold hair, he was more handsome than Lou had ever seen him before, and she began to regret that she had chickened out on her decision to attempt a seduction.

"You look nice," she told him, feeling her heart skip a little at the icy fires that danced in his blue eyes when his gaze raked her up and down several times.

"You're wearing that dress again," he replied simply, although this time, his voice held none of the censure it had contained the night she'd been wearing it for Albert.

"I like this dress."

"So do I," Mason agreed. Too much, he added to himself.

Lou's cheeks pinkened as her eyes widened in surprise. "I, um . . . I'll just get my purse."

Mason watched Lou as she collected her things, marveling at the change that had come over her during their stay on Sonora. She'd gotten some sun, thanks to their trip to the interior of the island and their occasional quick escapes to the beach. Her ivory skin was touched with just a hint of bronze, and her pale brown hair was lit with sunny, silver highlights. But that wasn't what made her lovelier now than she'd ever been before, he thought. Something else in Lou had changed this week, something of colossal magnitude. When she turned back to smile at him with a radiant, confident smile, it finally hit him what it was. Lou Lofton had come out of her shell. She had at long last succeeded in leaving the poor, scared, lonely mountain girl behind, and had allowed herself to become the self-assured, knowledgeable woman she'd been struggling to be for years. He wasn't sure exactly when it had happened or how, but with no small amount of guilt, he realized it had been through no help from him. In fact, now that he thought about it, he understood that the changes in Lou had probably come about despite him. When the hell had it all occurred, and what was he going to do about it now?

"So what do you have planned for me this evening?" Lou asked innocently as she preceded him through the door and down the corridor toward the elevators.

"What?" he asked absently, distracted by the licentious thoughts her question aroused in his muddled brain.

"You promised we'd do the whole tourist thing," she reminded him. "I was just wondering what that might involve."

"Oh, that." He was surprised to discover that he wasn't as relieved as he thought he'd be that she wasn't referring to plans of a more intimate nature. "I thought we'd start with dinner at a little place up the beach, then maybe go to a show, hit a casino or two, go dancing, whatever suits you. Any of that sound good?"

When Lou smiled at him, Mason's heart dropped into his shoes. Where had she learned to smile like that? he

wondered. It was as though she knew everything he was
thinking and was more than willing to go along with
whatever he proposed.

"All of it," she replied enthusiastically as the elevator doors closed behind them. "Let's do it all."

Mason wanted to laugh maniacally at her willingness
to explore the gamut of human experiences with him,
especially when he realized all he had to do was push the
Stop button on the elevator's panel to completely iso-
late them from the rest of the world. Then when he had
Lou alone, he could perform all the erotic activities with
her that had been plaguing his dreams for the past few
nights. As the elevator slowly descended, he relived in
his mind each and every one of the feverish, disturbing
visions that had accompanied his sleep, and he noted
how perfect and slender Lou's throat was, how it just
called out to him to place a soft kiss right at the juncture of her neck and shoulder, and then . . .

It was a good thing the Hotel San Sebastian only had
four floors, Mason thought when the elevator doors
opened once again with a muffled *ding*. Otherwise, he'd
be having some significant difficulties explaining to Lou
why he was nibbling on her earlobe. When they exited
the hotel lobby and entered the street, Mason tucked
Lou's hand into the crook of his arm as if it were the
most natural thing in the world to do. He told himself
it was because he wanted to avoid losing her among the
throngs of people that crowded into the streets of
Madriga to celebrate their first election and not because he simply wanted to have her close to him.

Despite the darkness that had settled over the city, the
temperature hovered at just below eighty degrees and a
warm breeze rustled the palms that lined the avenue and
nudged Lou's hair onto her forehead. She brushed the

silky strands back into place, wondering about the curious expression on Mason's face and the unmistakable heat that still smoldered in his eyes. Something about him was different tonight, she thought. Something in him had changed. His dark mood had lifted, and now he seemed to be back to his easygoing self again. Gradually, she began to relax, too. It was a beautiful night, clear and balmy, with the clean, salty scent of the sea hanging in the air to remind her of her exotic, romantic surroundings. For a fleeting moment, Lou thought this must be how it felt to be on a honeymoon, then wondered at the whimsical turn of her reflections. She was here on an assignment for the newspaper, she reminded herself. She was a reporter, not a honeymooner.

"I thought we might have dinner at La Mer," she heard Mason say from what seemed like a thousand miles away, and she pulled herself out of her rambling reverie. "It's well-known locally for its seafood. But I promise, this time I'll skip the conch fritters." He turned to her then with an affectionate smile, and she would have given the world to know what he'd been thinking about for the past several minutes. "I think you're really going to like it."

Lou smiled back a little uncertainly, then nodded. "That sounds nice."

Actually "nice" was something of an understatement for the restaurant they entered, and Lou more than liked it. Situated at the end of a pier and built so that most of the structure lay below sea level, La Mer was an eating establishment like none she had ever visited. The maître d' led them through a dining room decorated in muted, calming shades of pale green and lavender to a table by a window that, instead of looking out over the ocean, looked out into it. Beyond the window lay a small reef dotted by corals of purple, yellow and pink whose population consisted of small damselfish darting around in a blur of red, blue, orange and green, seemingly unimpressed by the strange denizens on the other side of the glass. Lou had never seen anything like it and was delighted that Mason would bring her to such a place.

"It's wonderful, Mason," she told him with a shy smile after they had been seated and ordered cocktails. "I like it very much."

"I kind of thought you would. This place suits you. It's full of life, color and mystery, and sitting here makes me feel like nothing in the world will ever go wrong again."

Lou was stunned by his uncharacteristically candid statement. Never had Mason let her know she had such an effect on him. "That's very sweet of you to say," she told him quietly, not sure she trusted her voice to rise to its usual timbre. "I... Thank you, Mason."

He seemed genuinely puzzled. "For what?"

How could she tell him? Lou wondered. How could she ever begin to list everything she had to be thankful for because of him? She decided it would be impossible even to try, so she just shook her head and smiled sadly. "For surprising me," she said simply.

And way back in the corners of her mind, Lou couldn't help but hope that this would only be the first of a number of surprises he had in store for her this evening.

Chapter Eight

The Copa Playa Bar and Nightclub was as excessive
and showy a tourist attraction as anything Lou had seen
since arriving on Sonora. There were flashing strobe
lights that changed her dress from red to purple to orange, glittering mirror balls that threw fractured bits of
shimmering light everywhere, and a dance floor that
seemed to shift and undulate more than the people
crowding onto it. The people themselves put on something of a show, too, dressed in everything from the
standard tropical wear of Hawaiian shirts and jeans to
outfits that she herself would consider too skimpy to
even be swimwear. The festive atmosphere that was already so common on Sonora was made even more so by
the triumph of democracy sweeping across the island,
and the Sonoran nationals were going out of their way
to commemorate the occasion with a massive celebration that night.

Mason had suggested he and Lou end the evening helping them do so, dancing off what was left of their massive dinner at La Mer before returning to their hotel less than a block away. However, why he had done so remained a mystery to Lou because ever since dinner, he had been annoyed about something. As far as she was concerned, returning to the hotel hours ago would have been preferable to watching him slip farther into his dark mood. But when she had suggested just that, Mason had refused, once again citing the fact that it was Lou's first time out of her native country and he didn't want to hinder her enjoyment of the trip.

Lou sighed and rattled her swizzle stick around in her quickly diluting drink. He would never understand that where she was had nothing to do with how much she was enjoying herself. She could be happy doing anything as long as it was with Mason. Glancing over she saw him staring down into his own drink as if it had turned into a loathsome insect. Lou shook her head and reconsidered. She could be happy doing anything with Mason as long as he wasn't in a lousy mood.

As if he could feel her assessing him, he snapped his head up to meet her gaze. For a long moment he said nothing, only looked at her as if she were the one to blame for his having such a terrible time this evening. Finally, he lifted his drink to his lips, took a mighty sip and gritted his teeth. Lou knew the feeling. For all its expensive paraphernalia, the Copa Playa Bar and Nightclub poured pretty cheap liquor.

"Having a good time?" Mason asked, still clenching his jaw. He had to shout to be heard, but his tone of voice made Lou feel that he couldn't care less what her answer would be.

"Swell," she yelled back in response over the thumping bass line of the heavy-metal music blaring from the speaker behind her. "The time of my life."

"What?" he asked, putting a hand up to his ear.

"Terrific," she said a little more loudly. "But I'd be having more fun if we were dancing."

He shook his head. "I hate dancing."

"Then why did you suggest we come here?" Lou wanted to know, thinking it was an excellent question.

Mason shrugged. "I figured you'd enjoy it."

"How can I enjoy it if I'm not even dancing?"

"Why does anyone enjoy going to a nightclub?"

"Because they dance," she informed him.

"Then go ahead and dance," he encouraged her. "Hell, I'm not stopping you."

As if he'd been waiting for such a cue, a young man stepped up on the other side of Lou and tapped her on the shoulder. When she looked up at him, it was into a pair of laughing green eyes below a thick thatch of unruly, sandy-colored hair. The newcomer was probably younger than she was, she thought, certainly no older, and he was smiling as if he'd been turned loose on the world for the first time.

"Want to dance?" he asked her, offering no indication that he even saw Mason seated at the table across from her.

Lou's initial instinct was to decline, but suddenly, some perverse sense of poetic justice made her reconsider. It was as if the gods had offered her this young man as a sign to rebel against Mason. Risking a quick glance in his direction, she saw him fixing her with an impressive scowl and grinned.

"Sure, I'd love to dance," she replied to the offer. "My big brother here won't mind, will you, bro?"

Before he had a chance to say anything, Lou was up and out of her seat, heading toward the dance floor hand in hand with her new escort. He tugged her gently through the throngs of writhing bodies, then spun her deftly around once before assuming the stance of a truly expert dancer.

"My name's Billy," he introduced himself, still smiling his dazzling smile.

"I'm Halouise," she replied, smiling back.

"Nice to meet you."

Billy clearly had no other motive than to trip the light fantastic with Lou, and he was indeed a very good dancer. The two of them worked up a sweat that had little to do with the heat of the club, their bodies swaying and gyrating to a number of lively reggae tunes and sambas that followed one after another. By the time the disc jockey chose a mellower number, a decidedly American tune, they were both laughing and giddy and ready to slow down. Lou stepped into the circle of Billy's arms with a natural grace, a gesture he didn't seem inclined to dispute. Just as they took their first few steps, however, a large hand clapped over Billy's shoulder next to Lou's slender one, and they both looked up to find Mason impeding their effort to dance.

"Mind if I cut in?" he asked, although there wasn't an ounce of inquisitiveness in his question. It was clearly a statement that brooked no argument.

Billy had the decency to look regretful of the interruption, but was obviously too much of a gentleman to decline an older brother the opportunity to dance with his sister. "No, of course not," he said to Mason as he released his partner and stepped aside. Turning to Lou, he added, "Maybe we can pick up where we left off later?"

"I don't think so," Mason answered for her. "Mom and Dad would never forgive me if I let little Halouise stay out too late. She just catches her death of cold when she's out in the night air, don't you, Halouise?"

Lou made a face at him, but told Billy, "Thanks, but I don't think so. We really should be getting back to the hotel soon."

Billy smiled at her wistfully. "My loss," he said as he disappeared into the crowd.

"Your gain," Mason muttered in his direction after Billy was gone. "You get to live."

Lou offered him a withering look. "Mason—" she began, but was quickly cut off. Not by any verbal argument she might have expected him to throw at her, but by the physical presence of him when he yanked her body flush against his. Suddenly Mason surrounded her, and she was nearly overcome by the feel of him everywhere. His big arms were wrapped possessively around her waist, pulling her close, her breasts were crushed against his chest, her legs nearly tangled with his. Even in her high heels, she had to look up to see his face, and the expression clouding it was less than reassuring. It was a look she'd seen him offer other women often enough, but one he had never turned on her—the look of a predator, pure and simple.

"Mason?" she tried again. This time her voice had lost all of its venom, and what she had intended to be a threat came out sounding like a plea.

Mason loved the breathy, restless quality Lou's voice had adopted when he'd pulled her close, but didn't reply to her unvoiced question. Instead, he pressed one hand intimately over the small of her back, then ran his open palm slowly over the little red dress that had been taunting him all night, up along the length of her spine until he came into contact with the bare flesh between her shoulder blades. His fingers inched up to her nape, along the slender column of her throat, then settled in her hair to tuck her head into the hollow below his chin. He felt as much as heard her sigh in contentment, and he smiled that her feelings seemed to reflect his own.

Holding Lou like this seemed like the one thing to go right in a night full of wrongs. Ever since encountering her at her door to find her wearing the dress that blatantly cried out her womanhood, Mason had been more than a little agitated. Everything about her tonight somehow seemed different. He'd sat across from her at the restaurant, watching as she sipped her wine and tasted her food, only to become entranced by the crimson ring of lipstick on her glass and the way her tongue flicked out over her upper lip from time to time. It hadn't helped matters at all when he'd felt himself growing hard just observing her while she ate. God help him, all he'd been able to do throughout dinner was fantasize about what it would be like to sweep away their dinner dishes with a forceful hand and make wild, passionate love to Lou on the table.

His fingers clenched now at the memory, a gesture that only brought her body into closer contact with his own. It wasn't true that he hated to dance as he'd assured Lou earlier, Mason thought while the two of them swayed slowly to the hypnotic music. The reason he had turned her down then had been the very reason he wished he'd been able to stay seated now. Being this close to Lou simply played havoc with his senses. He didn't want to respond to her sexually, but he did. He couldn't help himself. He wasn't sure when it had happened, or how or why, but sometime during this trip— or maybe even before it, he wasn't sure anymore—Mason had begun lusting after Lou. Lusting after her as he had no other woman he had ever known, and there had been times when he'd felt pretty damned lusty. As he'd watched her dancing with another man, he'd realized something else that was extremely disconcerting. Not only did he want her in the worst possible way, over and over again, but he wanted to make sure no one else had her besides him. So what kind of creep did that make him, he wondered, wanting to take advantage of a naive kid he'd sworn he would always look after?

At the moment, that wasn't a question that was uppermost in Mason's mind. What *was* uppermost in his mind was the way Lou's body felt pressed against his. He was inundated with memories of that night in the jungle when they had both been overcome with whatever madness it had been that resulted in their heated embrace. He wanted more than anything to relive that now, but tried to talk himself out of it. Lou was an innocent, he reminded himself, barely out of school. She trusted him. He was supposed to be her protector, her friend, her counselor. Ah, a little voice piped up in the back of his feverish brain, but Lou is also a woman and a college graduate. She wants you. You could still be her protector, friend and counselor, but you could also be her lover.

No way, he insisted. It was too bizarre to think about. But wasn't it something he had in fact been thinking about ever since they'd come to Sonora? the little voice countered. Wasn't making love to Lou what had been on his mind that morning she came to check on him wearing her lacy lingerie? Wasn't making love to Lou what he'd been obsessed with all evening? Wasn't it precisely what was on his mind at this very moment? Almost as if it were an involuntary action, Mason moved his hands over Lou's back, telling himself his gesture was only an experiment. He just wanted to see how Lou would react, he thought. Just wanted to see how far things would go before one of them would put a stop to it. He only hoped Lou had as much willpower as he was certain he had himself.

Because the dance floor was so crowded and because every couple on it seemed to be utterly wrapped up in themselves, it was easy for Mason to mask his movements. He started at her shoulder blades, then quickly swept his open palms across the bare skin exposed above the zipper of her dress, all the while telling himself he was only imagining the accelerated heartbeat he felt mingling with his own. His hands settled at Lou's waist only momentarily, then began to wander off in separate directions. While one dipped down to cup her fanny, the other crept upward to linger below the swell of one breast. He knew this time he wasn't imagining the pounding of Lou's heart he felt below his thumb, and he wondered crazily what she was thinking about. Hoping to raise some kind of response from her, he dug his fingers into the soft flesh of her derriere and pushed her more intimately against him.

She gasped, and he felt her clench her fingers into convulsive fists before opening them to flatten her palms against his back again. Then slowly, Lou began to do a little exploring of her own. Before he knew what was happening, she was touching him as intimately as he held her, moving her body in the motion of a harmless dance, a gesture that was anything but harmless. The sensation of her abdomen rubbing against his only aroused Mason that much more, and when he felt her lips press little butterfly kisses along his neck and jaw, he feared he would completely lose control. And that was the last thing he wanted to have happen. At least not on the dance floor with the rest of the world looking on. When he lost control, he wanted it to be in the privacy of a hotel room.

"Lou," he rasped out, trying to keep his voice steady, alarmed at the avenue his thoughts had taken.

"What?" she whispered hotly against his throat.

"We have to get out of here."

"Why?"

Because if we don't, he thought wildly, I'll take you right here on the dance floor and really give these folks something to remember about their night out. "Because it's getting late," he told her instead.

Lou could only shake her head in silent denial. Why did he keep doing this to her? Why did he keep tormenting her this way, getting her all worked up only to reject her? If he was just trying to prove that he had complete control over her emotions and could make her senses catch fire by simply touching her, then he had nothing to prove. She would readily admit that was the case. Couldn't he understand that? Couldn't he see what he was doing to her when he drove her to this point and pulled back again?

Well, this was the last time it would happen, she thought. She'd had enough of his body language saying one thing while his verbal language said something else entirely. Pushing herself away from him with as much force as she could muster, Lou met his gaze levelly and said, "What if I'm not ready to go?"

He lowered his eyebrows in confusion and consternation. "What do you mean not ready? It's after midnight."

"And the night is still young," she assured him with what she hoped was a flippant toss of her head.

"Lou, it's late," he insisted.

Her lips thinned. "Quit treating me like a child, Mason. If I want to stay, I'll stay."

"You will not stay," he warned her.

"I will, too."

"Will not."

"Will, too."

"Lou—"

"Mason—"

They stood toe to toe, glaring at each other for long moments until Lou finally took the initiative. Drawing in a deep breath, she asserted, "You can't make me leave."

Mason had no idea what she was up to, but he'd had enough. All he wanted was to get back to the hotel with Lou so he could further analyze the strange attraction that seemed to have overcome them both since arriving on Sonora. However, the way things were going now, they would probably only wind up calling it a night before turning in. Still, if his dreams wanted to pick up where reality was evidently going to end things with Lou, that would be fine. Hell, why should tonight be any different? He was beginning to look forward to his feverish dreams about her. With a heavy sigh, Mason ran a big hand restlessly through his hair and glared back at her.

"I can't make you leave?" he asked in a deceptively quiet voice. "Is that a dare, Lou? That sounds like a dare to me."

"Mason—"

Before she could say anything more, he grabbed her wrist and tugged with just enough force to bring her body against his once again. Then he hooked one arm around her waist and hefted her up over his shoulder, ignoring the cheers and jeers of the audience they'd garnered among the dancers, and refusing to acknowledge Lou's colorful protests. Wrapping his arm firmly around her legs at the knees and clapping his other hand soundly over her bottom, Mason carried his loudly objecting burden to the coat-check room and retrieved Lou's purse, then waved goodbye to the bartenders and bouncers and disappeared into the night.

"I can't believe you did that to me," Lou said softly when they were back in her hotel room. They had ordered nightcaps from room service and now stood out on the balcony overlooking the ocean, drinks in hand. The moonlight sparkled on the dark waters of the Caribbean like a handful of diamonds that had been cast down from the heavens, and from a distance, she could hear the lively strains of the salsa band that had serenaded them on the beach so many nights before, when she had dared to kiss Mason for the first time. The memory of that fiasco did little to make her feel better now. "Of all the humiliating, demeaning, childish things you've ever done to me—"

"Hey, when you behave like a child, you get treated like a child," Mason pointed out.

"I wasn't behaving like a child."

"You offered me a dare. You know better than to do that."

"All I said was that I wasn't ready to leave yet," she reminded him. "Maybe I wanted to stay and dance for a little while longer. Is that such a crime?"

"So dance," he told her.

"What?"

"Dance," he repeated gruffly. "You want to dance so badly, then dance."

Lou took a nervous sip of her brandy and continued to gaze out at the ocean. "There's no one to dance with," she mumbled.

Mason set his own drink on the balcony railing before taking a step away. When Lou looked over at him, he was standing with his arms spread wide as if in invitation.

"I'll dance with you," he offered quietly.

Her heartbeat kicked up the funny rhythm it had pounded out all night, and her breathing became a little shallower. Lou knew exactly what would happen if she went into his arms. She would start thinking about how wonderful it felt to be close to him, then he would start touching her again in that frustratingly intimate way that she didn't understand. And then she'd start kissing him and making a fool of herself. "No, I . . . I don't want to."

"Come on," he cajoled softly. "Dance with me."

As if to punctuate his invitation, the salsa band in the distance began a slow number meant to bring lovers close, and Lou was helpless to refuse him. She promised herself that this time she wouldn't let it go any further than a dance, and she only hoped she could trust herself not to go back on her word. Reluctantly, she set down her drink and went to meet Mason's embrace—and immediately regretted her action. As his arms encircled her waist and he pulled her to him once again, Lou knew without question that she would grant him anything he asked of her. What was it about him that made all rational thought flee her brain whenever she was this close to him? It was as if he exuded some magical aura that enchanted and ensnared her, as if he held some power over her that she was helpless to resist. Is that what love did to people? she wondered. Completely scramble their brains?

She had taken off her high heels as soon as they'd entered the room, so now Mason stood nearly a foot taller than she was. As Lou nestled her cheek against his hard chest, she heard him murmur something that sounded like, "Now that's more like it."

Several silent moments ensued as their bodies swayed gently to the distant strains of mellow music. Finally, Lou could stand it no longer, and said quietly against his shirt, "Mason?"

"Hmm?"

"Why were you so mad at me tonight?"

Her question startled him, but he made no move to distance himself or disrupt their dancing. "I wasn't mad at you, Lou," he told her softly, before adding silently to himself, I was mad at me. "Why would you think that?"

He felt her shrug. "I don't know. Sometimes . . . sometimes the way you look at me makes me think I've done something to annoy you."

Mason drew a deep breath. This conversation wasn't nearly as harmless or unimportant as its tone suggested. How could he tell Lou that sometimes when he looked at her she *did* annoy him? But not because she was making him mad. Because she stirred feelings in him that he wasn't sure he should be having.

Feeling more frustrated than he'd ever been in his life, Mason sighed and said, "Lou, that's not true at all. No one's ever made me feel as good as I feel when I'm with you."

She lifted her head from his chest and smiled up at him, the happiest, most radiant smile he'd ever seen. "Really?" she asked innocently.

How could he lie to her? "Really."

Something in her expression unraveled him then, but Mason wasn't sure what. He only knew he wanted to be closer to Lou, so he lifted his hands to frame her face, then leaned down to take her lips softly with his. It was a kiss that started off gently, chastely, with none of the urgency or hunger he had experienced that night in the jungle upon waking to find Lou's body intimately entwined with his. For a long time he only cupped her jaws with his rough palms, stroking her cheeks with his thumbs, rubbing his lips softly over hers. It occurred to him vaguely that there was something hypnotic about kissing Lou this way, that his heart hummed and his blood sang as if in harmony with the music of the universe. It was an odd sensation, one he'd never experienced before. As if for the very first time in his life, everything was exactly as it was supposed to be.

When Lou spread her palms open on his chest, Mason felt a shimmer of heat race through his body, setting little fires everywhere it went. His heartbeat lunged forward in an irregular rhythm, and his breathing became ragged. He took a step toward her, dropping his hands to her waist as he went, and dared to venture farther in his exploration of her tempting mouth. As his tongue darted out to taste the swell of her lower lip, Mason felt indecision tearing him apart—he prayed Lou would deny him entry even as he desperately hoped she would not. When she uttered a helpless moan and tentatively opened her mouth to encourage his penetration, Mason tasted her as deeply as he could. As her tongue tangled intimately with his, he was stunned to realize that they were both trembling. It was a reaction he had never known with another woman.

Even as he knew it would be madness to continue, Mason wrapped his arms tightly around Lou and pulled her body against his with possessive insistence. He wanted to feel every part of her, wanted to be intimately acquainted with all the curves and valleys that had fascinated him since the night he'd first become so achingly aware of them. He wanted to live out every fever dream he'd had about Lou, wanted to make every fantasy he'd entertained a glorious reality. He wanted to make love with her into the next century and beyond. He wanted ... he wanted it all.

"Lou," he finally rasped out when he was able to tear himself away from her for a moment.

She stared up at him with an expression that said she was no more aware of their surroundings than he was. Her eyes were glazed and starry, and her cheeks were flushed with the heat that comes from an indulgence in dangerous loveplay. Her lips were red and swollen from the intensity of their kisses, and it occurred to Mason that she had never looked lovelier than she was at that very moment. Oh, man, did he want her. He wanted her worse than anything else in the world.

"Lou ..." he tried again, but his voice still came out sounding breathless and uncontrolled. "We have to go inside now."

She shook her head slowly, drawing her eyebrows down in confusion before gripping his shirt in both hands. "Why?"

Mason cupped his hands over her shoulders forcefully, but pushed her away from him only far enough so that he could meet her eyes levelly. He wanted to make sure she understood exactly what was about to happen, wanted to give her every opportunity to back out if she wasn't ready. Unfortunately, he wasn't at all sure how he would react if she did just that. "Because I'm going to make love to you," he asserted in a low, gravelly voice. "And I'd rather have you all alone to myself, away from prying eyes when I do it. I'm kind of old-fashioned that way."

Lou felt her knees buckle at hearing Mason's roughly uttered intentions, and she remained standing only by sinking her fingers into his big biceps to hold herself up. It's going to happen, she thought wildly, feeling a shiver go through her body that had nothing to do with the cool evening breeze. It's finally going to happen. What was she supposed to do? Making love with Mason was something she'd been fantasizing about for six years, something she had rehearsed in her mind thousands of times. And now she couldn't remember a single thing about how she had seen it happening. All she could do was look into Mason's eyes and pray that this wasn't some terrible joke.

She was unable to speak, so she only nodded her agreement. Slowly, Mason danced her back into the room until the distant music completely faded away. He turned her loose long enough to close the French doors behind him, then stood gazing at her as if she were something come to him from a dream. A flash of panic threatened to overtake her as he took a few measured steps in her direction, but Lou reminded herself that what was about to happen was something she had wanted for too long to let it slip away simply because she was a little apprehensive.

Mason didn't say a word as he approached her, only gazed at her as a starving prisoner beheld a sumptuous banquet that was to be his last meal. No man had ever made Lou feel sexually attractive before, she realized, but with one look, Mason had managed to make up for years of having missed that experience. Instinctively, she placed her hand behind her back and reached for her zipper, but Mason paused in front of her and lifted a hand to stop the action.

"Don't," he instructed her softly. "Let me."

Obediently, she dropped her hand back to her side and stood still before him, her eyes never leaving his as she wondered what he wanted her to do. Mason's eyes grew warmer as he circled her waist with his arms once again. This time, however, when he pulled her close, it wasn't for a dance. Instead, he lifted his hands to the top of her dress and with an agonizingly slow gesture, began to draw the zipper down toward her waist. Lou felt her dress gaping open as he went, felt Mason's warm fingers skimming over her bare back all the way down to where the opening ended just below the small of her back. Gently, he gripped both sides of the fabric and pulled them apart, pushing the dress down her body until it pooled in a puddle of red around her ankles.

Lou felt heat darken her cheeks as she watched Mason watching her. She hadn't bothered with any hosiery because of the heat and the light tan she'd acquired while on Sonora. And because her dress was sleeveless and she hadn't wanted to worry about bra straps showing, Lou had chosen to wear a strapless bra. A red lace, demicup strapless bra, she recalled now. With matching bikini panties. The look on Mason's face as he studied her from head to toe let her know in no uncertain terms that her selection of lingerie came as something of a surprise to him.

When Mason first saw exactly how perfect and luscious Lou was under the little red dress in her little red underthings, he wanted to cry out in celebration. Then it occurred to him again that she seemed to wear some

awfully progressive underwear for a shy kid who'd
come from the mountains, and his frown returned.

"Dammit, Lou, where do you get this stuff?" he
whispered roughly. "Why? Why do you get this stuff?
Is there . . ." He took a deep breath and prepared himself for the worst. "Is there someone you've been seeing? Someone I should know about?"

He was so blind to the obvious, Lou thought with an
affectionate smile. Inhaling a shaky breath, she told
him, "I wear this stuff because I like it, Mason. I never
had nice clothes—or nice underwear—when I was
growing up. And as for your other question—" She
lifted one shoulder in an uncertain shrug. "You already know everything there is to know about him."

He nodded absently, unwilling to consider the implications of Lou's statement at the moment as he was too
fascinated by a tiny mole at the very top of her left
breast. He'd never known she had one there. Impulsively, he lifted his index finger to stroke over it, nearly
losing control when he heard Lou's quick intake of
breath and saw her close her eyes. Gratified that he evidently pleased her as thoroughly as she did him, Mason cupped his hand fully over her breast and took a
final step that brought his body into contact with hers.
When he gently squeezed the warm flesh in his palm,
Lou's eyes flew open again and he smiled at her as he
circled her wrist with his fingers and placed her hand
over the knot in his tie.

"Now it's my turn," he announced softly.

Lou understood his meaning, but had no idea how to
go about undressing a man. Telling herself to relax, she
tried to ignore the incredibly erotic sensations he
aroused in her as he continued to caress her breast during her attempt to disrobe him. She raised her other

hand to his throat and deftly loosened the knot, un-threading the loops of silk completely before tossing his tie to the floor. Then she went to work on his buttons, slipping each pearly circle through its matching but-tonhole with the fascination of a child seeing it done for the first time. When she reached his waist, she looked up at Mason's face questioningly only to find that his eyes were alight with a dark blue flame. She swallowed with some difficulty when he aided her by yanking his shirttail free of his trousers and shrugging out of the garment.

Lou had seen Mason without his shirt before, but only in harmless situations such as days spent at the beach or those spent painting her apartment during the summer months. Knowing his chest was bared now so that she could touch it and explore it and do her best to arouse its owner was a realization that brought with it a certain degree of power that Lou found she rather liked. Lifting a hand to spread her palm over the warm flesh spattered with coils of dark gold hair, she discov-ered Mason's heart was racing in much the same way as her own. The knowledge that he was as excited by what was happening as she, encouraged her further, and she flattened her other palm over the muscles rippling po-etically across his hard abdomen. Bending her knuck-les to rake her short fingernails playfully along the solid cords of sinew, Lou discovered to her delight that the closer her hands drew to Mason's belt, the hotter his skin became. When she finally paused at his buckle and began to undo it, his big hand clamped down over hers to cease her motions, and she looked up at him, con-fused.

His tortured expression almost silenced her, but Lou managed to whisper, "What's wrong?"

"This is the point of no return, Lou," he told her in a low, dangerous voice. "We're not playing games anymore. When this belt comes off, the pants are coming with it. And then no one gets out of this room until we're both completely satisfied."

Lou swallowed hard again. "That could take days," she told him with uncharacteristic frankness.

Mason smiled grimly. "Or weeks."

Her eyes widened at the prospect. "It's a good thing room service here is so efficient."

"Last chance, Lou," he said, ignoring her attempt to ease the sexual tension that was bearing down on them like a freight train. "When the zipper goes, I go. And I won't stop until we're both too crazy to know what's real and what's fantasy."

Lou looked at him for several moments before replying, thinking long and hard over what she was about to do. When she finally did respond to Mason's warning, it wasn't with words, but with actions. Impulsively and with maddening slowness, she raked her fingernails up the expanse of muscled torso and chest, then brought her hands back down to the buckle of his belt. Her eyes never left his as she tugged the leather free from its bonds and undid the button at his waistband. Then, fully aware of what she was about to do and welcoming the consequences with all her heart, Lou dropped to her knees before him. Leaning forward to grab the tongue of his zipper with her teeth, she pulled it insistently until it was down as far as it would go.

she straightened her body at the realization of her ink dry skin would need smoothing it, but the eyes—it has lost all of the float beyond them. The perfection of the... Her ... as Mason's eyes rested for a ... when ... A helpless groan the wilderness she had known ... to the portrait the ... The sound of ... to recapture Mason... Very ... he ... and helped ... by to reclaim the first meaning ... With his arms ... he tipped back his head ... gently open a mouth at the sound of her quickening breath ... paced over. She swished up to ... slowly down at her hip ... then he told her ...

Chapter Nine

"I can't believe you did that," Mason rasped hoarsely as Lou released his zipper and settled her hands on his hips.

Frankly, she couldn't believe she'd done it, either, but somehow, the action had just seemed appropriate. Gripping his waistband firmly in both hands, she pulled her body up sinuously along the length of his, circled her arms around Mason's neck and kissed him with all her might. She wove her fingers passionately through his hair, crowded her body as close to his as she could and gave him everything she had to give.

At first, Mason seemed to be too stunned to respond. He stood stock-still as she pulled at his mouth with hers, and he made no move to help her out in any way. Then as if someone had put a lit match to his heart, he wrapped his arms around Lou's waist and squeezed her with crushing familiarity. She felt his fingers wander up her back to the fastening of her bra, deftly unhooking and removing it, then the scrap of red lace fell to the floor beside them. The sensation of her bare skin against his was almost too much for her to endure. And when Mason only pressed her closer, Lou was helpless to prevent the wild little cry that escaped from the back of her throat. The sound only seemed to intensify Mason's ardor, because he leaned forward purposefully to deepen the kiss, bending Lou's body backward over his arm as he did so. With his free hand, he cupped her breast and gave it a gentle squeeze, and at the sound of her quickly indrawn breath, pulled away long enough to gaze hungrily down at her face.

"You are so incredibly beautiful," he told her solemnly. Yet his eyes indicated he was anything but solemn.

When Lou only sighed in response, he smiled ferally and lowered his head to place a maddeningly gentle kiss below the curve of her breast. Electricity shot through her as though she were a live wire on a lake, and she could only roll her head backward, pleading silently for more. Mason didn't disappoint her. Leisurely, almost as if he were distracted, he rubbed his partially opened mouth across the satiny skin of her breast, at times teasing her with his tongue or closing his lips over the warm flesh to taste her. When he finally arrived at the center, he nudged her to life with butterfly soft kisses before drawing her fully into his mouth. All Lou could do was feel the shudders of pleasure ripple throughout her body, making her go hot and weak all over. As Mason's tongue ministered to Lou's breast, his open palm skimmed down over the smooth skin of her belly, pausing only when he encountered the barrier of red lace panties. Without awaiting her encouragement, he

dipped his fingers inside to touch her, an action that
sent Lou's senses spiraling completely out of control.

If there had ever been any doubt in her mind that she
wouldn't be able to go through with this night with
Mason, the way he was holding her now, the way he was
making her feel drove all her fears away. Nothing had
ever felt better, more right, more perfect than being here
with Mason like this. Nothing. And deep down inside,
Lou knew somehow, that as the night wore on, it was
going to exceed her most wondrous dreams.

She gasped when Mason lifted her off the floor without altering his movements and carried her to the bed.
As she teetered on the edge of delirium, torn between
pleading with Mason to put an end to his hungry, demanding onslaught and begging him never to stop, he
made the decision on his own. Laying her on her back
with infinite gentleness, he placed his hands on the
mattress on either side of her head and loomed over her,
studying her with great care. His body was covered with
a slick sheen of perspiration, and his chest rose and fell
with his ragged breathing.

"I have never wanted a woman as much as I want you
right now," he vowed roughly. "Never."

Lou stared at him for a long time before replying,
marveling at the undisguised emotion in his eyes and
loving him more than ever. Finally, she whispered,
"Then take me, Mason. Take me now."

He remained standing only long enough to strip off
his shoes, trousers and briefs, then with a muffled
growl, he threw himself onto the bed beside her. He
kissed her quickly, deeply, on the mouth, then followed it with a line of kisses along her jaw, down her
throat and over her heart. He nipped playfully at the
tender skin of her breast before trailing his tongue down

along the warm expanse of skin on her abdomen, dipped momentarily into her navel and paused at the scrap of red lace that was the only thing left hindering their consummation. With a quick, mischievous glance into her eyes, he buried his hands below her buttocks and clamped his teeth down on the elastic that held her panties in place, then lifted her hips so that he could drag the offending garment down along the length of her slender legs. Lou began to emit a throaty chuckle, but Mason proceeded to cut it off by fastening his mouth over hers once again. After that, Lou felt herself descend into a smoky silver haze of passion.

Mason was everywhere she turned—on top of her, beside her, in front of her, behind her. His mouth tasted every part of her, his fingers touched her in places she'd never touched herself. Surprisingly, she found herself exploring his body with equal fervor and curiosity, and she was amazed at the differences she found. The muscles stretched across his back and over his torso bunched and flexed instinctively whenever she ran her fingers over them, and the ripples of sinew cording his arms and legs became harder and larger with every stroke of her palm. When Mason circled her wrist with his fingers and drew her hand downward over his stomach to his thigh, Lou didn't resist. Instead, she cupped what she could of him in her palm and was stunned by the silky strength she encountered.

As if her gentle caress were more than he could bear, Mason jerked savagely and rolled Lou onto her back, insinuating himself purposefully atop her. With a mighty thrust, he entered her, and Lou cried out at the exquisite pleasure that accompanied his penetration. Quickly he unsheathed himself, lunging forward again to drive himself even deeper. And then he was completely inside her, filling her, and she knew once and for all how incredibly close two human beings could be.

Lou feared for a moment that she'd given voice to her love for Mason then, so helpless was she to keep her feelings inside when they were so utterly out of control. If he heard her, however, he offered no indication. Instead, he continued diligently in his possession of her body, steadily building his rhythm until it was a force that propelled them both into a state of sensual frenzy. Lou met his demanding strokes as eagerly as he made them, insisting on more and rejoicing when he obliged her. They both cried out at the peak of their culmination, then tumbled wildly over the precipice into languid satiation. For long moments they only lay beside each other, gasping for breath, scrambling for thought, startled by the heights that they had hit.

Lou turned to look at Mason, puzzled by the expression on his face when his eyes met hers. Had she not known better, she would have thought he looked almost...fearful. She lifted her hand to his face, brushing back a lock of damp hair from his forehead before laying her palm softly against his cheek. Immediately, his own hand covered hers and he brought her fingers to his lips to kiss them.

"Mason," she whispered, not sure what she wanted to tell him, but somehow needing to hear him speak.

"Ssh," was all he said, placing his other hand gently over her mouth. "No talking. Not yet."

"But—"

Before she could say anything more, he was kissing her again with all the hunger and need that she would have sworn they had just put to rest. But as his lips plied at hers, she was surprised to discover that she, too, still had wants and requirements left unassuaged, empty places that needed to be filled. Mason was right. There would be time for talking later. Now they had something more important to address. As he rolled over to cover her with his hard, hot body once more, Lou encircled him in an embrace she never wanted to end. And as Mason buried himself inside her warmth again, Lou wrapped her arms tightly around him, swearing once and for all that she would never let him go.

Later in the night when it was still full dark, Lou awoke to find herself held warm and safe in Mason's strong arms. His heart was beating quietly and steadily against hers, and his soft, shallow breathing stirred the wisps of hair that had fallen down on her forehead. At first she was sure she must still be asleep, was certain that the sensation of supreme happiness swelling her heart could only be found in her dreams. Then she dared to lift a hand to his cheek, stroking her thumb over his prominent cheekbone, and when he inhaled more deeply and mumbled something in his sleep, Lou knew that she was indeed awake.

"I love you, Mason," she whispered quietly against his throat before closing her eyes to sleep once again. "I love you."

Mason awoke before Lou did some hours later. The room was pale and gray in the first light of the morning, and through the silence he could hear a gentle rain pattering halfheartedly against the windows and French doors. At first he wasn't quite sure where he was and couldn't exactly remember what had led up to this hazy moment just before dawn. Then he turned to the woman sleeping curled up against him like a child and remembered all too well.

He had made love to Lou last night. And it had been the most intense, most erotic, most incredible encounter with another human being he'd ever experienced. He had eagerly enjoyed things with her that he'd never even wanted to explore with other women before. Good God, how had that come about? he wondered now. How had things escalated to such a point between them?

Gazing past the sleeping figure beside him, Mason saw the little red dress in a heap on the floor where it had fallen when he'd pushed it from Lou's body. A few feet away from it lay the red bra that had driven him to near madness. He couldn't see her panties from his position in the bed, but he recalled with alarming clarity that he had removed them from her tantalizing hips with his teeth.

"Oh, hell," he muttered almost silently. How could he have done such a thing?

Lou stirred beside him, inhaling a deep, contented breath before snuggling closer. The crisp, white sheets were now a tangled mass of rumpled fabric at the foot of the bed, and both of their naked bodies were fully exposed to Mason's view. Lou was pressed against him from head to toe, with her head tucked into the hollow created between his chin and shoulder, and her slender calf draped loosely across his shin. One of her hands was curled into a loose fist against his chest while the other lay harmlessly cupping his upper thigh. He pillowed her head with one arm, curling his hand over her opposite shoulder, and spread his other hand open across her bare bottom. There was something altogether disconcerting about seeing himself and Lou entwined in such a blatantly sexual pose, but worse than that, he realized much to his dismay, there was also something incredibly reassuring about it.

No, that was wrong, he corrected himself. There was absolutely nothing reassuring about having taken advantage of Lou because he hadn't been able to control his own lusty response to her. How could he have allowed himself to behave this way? He'd known she had a crush on him. Hell, he'd always known that, ever since she'd come to stay with him in Washington six years ago. It hadn't been a surprising reaction from a nineteen-year-old girl who'd grown up in the mountains and never had a decent example of a man set before her. But Mason had always assumed that when she went to college and got out in the world, her crush on him would fade and go away and she'd find a nice guy her own age with whom she had something in common before settling down. But that hadn't happened. Instead, she had nurtured her crush on him all this time and had come to rely far too much on him for her own happiness.

And he hadn't exactly discouraged her, Mason realized guiltily. There had always been something revitalizing in the knowledge that Lou cared for him so deeply, something that had just made him feel good inside. But she was only a kid, he reminded himself brutally. A kid who was eleven years his junior. A kid he had promised himself he would take care of and look out for. A kid he had sworn would never be hurt again.

Suddenly he remembered that he had awoken one other time in the night, while it was still dark and Lou was asleep beside him. He had thought for a moment he heard her speak, had almost sworn she had told him she loved him. Looking down at her now at the satisfied smile that curled her lips, at the possessive way she wound her body around his, he knew at once that what he thought he'd heard had been real. Lou thought she was in love with him. Now he was really in trouble.

Dammit, how could he have allowed this to happen? he asked himself again. Why hadn't he been able to control himself around her? Then in a desperate attempt to lay the blame elsewhere, he glanced down at Lou once more and silently demanded to know why she had to change so much over the years. Why couldn't she have remained the kid who'd come down from the mountains? Why did she have to grow into an intelligent, independent woman who could tie a man's libido in knots? Hell, why couldn't Lou have stayed nineteen forever?

Feeling more and more panicked with the passage of each minute, Mason wondered wildly how he was going to get out of this one. There was no way this thing with Lou could go any further than it already had. She thought she was in love with him, for God's sake. Couldn't she see what an impossible situation that would be? Not only was he eleven years older than she was, but he was also not the kind of man to settle down with one woman. Lou wanted and deserved everything the world had to offer her—a successful career, a wonderful home and a man who would spend his life being utterly devoted to her. She'd even said she wanted children eventually, and Mason was sure there was some fabulous guy out there who would be more than willing to provide her with them. But that guy wasn't him. She was just getting started with her career. It could be ten years before she was ready to start a family. By then he'd be forty-six, he reminded himself. Not a good age to begin a family.

But what difference did it make when beginning a family at any point in his life was the last thing on earth that he wanted? he reminded himself. He liked the way he was living now, liked it just fine. He had the freedom to come and go whenever he wanted, could pursue any story anywhere in the world, regardless of how hot the political climate might be. He could take risks. Why would he want to be saddled with a wife and kids? The more he thought about it, the angrier he became, and the angrier he became, the more he blamed Lou. She was trying to trap him, he thought. Yeah, that's it. All these years she'd been pining away for him, and she'd seen her chance to snare him once and for all when he'd been forced to accompany her to Sonora. It was her fault last night had happened, he convinced himself. She had been planning it all along. Why else would she have packed that red dress she knew drove him wild? Why else would she have brought all that damned sexy lingerie? She was responsible for their current predicament, not him. So she was just going to have to be the one who faced up to the consequences.

Oh, who was he kidding? he asked himself. He and he alone was to blame for what happened last night. Glancing down once again at their nude bodies so closely interwoven, he sighed in defeat. She had insisted he stop treating her like a child and accept the fact that she was a grown woman. There was certainly no denying now that he had succeeded in doing that. If he searched his brain to the end of time, he knew he'd be hard-pressed to think of another female who was more of a woman than Lou Lofton. Dammit, he was supposed to look after her, he berated himself. He was supposed to make sure she stayed out of trouble. Instead, he had selfishly dragged her down to satisfy his own eager desires. Well, one thing was certain. This could never, ever, happen again.

As slowly and carefully as he possibly could, Mason disengaged himself from Lou, praying anxiously that she wouldn't wake up until he was safely away. He needed to be alone for a while to think all this through. This was to have been their final day on Sonora. They were supposed to be catching a flight back to Washington in roughly twenty-four hours. As Mason searched for his clothes, groaning inwardly when he remembered how they'd been removed by Lou's tentative hands, he resolved that this situation would be settled between them before they boarded that plane.

When he had all of his belongings secured, Mason took one final moment to watch Lou as she slept. She was lying on her stomach, her arm stretched across the empty place on the mattress where he had lain only minutes before. In sleep, she seemed to look younger somehow, took on once again the innocent appearance of the nineteen-year-old Halouise that had stumbled into his office all those years ago. The realization and memory only made Mason feel that much worse about having taken advantage of her. Before he made his way through the connecting door into his own room, he paused to pull the sheet cautiously up over her unconscious form, torn between wanting her to awaken so that he could make love to her one more time and wanting her to remain asleep so that he could make a silent, hasty retreat.

You're a coward, Thorne, he told himself as he began to make his getaway to his room. Lou doesn't deserve to be abandoned this way. Then he recalled how she had quietly declared her love for him in the darkness of the night some hours ago, and a great fist clenched his heart. No, Lou didn't deserve to be abandoned this way, he agreed. But he realized he had abandoned her long before this—that night in her apartment when he'd admitted for the first time that she wasn't a little girl anymore. That was the moment he'd finally ceased seeing her as a helpless, innocent kid from the mountains, and that was the moment when he'd first let her down.

"I'm sorry, Lou," he said softly as he pushed the connecting door closed on her slumbering form. "I'm so sorry."

When Lou awoke, it was to find herself lying alone in her bed wearing naught but a rectangle of sunlight that filtered through the filmy curtains on the French doors. She realized absently that she was thoroughly exhausted and that every muscle in her body ached as if she had driven it to its extreme. Then she recalled how she had spent the majority of the night and understood why. She felt heat seep into her face and chest at the memories replaying in her brain. For once she wasn't remembering dreams about how Mason had made love to her, but actual events. Lou smiled. Reality had far exceeded fantasy. It had been the most heavenly night she had ever known. She'd never felt closer to anyone in her life, had never felt more cherished, more desired, more . . . loved.

Flexing her fingers open over the empty place on the cool sheet that had been hot from Mason's body not long ago, Lou wondered where he had gone. She listened for the sound of the shower and heard nothing, scanned the part of the room she could see for signs of his presence, but saw none. Pushing herself up from the mattress to turn over and struggle into a sitting position, she groaned softly. Yes, she definitely ached. But it was kind of a nice ache, really. One she wouldn't mind waking up with more often. Surely after she and Mason had made love a few more times, the kinks would be worked out and she'd awaken every morning feeling languid and relaxed and completely satisfied.

Her smile broadened at that. Lou wasn't sure she'd ever be completely satisfied where making love with Mason was concerned. Certainly she had little experience with which to make comparisons, but even she was sure it didn't take much to realize that Mason Thorne was a magnificent lover, one who would always leave a woman wanting more. The realization sent a thrill of excitement racing through Lou's body. These were thoughts she'd never contemplated before. Of course, she'd never had a lover before either, not really. What a strange concept. I have a lover, she told herself with a nervous chuckle. And how unbelievably fortunate I am that he's the one man I've always wanted, the only man I've ever loved.

But just where was that man now? she wondered. Scooting across the bed, Lou sank her toes into the plush gray carpet at the same time she noted her dress and underthings lying scattered about on the floor. Her pulse rate accelerated as she recalled how that had come about. She was stunned by the memory of how wantonly she had behaved, how she had allowed herself to be so utterly governed by her passion. Of course, Mason had had a lot to do with that, too, she reminded herself, thinking of the numerous ways he had touched her to make her feel things she had never felt before. She would have solemnly sworn before last night that she loved Mason as much as her heart would possibly allow, that nothing could ever make her love him more. How wrong she'd been. What they had shared together last night had simply strengthened her feelings for him tenfold, had assured her that her love for him would only grow every time they made love. What she had felt for him previously seemed almost childish now in its intensity. She hadn't truly known what love was before last night. How could she have known it would be like this?

Wrapping the bed sheet around herself like a sari, Lou wandered over to the connecting door and rapped softly three times. "Mason?" she said quietly. When she received no answer, she repeated her knocking and called his name once again, but still heard no reply. Automatically, she dropped her hand to the knob and turned it, only to discover the door was locked. A numbing cold settled into her stomach at the realization. Mason had unlocked this door as soon as they'd arrived at the hotel, and it hadn't been locked again since the morning Lou had taken advantage of his queasiness to sneak away into town. There had been an unspoken agreement after that that each would have full access to the other's room with complete courtesy and respect for each other's privacy. They had trusted each other not to take advantage of the agreement. Yet now the door was locked. And Mason had been the one to lock it.

Lou was afraid to consider what his action might mean. Perhaps it was only an accident, she told herself. Perhaps when he'd gone to his own room this morning to dress, he had unintentionally and mistakenly latched the door behind him. She pushed away the realization that it would be difficult to accidently jam a dead bolt into place, and instead focused on the fact that Mason apparently wasn't in his room anyway. So where could he be?

When her stomach growled, Lou had her answer. Breakfast, of course. He must be downstairs in the restaurant having breakfast. Naturally, it would have been very romantic if he had ordered something from room service—like coffee and croissants or maybe champagne and strawberries—for them to enjoy in the privacy of their chamber, but she supposed it was only to be expected that Mason might be as nervous and uncertain after their close encounter last night as she had been before it. Trying to ignore the creeping uneasiness in the corners of her brain that would not be soothed, Lou threw off the sheet and headed for her own shower. Surely she would find Mason in the dining room, and then her doubts and concerns could be put to rest.

But when Lou went down to the dining room a half hour later, showered and shampooed and dressed in her breezy yellow sundress, she could detect no sign of Mason. Inquiring at the desk, she was told Mr. Thorne had been down hours ago for breakfast, had left the hotel without leaving a message for Lou and hadn't yet returned. Her heart sank at the news. Why had he taken off this way without telling her where he was going? Why hadn't he even woken her up this morning? Why was he trying to avoid her?

Answers to those questions came readily enough to Lou, but they weren't the ones she wanted to hear. She wasn't sure what exactly to make of Mason's behavior, but she did know one thing: it wasn't the behavior of a man who was utterly devoted to the woman he'd spent the night making love to.

"When Mr. Thorne comes back," she said to the desk clerk, "will you give him a message for me?"

"Certainly, Miss Lofton."

"Will you please tell him I've gone into town for a little while, but that I'll meet him for dinner tonight at seven?"

The desk clerk scribbled the information on a card and looked up at her with a warm expression. "I'll see to it myself that Mr. Thorne receives your message."

Lou nodded, feeling anything but warm and genial herself. "Thank you."

"It is good news, is it not, about our new president?"

Lou had started to turn away, but the desk clerk's question made her pause. "What?" she asked.

"The final votes have been tallied, and General Papitou is now President Papitou," he announced, clearly very pleased. "Life on Sonora will now truly be free."

Lou smiled. "Congratulations. I'm very happy for you and your countrymen. I know President Papitou will bring only good things to the island."

The desk clerk smiled back. "It is a great day for everyone who calls Sonora home."

With final good wishes, Lou bid him farewell, wanting to say that it was a great day for herself, too, but not altogether certain that such a statement would be correct.

For the remainder of the day, she wandered through the streets of Madriga, exploring the open market in the center of town for mementos and souvenirs of her time there. She wanted to get a gift for Emily and Mick Dante to thank them for cat-sitting Roscoe while she was gone, and she wanted to find something special for the baby that would be arriving soon. When she stumbled onto a stall in the marketplace that boasted tiny woven blankets and handcrafted baby clothes, Lou couldn't help but slow her steps. She wound up buying a number of things from the vendor, telling herself it was because she didn't know the sex of the baby and wanted to be prepared for either, and not because she was so thoroughly enchanted by each and every item up for sale.

As she passed by another stall selling jewelry, her eyes lit on a scattering of semiprecious gems that were exactly the same pale blue color as Mason's eyes. For long moments, Lou only stared down at the stones, remembering how his eyes had changed in the heat of passion and with the languid relief that followed it, recalled how dark and endless their depths had seemed when Mason had first claimed her body with his. Impulsively, she lifted one of the stones carefully into her hand, considering how warm and smooth and hard it was, thinking it reminded her of the muscles her fingers had encountered when exploring Mason's body the night before. When she caught the vendor's eye, she asked how much the gem in her hand cost, and when he told her, she closed her fingers possessively over it. It was a fair price, Lou thought, even if she did have no idea what she would do with a loose stone the color of a summer sky.

By the time she returned to the hotel, she had used up the remainder of her film and nearly exhausted her supply of traveler's checks. As hard as she'd tried, however, she hadn't quite been able to dispel the feeling of foreboding that had accompanied her throughout the day. And now as she approached the hotel desk, her uneasiness was only magnified to a point where Lou couldn't shake the certainty that her world was about to shatter.

"Did Mr. Thorne return?" she asked the same clerk who had manned the desk several hours earlier.

"Yes, he did, Miss Lofton. He said to tell you he'll be up in his room packing when you return."

Lou nodded absently, a feeling of melancholy settling over her like a shroud. Mason was packing for their return to the States tomorrow, something she hadn't had the heart to do just yet. Why couldn't they stay on Sonora for just a little while longer? she wondered as she waited for the elevator. Just long enough to explore the new developments in their relationship alone, without any interference from the outside world. She feared for some reason that once they were back in Washington, they might not have the opportunity to get closer as they had here. There would be too many distractions with work and friends and their conflicting schedules, too many reasons why they didn't have time to see each other.

As the elevator ascended to the fourth floor and Lou stepped into the hallway, she realized she was apprehensive about seeing Mason now, so many hours after having made love with him. If they could have awakened together this morning, blissfully groggy from the night's passion and eager to enjoy each other again, she wouldn't have had time to consider all the implications of their new intimacy, would have been too preoccupied to worry about what was going to happen next. The fact that Mason had left her to go into Madriga alone had lessened their sensual experience and made Lou feel cheated somehow. It was as if what they had shared together meant nothing to Mason, while it had meant the world to her. Was that the case? she wondered. Had their hours of passion been just another night to him?

Instead of going directly to Mason's room, Lou decided to go to her own first. She wanted a moment to prepare herself, to gather her thoughts and collect her wits. She didn't want to seem overanxious or possessive when she saw Mason for the first time after making love with him, because she knew such a response would be the last thing he would want to see. However, when she entered her room to find that the connecting door to his had been thrown open wide in anticipation of her arrival, she realized with a sinking heart she would be denied the luxury of a little privacy before their encounter.

"Mason?" she called out as she placed her purchases on the bed, willing her heart to slow its impatient tattoo and trying to affect a casual posture.

"In here," he replied briskly to her summons.

Lou took a deep, fortifying breath before approaching his room, then paused at the door to observe him before entering the suite identical to her own. His small canvas carry-on was unzipped and spread open on his bed, his clothes spilling from inside and scattered about the bedspread. Mason stood with his back to her at his dresser, stuffing travel-size toiletries into his shaving kit before turning to toss it onto the bed alongside his other belongings. When he did so, he stopped abruptly to stare at her, seeming for a moment as if he were preoccupied by thoughts of something else. Lou held her breath, waiting anxiously to see what he would do, at once expectant and apprehensive about how he was going to react.

"I have to leave tonight," he finally said to break the awkward silence that had begun to loom over them.

Of everything Lou had anticipated hearing him say when she saw him again, the statement he uttered had been nowhere on her list. "Tonight?" she repeated, shaking her head in confusion. "But our flight to Washington isn't until tomorrow morning."

"I'm not going back to D.C."

Her confusion compounded. "What do you mean? Why not?"

"Well, not right away anyway," he qualified. "I'm taking a few vacation days to spend in Belize, and then I'm catching a flight to a location I can't reveal to pursue a story that's started to break there."

"But—"

"I should be back in D.C. by the time Emily's baby is born, though," he added, cutting Lou off before she could protest. "That's still what...three weeks away?"

"You'll be gone for three weeks?" she asked, now completely puzzled by his offhand behavior.

Mason's expression indicated he was giving her question only minimal consideration. "Yeah, about that."

"But, Mason..." Her voice trailed off when she realized she had absolutely no idea how to go about broaching the subject of their activities of the evening before. What was wrong with him? she wondered. What had happened in the past twelve hours to change him so completely? Last night he had gazed at her as if she were the one woman on earth who could give him everything he wanted out of life. Now he was looking at her as though she were just someone else he worked with.

"But what?" he responded with a careless shrug. "Can't you make it back to Washington by yourself? You're the one who keeps pointing out that you're a grown woman who can take care of herself." He picked up a pair of socks from the pile of clothing on the bed and proceeded to roll them into a ball as he added non-chalantly, "Hell, you more than proved that last night."

A cold hole opened up in the pit of her stomach as Lou gripped the doorframe in an effort to keep her knees from buckling beneath her. "What...what do you mean by that?" she demanded on a shallow breath.

Mason's fingers clenched convulsively on the socks he wadded up in his hands when he heard the plaintive quality her voice had adopted. He didn't want to do this to Lou. He didn't want to hurt her. But he had no choice, he told himself viciously. There was no other way. If he showed her any kind of encouragement, offered her even the smallest sign that he returned her feelings of love, she would never get on with her life. He had to spell it out for her in capital letters that he wasn't the kind of man she should waste her time on, that he had no desire to include her in his life in any other role than the one she had been playing for six years. He had to show her that he didn't love her. Not in the way she wanted him to.

Forcing himself to face her fully and assume a bland expression, he said matter-of-factly, "I mean that your performance last night was a damned convincing one. You wanted me to view you as a woman, and by God, you managed to succeed very nicely."

Lou felt all the air leave her lungs in a painful surge. "My performance?" she asked with a gasp. "I wasn't performing, I—"

"No, wait," he said, holding up a hand to stop her protest. "Let me guess." Placing a finger against his cheek, he gazed up toward the ceiling and feigned thoughtfulness. "Let's see now...You weren't performing last night. You meant every word, every gesture, every action and it wasn't having sex, it was

making love. Oh, yeah, and it was the most incredible
thing that ever happened to you, the most devastating
experience you've ever had. Is that what you were going to say?'' he recited carelessly. ''That is the standard
spiel, after all. Or are you one of those women who just
skips over all that and gets to the part about how I'm
the only man you've ever loved?''

As he stood there looking at her as if she were the
shallowest kind of woman, Lou felt her stomach tighten
into a cold fist, felt her eyes burn from the tears that
were pooling there. He had anticipated every word and
emotion she had been about to declare, and had turned
them around until they sounded like the most superficial kind of rot. How could he do that? she demanded
silently, helplessly. How could he make light of what
they had shared last night? How could he think she was
like other women he had known? Dammit, she thought
as she swiped quickly at her eyes, how could he?

''Yes, that's exactly what I was going to say,'' she told
him miserably as she choked back a sob. ''Not because
I was trying to feed you a line, but because I really
meant it. I do love you, Mason,'' she whispered
hoarsely. ''I've loved you for nearly six years. Can't you
see that? Can't you *feel* it?''

Mason hadn't been expecting that she would admit
that so adamantly. And to hear her utter it now with
such vehemence was nearly his undoing. Just for a moment, he allowed himself to feel tenderly toward her.
Then he remembered that neither of them could afford
such a response from him, and he forced himself to
chuckle.

''That's pretty good, Lou,'' he told her as he began
packing his things once again. He focused his attention
on the task at hand as he continued, not wanting to see

her expression as he drove the final nails into her heart. "You almost had me believing you there for a minute." He tried to inject a note of indifference into his voice as he continued, tried to ignore the pain eating up his own heart inside. "Look, don't lose any sleep over this, okay? It's perfectly understandable that you were curious about how it would be between us, and now you know. Lots of women your age experiment with sex before settling down with one man. Don't feel like you owe me anything because you set your sights on me temporarily. You forget who you're talking to. This sort of thing happens to me all the time."

All the time. The words echoed in the empty places of Lou's heart over and over again. She was sure what he said was true. This sort of thing probably did happen to Mason all the time. But it never happened to her.

"Mason, it wasn't like that," she tried again in a very small voice. "It wasn't like that at all."

He glanced up at her with an indulgent smile. "Okay, whatever you say. Anyway, I have to catch a cab in a few minutes. I called Michaud, and he said he'll be glad to give you a ride to the airport tomorrow." After zipping his bag shut, Mason looked up at Lou one last time with an open expression that she decided could mean just about anything. "You know, I guess I owe you an apology about that. Maybe I was wrong about Albert. He might be a decent enough guy after all. He seems to honestly like you. You know, *he* might be just the ticket for a woman like you, Lou. Exotic, foreign accent, no doubt very experienced. And surely more than willing."

Mason's callous comment made Lou feel sick to her stomach. Not only was he trying to foist her off on a man he had recently claimed untrustworthy, but he was suggesting that he thought her promiscuous enough to allow such a liaison to occur. She felt hot tears tumble down her cheeks as she shook her head at him hopelessly.

Pushing herself away from the door, she mumbled weakly, "Oh, Mason, how could you?"

Before he could respond, she stepped back into her room and slammed the door on him. Mason's shoulders sagged with a dubious sense of relief. He, too, felt sick to his stomach, knowing the look on Lou's face would haunt his dreams for years to come. If she only knew what his cruel comments had cost him, he thought. If she only knew how much he honestly did care for her. But she would misunderstand, he told himself. And as cruel as it had been to reject her this way, it would be crueler still to let her go on thinking she had a chance to become a more important part of his life.

Trying to ignore the jab of pain that slashed through his heart, Mason hefted up his bag and headed for the door. It would be three weeks before he saw Lou again, and by that time, he was sure the hurt would be mended. He refused to consider whether it was her pain or his own he was trying to dismiss.

Chapter Ten

Lou's trip back to the States was long, quiet and completely uneventful. Paul Kelly met her flight at Dulles, full of praise and promise about her outstanding articles for the paper and the positive responses they'd received from the public and press circles alike. The newspaper was awarding her a desk in the newsroom, he declared proudly, and she would be working under Charlie Atwater on the Caribbean beat. Upon Charlie's retirement in a few years, Paul added, that part of the world would be hers to cover on her own. It was everything Lou had always wanted from her career. But for some reason, Paul's announcement didn't even come close to filling the empty void that was still yawning open deep inside her.

When she arrived at her apartment, Lou gave her plants a thorough watering, feeling lonely and sad without the presence of Roscoe to cheer her up. She was honest enough to admit, though, that even the presence of her cat would do little to alleviate the melancholy that had been her constant companion since parting ways with Mason the night before. Everything would be different between them from here on out, she realized disconsolately. Nothing would ever be the same again. She had gambled that Mason might come to care for her as deeply as she loved him, and she had lost it all. She'd had to discover the hard way that she meant no more to him than any of the other women he'd ever dated. The night that had been a dream fulfilled for her had been nothing to Mason except another conquest to add to his list of hits.

That perhaps hurt worse than anything else, Lou thought as she fell back onto her couch and stared blindly at the ceiling, that he now viewed her in the same light as every other woman on the planet. She had always taken some consolation in the knowledge that Mason's feelings for her—although not precisely the ones she desired from him—were at least unique. Maybe he had always viewed her as a little sister who needed constant supervision and protection, but at least those feelings had been special ones, reserved for her alone. Now he could simply lump her in with the rest of the women he'd known, those who had been interested in him sexually and had assuaged their curiosity by going to bed with him. It was simple enough to understand; Mason had said so himself. People did things like that every day. Unfortunately for Lou, however, she wasn't one of them. But evidently the man she loved was.

Gripping one of the throw pillows tightly to her heart, Lou allowed herself the luxury of reliving every moment she'd spent on Sonora. Where had she gone wrong? she wondered. How could she have so completely misjudged Mason's feelings for her? When had things gone so utterly awry? And why couldn't he love her the way she loved him?

As frantically as Lou searched for answers that might put her past experience into some kind of satisfactory perspective, she could find none. So instead, she began to consider her future, began to worry about how she was going to get through the rest of her life loving a man who did not return her affection. Every day she would sit at her desk at the newspaper, and every day she would see Mason working on something that did not involve her. Through the newsroom grapevine, she would hear all about the women he was seeing, and she would know that each one stood as an example of how very little their night together had meant to him. And despite everything he had put her through, despite all the cruel things he'd said to her in parting, Lou was quite confident that she would still be doomed for the rest of her life to compare every eligible man she met with Mason Thorne. She was also quite confident that none of them would ever come close to measuring up.

She thought for a moment. Paul had told her that some of her stories and articles about Sonora might possibly be seriously considered as Pulitzer material. That meant she'd done an extraordinarily good job in covering her assignment, right? That also meant she probably had a very good chance of finding a news job with another paper, didn't it? She could go anywhere she wanted; there was nothing in Washington to tie her down now. All these years, she'd been hanging around because she was in love with Mason. All these years, she'd stayed here because of some misguided fantasy that maybe one day he would feel as deeply for her as she did for him. She'd spent a lot of time lately insisting that she was a grown-up, adult woman, Lou reminded herself, and maybe now it was about time she started acting like one. And the first order of business was to accept the fact that Mason did not, would not and perhaps even *could not* love her the way she loved him. Facing that ugly truth would go a long way toward helping her break free from her adolescent, schoolgirl dreams.

The next order of business was to think about exactly what she wanted to do with her life, both in relation to her career and her personal needs. Mason himself had told her he expected her to settle down with one man eventually, hadn't he? Thereby insinuating he was sure it would be a man other than himself. That meant the world was open to her, didn't it? She could pick and choose from an enormous spectrum of jobs and companions, could virtually pack up and leave tomorrow if that were what she had a mind to do. Truthfully, Lou did love Washington and thought it was probably the most perfect place in the world to live. It was a city that boasted everything—parks and museums, artistic functions and big business, restaurants and festivals, city excitement at her doorstep and rural relaxation, not to mention having the seashore within a short drive. It would be difficult to leave it all behind. But she could do it if she had to.

And breaking away from Mason meant breaking away from Washington, D.C. It was indeed something she had to do if she wanted to avoid being hurt and depressed and lonely for the rest of her life. How was she supposed to go on here with things the way they were between herself and Mason? How could she ever expect to get on with her life if she were mooning over a man who didn't want her? How was she going to marry and have children if the constant reminder of what she really wanted and couldn't have was working right beside her every day in the same room?

Pushing herself up off of the sofa, Lou went to her hall closet and retrieved the electric typewriter Mason had given her as a gift upon her graduation from college. How oddly fitting that a present from him would be instrumental in helping her to make big changes in her life and leave her past behind. When she was seated at her dining room table with paper in the roller and a notebook by her side, Lou began to type. The first word that appeared on the stark white paper was "Résumé." The last ones, she was sure, would be "Willing to relocate."

Mason was cold. He was cold, wet, irritated, infuriated and generally ticked off. He was also very, very lonely.

What was it with guerrillas who tried to overthrow small governments? he wondered idly as he hunkered down in the rain beneath a huge banana tree. He was squatting in a grove knee-deep with mud, somewhere so far in the jungles of Central America that he wasn't even sure what country he was in anymore. Why did guys like that have so much damned trouble getting organized? It wasn't like they were trying to bring down the president of the United States or the British prime minister here. In this particular instance, they were going after a seventy-eight-year old megalomaniac alcoholic who spent more time in his mistress's bed than in the capital city. These guys weren't even established enough to have provided tents for everyone. Why couldn't they just get it together and get it over with?

Then he could go home where he had dry clothes and access to a shower. Then he could go home to be with Lou.

It surprised Mason to realize that what really lay at the bottom of his resentment had very little to do with his current situation. More often than not, his travels had led him into some predicaments that were at best annoying. It was the nature of his job. News stories seldom manifested themselves in convenient, predictable, comfortable surroundings. They tended to come up at the worst possible times, in the worst possible locations under the worst possible circumstances. It was part of what made those stories . . . well, newsworthy. And never before had Mason been one to complain. Not with any amount of real petulance anyway. Not until recently. But even he had to admit that the actual reason he wanted to be so far away from this story wasn't because it left him in a jungle swamp that was cold and wet, and it wasn't because it would probably drag on for weeks, maybe months. The actual reason Mason wanted to be far away was because he felt strange being here without Lou.

He didn't know why that was, frankly. He had never missed Lou when he'd been on assignment before. Well, that wasn't entirely true, he admitted. He'd missed her sometimes. A little bit. But he'd always known he would be going home to find her waiting for him at the airport, had always known they would go out to dinner afterward and he would be able to tell her all about the things he'd seen and done, and listen while she described her experiences during his absence. But this time, Mason realized with no small amount of panic, he wasn't at all certain Lou would be there for him when he got home. And if she wasn't there for him this time, he had no one to blame but himself for behaving like such a jerk.

A branch snapped above him and Mason glanced up, only to be doused in the face with a stream of cold rainwater. He sighed wearily as he wiped his face with his hands. Think warm thoughts, he instructed himself. Think about your two days in Belize.

Actually, it hadn't been as much of a vacation as he had planned. Yes, the beaches had been plentiful, the restaurants wonderful, the sunsets delightful and the women beautiful, but something about his time there had left him wanting more. Everything had been perfect, and yet it hadn't been enough. That realization confused Mason no less now than it had when it had struck him the first time while he lay on the beach beside a ravishing redhead. The redhead herself had been something less than perfect, too, and as much as he had wanted to be captivated and enthralled by her, Mason had instead wound up resenting her because she wasn't Lou. That had really scared him, he remembered now. Because he had begun to worry that maybe, just maybe, he might have been wrong about Lou. Or worse still, he might have been wrong about himself.

It was true that he had entertained some doubts after leaving Lou at the hotel in Madriga nearly two weeks ago. He had been so sure that she would get over him in no time, that she would be able to get on with her life and be very happy once she worked through her silly notion that she was in love with him. He had been so certain that what she felt for him was nothing more than an extreme case of gratitude and puppy love, a leftover adolescent response that she would surely reject once she realized how unrealistic her emotions were. Now he was beginning to wonder if maybe he'd shortchanged

Lou in that department, just as he had been short-changing her all along. Who was he to say what she felt? Who was he to presume to know her better than she knew herself? Hell, he was the last person on earth who should be trying to figure out a woman.

And then there was this preoccupation with analyzing himself lately, Mason recalled warily. Try as he might to dismiss the haunting images of making love to Lou that night on Sonora, he knew there was little chance that his dreams and fantasies about her would be coming to a conclusion anytime soon. And try as he might to keep insisting that what he felt for her was no different than what he'd felt for other women in the past, deep down, he knew that was completely untrue. He'd always had special feelings for Lou. Despite his belittling of the phrase when he was trying to push her away, he admitted now that in many ways, Lou was the only woman he had ever loved. But it wasn't romantic love. At least, he'd never thought it was. And he still didn't, he told himself. At least, he didn't think he did.

"Señor Thorne?" he heard a voice call out from the rainy darkness as he grew more and more confused by his own thoughts.

"Yes?" he answered absently.

"We are ready to move out now."

Great, he thought. The guerrillas are ready to move out. Maybe they'd even cover a couple of miles this time if no one got tired or stubbed his toe. Pushing himself up from the ground with a resounding grunt, Mason went back to the compound to retrieve his gear. This story was going nowhere, he said to himself. These guys couldn't overthrow the old neighborhood, let alone a small country. Paul must have been nuts to send him on this assignment. Then Mason remembered that after his original story on Presidente Ramiriz and the senators had fallen through, he had begged his editor to come up with something else for him to cover, something that would be sure to keep him out of the country for another couple of weeks. He grudgingly admitted that he had no one but himself to blame for his current situation. But it wasn't so much the professional predicament he was in now that concerned Mason as much as it was the personal one.

Boy, did he miss Lou.

"Lou, you have to come this weekend. Emily's positive the baby's going to be here by Sunday night."

Lou cradled the phone receiver between her chin and shoulder and shifted absently through her mail. "But she's still got another week to go," she protested to a pleading Mick Dante at the other end of the line. "Mason and I weren't planning on coming to Cannonfire until next weekend, and even that looks iffy for Mason if his assignment isn't wrapped up by then." And iffy for both of us depending on what happens when he gets back, she added to herself.

"I know my wife," Mick persisted. "If she says the baby is coming this weekend, the baby is coming this weekend, regardless of who says otherwise. And she really wanted the two of you to be here when it happened."

Lou relented. Mick and Emily Dante had done nearly as much for her as Mason had since she had left Hack's Crossing. Emily was like the big sister Lou had never known, and Mick was just about the most wonderful man she'd ever met. Just about. "All right, Mick, I'll leave work early tomorrow afternoon and catch the last train. Will that be okay?"

"I'll pick you up at the station myself."

Lou smiled. It was nice to know there were still some men in the world a woman could count on. "Thanks. I'll see you both tomorrow then."

When she hung up the receiver, she was still smiling. The last time she'd seen Emily had been two weeks ago, right after Lou's return from Sonora, when the two Dantes had brought Roscoe home. Lou would never say it to her face of course, but Emily was huge. Lou remembered she had wondered what it must feel like to be that pregnant and had been surprised to discover she was looking forward to finding out someday. Briefly, she had thought she herself might be pregnant after her night with Mason. They had both been too overcome by their desire to consider the consequences and take precautions. But a week after returning home, she had been assured no such consequence had come about. She told herself she should be relieved since getting pregnant now, especially by a man who did not want her, would do nothing but disrupt her career and her plans for the future. Still, there was a little part way down inside her that looked forward to the day—someday—when she brought another life into the world.

Two envelopes in Lou's hand stayed her thoughts in that direction. One was postmarked Seattle, the other Phoenix. Both return addresses were from newspapers to whom she had sent copies of her résumé and samples of her writing. Her heart skipped a little at the realization that once she opened those letters, her life might change irrevocably. These were the first replies she'd received to the dozen inquiries for employment she had sent out, and these were in the cities that were the farthest away from Washington, D.C. For a moment, Lou wasn't certain she even wanted to open them.

She almost didn't want to know if there might be a chance for her elsewhere in the world. There was still a very big part of her that wanted to remain and take a few more chances with Mason.

That's ridiculous, she told herself as she tore into the first of the envelopes. There were no more chances with Mason. He had made it crystal clear that there would be no gray area for her to lose herself in hoping. Scanning the words on the white vellum she pulled from the envelope, Lou began to smile uncertainly. They wanted to set up an interview with her. They needed a reporter who had ties to the Caribbean. Quickly, she set that letter on the table and ran her thumb under the flap of the other. This reply, too, was positive. They were very impressed by the fact that she had managed to be granted an interview with Marco Papitou as a part of her first assignment.

Lou held her breath as she stared thoughtfully at the letters lying side by side on her table. There was someone in the world who wanted her. Someone who needed her. She had overcome the first hurdle in gaining total independence, had taken one giant step forward in seizing control of her life. And she had done it all by herself, without any help at all from Mason Thorne.

What was she going to do? she asked herself. What was it that she really wanted? Actually, that wasn't the right question to ask, Lou realized, because what she really wanted was a lifetime spent loving and being loved by Mason, and now that was obviously beyond her grasp. Therefore, she should be asking herself what situation would be second best for achieving complete happiness. That, too, though, was a question that was unfair, she decided, because as long as she didn't have

Mason, she would never be completely happy, regardless of her situation.

You're stalling, Lou, a little voice in the back of her head piped up. Knock it off and make a decision.

Lou thought good and hard for a long, long time before she did just that, and when she finally did reach a decision, it was to pack her bag in preparation for a weekend spent in Cannonfire with the Dantes. She could think about her future when she got back, she told herself. Right now, there was a baby waiting to come into the world, and Lou wanted to be there when it happened, just in case she was needed.

"I am so glad you were able to come," Mick told Lou as they made the short drive from the Cannonfire station to the shorefront Dante homestead on the north side of town. "Emily would have been frantic if neither you nor Mason had been able to make it. As it is now, she's just mildly neurotic."

Lou grinned at the man in the driver's seat, thinking Emily Dante was probably one of the luckiest women alive. Mick was the epitome of tall, dark and handsome. Standing at six foot five, he was a solid mass of hard muscle, with rebelliously long black hair and eyes the color of dying charcoals. He was a dream of a man, straight from the pages of a romance novel, and he was utterly, unequivocally devoted to his wife.

"Yeah, well how would you feel if you were toting around another human being inside your body?" she challenged him playfully. "Of course, you'd probably never notice because you have plenty of room for one. Emily, on the other hand, barely has extra room in her for lunch."

Mick chuckled. "Okay, you're right. But this having babies business is all pretty crazy. I hate to think we're going to have to go through this again someday. About fifteen times, if Emily has her way."

"Oh, with the next one this will all be old hat," Lou assured him. "You guys will be pros."

Mick shook head head ruefully. "No way. I'll never get used to it. Never."

Lou studied him closely, knowing full well that despite his protests, Mick was more than likely the happiest man alive. He and Emily had wanted to start a family years ago, but had put it off, first because they were working on the house and wanted it to be perfect—not to mention safe—for starting a family, and then because they had bought the bookstore Emily had been managing. It had taken time to get the business running the way they wanted it, and just under a year ago, they had deemed the time right for having children. It hadn't taken long for them to find themselves in the family way. And both had made sure everyone knew that they were only getting started.

When Mick pulled the car into the driveway of the rambling old Victorian, Emily was sitting in the wicker swing on the porch, pushing it back and forth slowly with her toe, and fanning herself with the evening newspaper. Lou thought she looked absolutely radiant, dressed in dark green maternity overalls, bathed in the orange glow of the setting sun that struck fire in her dark auburn curls. Across the street from the house, Chesapeake Bay sparkled in the dying light, and the wind ruffled playfully through the leaves of the two big oak trees in the front yard. It was going to be a beautiful weekend, just perfect for watching a baby come into the world.

"Don't get up," Lou called out to Emily as the latter attempted to raise herself from her seat on the swing. "I'll join you."

As Mick unloaded her bag from the trunk to carry it to the spare room Lou always occupied on her visits to Cannonfire, Emily scooted over to create a place for her on the swing.

"Have you heard anything from Mason?" Emily asked as Lou tucked one leg beneath the other and set the swing into motion again with her own toe.

Lou shook her head, trying to ignore the pain that shot through her heart at hearing the question. "Not a word. I haven't spoken to him at all since we parted on Sonora."

Emily smiled derisively. "That's just like Mason. To take off without telling anyone where he's going and stay incommunicado the entire time he's gone. You'd think that after what happened to him in Hack's Crossing, he'd reconsider, but nooo.... He has to be Mason Thorne, investigative reporter on the go."

Lou chuckled humorlessly. "Yeah, that's Mason all right."

Emily glanced over at her with a puzzled expression. "Is there something wrong, Lou?"

Wrong? Lou thought. Gee, what could possibly be wrong? Just because the man she loved had completely rejected her and made it clear she had no business being a part of his life other than to replace the little sister he'd forfeited to marriage? Just because she was about to resign from her job after earning the international-news position she'd always dreamed of having? Just because she was going to have to leave the city she'd come to love? Just because her entire life was about to enter an unknown dimension she had absolutely no desire to explore? No, there was nothing wrong.

"No," she replied tonelessly.

But Emily wasn't so easily deterred. "What is it?"

"Nothing."

"There's something wrong."

"No, there isn't," Lou insisted.

"I've known you too long, Lou. In a lot of ways, I've watched you grow up. I can tell when something is bothering you. Your face is a complete reflection of your heart where your emotions are concerned. Now fess up."

Lou sighed, knowing what Emily said was true. She also knew that when Mason's sister put her mind to finding something out, there was little chance any secret would remain undisclosed. It would probably be best for all concerned if she just went ahead and made her confession now. "When we were on Sonora," she said slowly, trying to choose her words carefully, "Mason and I... That is, we... I mean he..."

"He seduced you," Emily guessed on a low whisper, her voice belying nothing about what her reaction to the news might be.

"Actually," Lou corrected her softly, looking down at the fingers she had tangled nervously in her lap, "I kind of seduced him."

"*What?*"

"It was the dress," she explained lamely, unable to meet Emily's intent scrutiny. "See, I have this red dress that I knew Mason...uh...responded to, and I packed it on purpose because I kind of hoped he might, you know... respond to it again. And he did. Real well."

"You and Mason made love?" Emily asked cautiously.

Finally Lou met the other woman's gaze and nodded miserably. "Uh-huh," she mumbled, feeling like a fifteen-year-old who'd been caught necking on the couch by her mother.

Lou wasn't sure how Emily was going to respond to the revelation and prepared herself for the worst. But when the other woman began to smile with genuine delight, Lou felt muscles in her body ease that she hadn't been aware of tensing.

"That's wonderful," Emily said, her green eyes bright with unmistakable pleasure at the prospect. "When's the wedding?"

Lou's eyebrows drew down in disappointed confusion. "There's not going to be a wedding. I'm moving. I'm going to be leaving Washington soon."

"But that's the silliest thing I ever heard," Emily said with a shrug. "You love Mason. Mason loves you. Now that you both finally realize that, I would think you'd be moving in together."

Lou widened her eyes in surprise before she objected, "Mason doesn't love me."

"Well, of course he does."

"Not like that. Not the way you think."

"Lou," Emily began, adopting a scholarly expression, "if there's one person on earth that I know through and through, it's my brother. He may be a geek sometimes, trying to deny his feelings, but he's as open as a book. He's been in love with you since the day you guys got back from Hack's Crossing. I could see it by the way he was looking at you in the hospital that afternoon. He just had to wait until you did a little growing up before he could let love take its course."

"No, Emily, you're wrong," Lou assured her adamantly. "What happened that day at the hospital was that I took your place in Mason's life. He knew that you and Mick would be spending the rest of your lives together, and he wasn't sure what he was going to do without a kid sister to look after anymore. So he adopted me and cast me into the role instead."

Emily smiled at Lou indulgently. "No, no, that's completely wrong. That may be what he told himself, but that isn't the case at all. He's in love with you, Lou. He always has been, and he always will be. He's just a little slow on the uptake sometimes, that's all."

Lou shook her head again. "I wish I could believe you, but it's just wishful thinking."

"Give him time," Emily told her gently. "You'll see that I'm right."

"He's had six years, Emily. Don't you think he would have realized it by now if he was going to?"

"Look, you said the two of you made love for the first time on Sonora, right?"

"Right..."

"And that was what? About two weeks ago?"

Lou nodded, telling herself not to let the other woman's analysis of the situation raise her own hopes.

"So, you know Mason. He has a thick skull," Emily pointed out with sisterly affection. "It takes time for realizations like this to penetrate his brain, especially with him fighting them all the way."

"But—"

"Give him time, Lou," Emily repeated.

Lou wanted to agree with Emily, truly she did. But she and Mason had known each other for six years. They had worked together, gone out together, shared meals together, even slept together. If Mason was going to admit that he was in love with her—if in fact he was, which Lou still considered unlikely—then he had been presented with hundreds, perhaps thousands of opportunities to do it. And he hadn't admitted any such thing. He hadn't even come close. Instead, he had taken her avowal of love for him and had assured her that it was nothing more than a common reaction he received from a number of women. Then he had suggested she try it on other men before settling down with one who wasn't him. That wasn't exactly the behavior of a man who was in love with her.

"I can't give him any more time," Lou told Emily resolutely. "I've sent out résumés to several newspapers across the country, and I received replies yesterday from two very good ones who are interested in talking to me. If I pass up these opportunities, I may not get any other ones."

"Lou—" Emily began warningly.

"I'm sorry, Emily, but I have to get on with my life. I can't keep hanging around waiting to see if Mason's going to come to his senses—if that's even the case. I just don't believe he feels anything for me other than a brotherly affection that will never change."

"I think you're wrong," Emily said simply.

"I wish I were," Lou replied quickly as she rose from the swing. "Now if you'll excuse me, I'll go unpack. I'm taking Monday and Tuesday off from work, so if you need me beyond Sunday, you've got me."

"There's someone else who needs you more than I do, Lou," Emily told her meaningfully.

"And he's always had me, Emily. He just doesn't want me."

In an effort to prevent any further argument, Lou rushed into the house, taking the stairs two at a time and hoping to reach the privacy of her room before she completely fell apart.

Chapter Eleven

Mason gazed blandly at the woman seated beside him in the seaside bar in Acapulco and frowned. What had she said her name was? Brittany? Britta? Briana? He couldn't for the life of him remember. He did recall that she had said she was from Sweden. Or was it Norway? Switzerland? Oh, well. It didn't matter anyway. He had already decided that as soon as he finished his drink he would be going back to his hotel. He wasn't having nearly as much fun here as he'd thought he would.

The guerrillas with whom he had been traveling had abandoned their plan to overthrow their government two days ago, deciding it might be better to wait until after the rainy season was over before trying again. They had invited Mason to return then, to cover the story of their glorious deeds of heroism and freedom fighting, but said that for now, they were just going to call time out and go home to be with their families.

Mason had thought it was probably a very good idea. He had briefly entertained similar thoughts, of returning to Washington to be with Lou and Emily and Mick, but when his heart had twisted painfully in his rib cage at the prospect of seeing Lou again, he had realized it was still too soon.

Why couldn't he rid himself of the continuous blur of memories about her? he wondered. How come every time he closed his eyes at night, it was to find visions of Lou dancing in his head—Lou seated across the table from him at the dinner table in her apartment, Lou working on some story at the newspaper, Lou laughing at something he said while they walked down the street, Lou breathless and naked beneath him in bed. It didn't make sense. No woman had ever stuck in his brain the way she had managed to plant herself.

And the pain, he marveled dismally. Was that ever going to go away? Every time he remembered the look on her face when he'd implied she meant nothing to him, it was as if someone were turning a rusty knife in his midsection. He had hoped that in putting distance between himself and Lou, it would take care of the bizarre emotions that had crept up from somewhere deep inside him. He had thought that if he could just stay away from her for a while, the brotherly love he'd always felt for her would come back and replace the new feelings that had taken its place. These feelings of sexual love, of...of *needful* love...feelings like none he'd ever known before, feelings he was none too crazy about experiencing now. Needing someone wasn't something Mason particularly liked. Taking care of Lou because she needed him was one thing, but feeling a need for her in return was just too disturbing, too scary to consider. He'd never needed anyone in his life. He didn't know how to need.

"Mason, is everything okay?"

The question brought him out of his reverie only long enough to glance up and remember he wasn't alone at the bar. He recalled vaguely that he was supposed to be entertaining his new friend. Taking a deep swallow of his beer, he replied quietly, "Yeah, great. Everything is just great."

"Do you want to tell Brigitta about it?" the beautiful blonde asked with a pouty little smile Mason was sure drove all the boys wild. Until a few weeks ago, it probably would have had the same effect on him. Now all he could do was compare her blatantly suggestive expression to Lou's laughing, open face, and he frowned. Lou never played the games that people always played with each other. She wouldn't be caught dead trying to entice a man with superficial little poses. She wouldn't have to.

"No, thanks, Brigitta," he replied, cursing himself for comparing her to Lou as he tried to embed her name in his brain so he wouldn't forget it again. "It's a long story."

Mason forced himself to focus his attention on the woman seated beside him and to forget about the one he'd left looking so forlorn and devastated on Sonora. He told himself Brigitta was everything he looked for in a woman—beautiful, experienced, interesting to talk to, someone who understood the rules of the game and would play by them accordingly. They'd have a wonderful time tonight, and in the morning they could go their separate ways, neither of them feeling cheated or expecting anything more. In that final respect, she was the complete opposite of Lou. And that, Mason assured himself, was precisely why he preferred women like her.

Yet for some reason, it wasn't Brigitta who kept usurping his thoughts. It wasn't Brigitta's face that superimposed itself at the forefront of his brain. And it certainly wasn't Brigitta he kept thinking about making love to. It was Lou, dammit. And somehow, slowly, he began to understand that there would never be another woman who could take her place.

"Brigitta, I've got to go," Mason said as he stood abruptly and threw some bills down on the bar to cover the costs of their drinks.

"But we just got here," she objected, clearly startled by the turn of events.

"I know, and I'm sorry to abandon you like this. But I really do have to go."

"Where?"

"Washington, D.C.," he told her. "Home. I've got to go home."

"And what's waiting for you there that you can't have here?" she demanded crisply.

Mason took a deep breath and met Brigitta's gaze levelly. "A woman," he said simply. "A woman who loves me."

He was unsuccessful in silencing the little voice down deep inside him that added, *A woman I love in return.*

"It's time," Emily announced quietly over breakfast Sunday morning as she poured herself another cup of decaffeinated coffee.

Lou glanced up quickly at the statement, all but forgetting about the spoonful of cereal she had been lifting to her lips. "Uh-oh," she remarked softly.

Mick rattled the newspaper section in his hand in an effort to unfold an article about the Chicago Cubs. "Time for what, honey?" he asked absently.

Emily spooned a generous helping of sugar into her cup and lifted it to her lips before responding, "For the baby. It's time."

Mick replaced his own cup carefully on the table and let the newspaper crumple into a heap in his lap. "What?"

"I'm going into labor," Emily clarified calmly. "It shouldn't be much longer now."

"Uh-oh," Lou repeated, setting her spoon back into the bowl.

For a long moment no one spoke, no one moved, no one breathed. Then Emily smiled serenely and placed her open hand across the floral overalls covering her ample abdomen.

"Oh, yes, it's time," she said again.

Mick leapt up and sprang into action. "Right. Suitcase is all packed and in the hall closet, car's gassed up, doctor's on call. Lou, you get Dr. Stenghal on the horn—her number is magneted to the fridge—and I'll take Emily's things out to the car. Emily, you just sit tight and breathe deeply."

"Are you doing natural childbirth?" Lou asked as she reached for the telephone. "Lamaze?"

"Oh, no, absolutely not," Emily replied mildly as Mick pushed through the kitchen door into the living room beyond. "The image I've always entertained of natural childbirth is squatting out in the jungle in the middle of a typhoon. I'm taking the fullest advantage of modern medical technology my doctor will allow."

Lou nodded sympathetically, imagining the pain of contractions.

"Let's go," Mick announced when he returned. To Lou, he added, "Everything set?"

"Dr. Stenghal said she'd meet the two of you at the hospital in twenty minutes," Lou assured him.

"The two of us?" Emily asked as Mick helped her out of her chair. "You mean the three of us. I want you to be there, too, Lou."

"Oh, I don't know," Lou balked. "I'm not real good with hospitals, even maternity wings. I'd just be in the way and—"

"It would make me feel better," Emily added.

Lou wanted to decline, feeling as if she'd only be an intruder on the happiest moment the Dantes had ever experienced. Frankly, she wasn't sure she wanted to be a witness to their loving celebration when her own love life lay in tatters. It would be too painful a reminder of what she herself might never know.

She started to refuse again. "I don't think—"

"Please, Lou?"

How was she supposed to turn down such a simple, caring request from a pregnant woman who was going into labor? Lou wondered. Wasn't that a capital crime against the American Way or something? Besides, Mick was looking anything but patient with his hands settled on his jean-clad hips and his chest rising and falling beneath his gray sweatshirt menacingly.

"Okay," she said, finally relenting, thankful she had changed out of her pajamas and into a pair of blue jeans and a pink short-sleeved blouse. "Lead on, Dantes. I'll be right behind you."

Mason had assured himself he'd been prepared to return to Washington Saturday night and find that Lou wasn't home. Really, he had. He hadn't *hoped* that

would be the case, naturally, but he had tried to prepare himself for it. And he'd been decent enough this
time not to have used his key to intrude into her apartment without her permission and lay in wait for her return. He'd told himself then it was because he had
respect for her privacy and not because he was terrified
that he might witness her coming home with some guy.
But now it was late Sunday morning, and she still wasn't
there. Never mind that he had telephoned her four times
during the night and received no answer. Never mind
that he had been waiting in the coffee shop across the
street since 7:00 a.m. for her to return home.

That didn't mean she had spent the night in someone
else's bed, he tried to convince himself. It probably only
meant she had turned off the phone and forgotten to
switch it on again before leaving very early to get
doughnuts or something because she hadn't had anything for breakfast at home. Then she might have decided to go to one of the numerous weekend events that
were always going on in the nation's capital this time of
year. It didn't mean she had been with some jerk of a
guy all night. It didn't mean she had already given up
on Mason.

But wasn't that what you wanted? the little voice that
had become his constant companion lately taunted.
*Didn't you tell Lou yourself that she should try out
other guys? Hadn't you made it more than clear that she
had no place in your own romantic plans for life?*

Yeah, but that was before, he argued with himself.
*Before she took up such a prominent place in my
thoughts. Before she became so damned important to
me. Before I realized I'm in love with her.*

All's fair in love and war, right? Mason thought now
as he stood at Lou's front door once again. He re-

moved his keys to her apartment from his pocket and inserted them into the lock. That was how the saying went, right? So this wasn't actually illegal entry, was it? No, it was . . . it was . . . Okay, so it was illegal entry, he admitted as he pushed the door inward. But it was for a good and noble cause.

Evidently irritated at being awakened, Roscoe emitted a low, throaty cat sound from his position on the couch as Mason closed the door behind him. If Roscoe was here, he deduced, then Lou couldn't have gone far. She always made sure there was someone taking care of her cat. Nothing was amiss in the apartment, he realized as he wandered through the small area. The refrigerator was as stocked as it normally was for a single woman living alone, and there was no indication she had planned for an extended stay anywhere. As Mason passed by the table near her kitchen, he glanced briefly down at a pile of mail lying there. He would have taken no more notice of it if his eyes hadn't lit on the return address of the envelope atop the pile and the fact that he realized immediately that it was the address of a newspaper in New York. Curious, he lifted the stack and sifted through it, discovering that there was yet another letter from a newspaper, this one from Florida.

That's funny, he thought as he placed the stack of mail back on the table in exactly the same way he had found it. Why would Lou be getting mail from other newspapers? Then he noticed that her typewriter was sitting out and that she had evidently been using it recently. Beside it were several sheets of typing paper, and upon closer inspection, Mason discovered two other letters that Lou had apparently received that week. He read them shamelessly, telling himself that just because he had acknowledged the fact that Lou was a grown woman with whom he had fallen deeply in love didn't mean he was going to stop looking after her. The words contained within those letters, however, caused him to slump into a nearby chair and shake his head in disbelief.

Lou was leaving him, he realized with no small amount of panic. She had evidently inquired about employment at other newspapers in the country and had received at least two positive replies. One from Phoenix and one from—

"Seattle?" he said out loud. "*Seattle?* That's a million miles away. She can't go to Seattle. I'll never see her again."

Of course, that was probably the whole point, he told himself. It was more than likely that she wanted to be as far away from him as she could possibly get. What had he expected? That he would come home to find Lou curled up on her bed crying her eyes out for him two weeks after he had spurned her? That he would just say, "I changed my mind. I love you," and have her leap into his arms? Well, yes, actually, that was what he had been hoping would happen. Of course, now he knew better. Six years ago, that might have been exactly how Lou would have reacted. Then again, six years ago, she'd been a frightened, insecure teenager. Now she was an adult woman and would behave as such in facing reality's little obstacles. She would pick herself up and get on with her life, precisely as he had always encouraged her to do. The problem was, he'd never intended that she get on with her life without him.

What was he going to do? What if she'd already accepted one of these offers? What if she was in Phoenix or Seattle right now telling them she had only to go home and pack her things and would start work at the end of the week? Where would that leave him?

It wasn't something Mason wanted to think about. Living without Lou? It was a concept he'd never even considered before. He'd just always assumed she would be there. He'd been so certain that their lives would remain eternally parallel, that one wouldn't do anything without the other's knowledge. Had he been wrong to make such an assumption? What did he base it on anyway? How could he have allowed himself to be so sure that theirs would be a lifelong, mutually sustaining relationship that satisfied them both? Had he ever taken Lou's feelings into consideration? Had he ever let her know that was how he felt? Had he ever offered her any indication that he wanted her to be around forever?

No, he realized belatedly, he hadn't done any of those things. Instead, he had told her to take it somewhere else. And now she was clearly planning on doing just that. He was such a jerk. How could he have let things get so messed up?

Mason's fingers clenched furiously on the piece of paper in his hand. Where was Lou now? he wondered. Seattle? Phoenix? Someplace even farther away? Wherever she was, he knew full well that it had been he himself who had sent her there. He only wondered now if he'd be able to talk her into coming back. Because suddenly, Mason knew that the only thing he wanted in the world was Halouise Lofton of Hack's Crossing, West Virginia. And it wasn't the kid who'd come down from the mountains six years ago he wanted, either. Nor was that who he was expecting to get. He wanted the woman Lou had become, every last inch of her. And he was fully prepared to do whatever was necessary to get her back. Because all at once, he realized that his life would be meaningless without Lou there to make it worthwhile.

He sat at her table for a long time, considering the repercussions of everything he had just begun to understand. Love was an awesome thing, Mason thought to himself. Completely incomprehensible and totally overwhelming. But actually kind of fun when you got right down to it. As long as you didn't do something to screw it up.

The sound of a key in the lock brought his body to attention with a snap. His pulse raced nervously at the prospect of seeing Lou now, when he was so utterly unprepared, with his heart baring itself for the world to see. But at the same time, he wondered if it might not be better just to let her know how he felt right off the bat. However, to Mason's combined relief and annoyance, it wasn't Lou who entered the apartment, but her across-the-hall neighbor, Mrs. Maloney, who had come to Washington fifty years ago as a war bride and still claimed an impressive cockney accent after all this time. When the elderly woman looked up to see a man seated at the table, her hand went up to splay open across her ample bosom.

"Oh, Mason," she whispered on a gasp. "You nearly gave me a heart attack."

"Sorry, Mrs. Maloney. I came in looking for Lou, but she isn't home."

"Well, I know that, you silly boy. I've come to feed her cat. Been picking up her mail, too. She's in Cannonfire this weekend, visiting your sister and brother-in-law."

Mason drew his eyebrows down in confusion. "But we weren't supposed to go until next weekend. The baby isn't due until then."

Mrs. Maloney shrugged. "Lou got a call on Thursday night from the pair of them saying they wanted her to come this weekend because your sister was sure the baby was going to be early. Lou told me to expect her back on Tuesday."

Mason stood and went to the phone in the kitchen. "Have you heard anything?" he asked. "Did Lou call?"

Mrs. Maloney shook her head. "No, nothing, love."

He quickly dialed the Dantes' phone number and waited for it to ring ten times before replacing the receiver. "There's no answer at the house."

With a mischievous grin, Mrs. Maloney said, "Maybe your sister was right. Maybe they're on their way to the hospital right now."

"Uh-oh," Mason mumbled as he hurried toward the front door. "I've got to go, Mrs. Maloney. Thanks for taking care of Roscoe."

"No worry," she called after him as he raced down the stairs. "Give my best to all concerned!"

Her final words were lost on Mason. He was much too preoccupied with other matters. His sister was about to have a baby. He was about to become an uncle. But even more important than that, Lou wasn't in another city being interviewed for a job that would take her far away from him. Lou hadn't left him, he realized as a flicker of hope sparked deep in his soul. Yet. He only hoped he would be able to make it to Cannonfire in time.

"Time?" Mick demanded gruffly as Emily cried out in the labor room of the Women's Center in the Cannonfire Hospital.

"Four minutes," Lou replied, fixing her gaze on her wristwatch as she totaled the passage of seconds between the other woman's contractions. Emily had been in labor for just over three hours, and Lou could nearly feel the tension that was so clearly tightening up Mick's muscles and stiffening his body. It was difficult for him to see his wife going through this, she guessed. He was a man who prided himself in his physical strength, and to know he was helpless to ease Emily's suffering during childbirth was probably tying him in knots.

"All right, I'm going after Dr. Stenghal," he muttered roughly as his jaw twitched in anger. "This has gone on long enough."

Lou nodded in understanding as he rushed out the door, then turned to smile reassuringly at Emily.

"Michael doesn't understand that the pain is something I can handle," Emily said as she inhaled another sharp breath. "He thinks I'm too fragile to go through with this. He forgets that women have been doing it for millions of years."

"Mason is the same way," Lou replied. "The whole time we were on Sonora, he was so sure he would have to be the one who kept me out of trouble. For some reason, he felt that he was responsible for keeping me protected from danger, had to be certain that I didn't get hurt. Naturally, I was perfectly safe for the duration of the trip. The only time I ever got hurt was when . . . was when he told me to get lost."

"Lou, he didn't mean it," Emily assured her, taking Lou's hand in her own with a gentle squeeze.

Lou smiled sadly. "That's just it, Emily. I'm sure he did."

The hand holding Lou's gripped harder as another contraction shook Emily's body.

"Oh, boy," the other woman whispered roughly. "That was rather a bad one. Time?"

Lou checked her watch. "Two minutes."

"They're getting closer."

"Too close," Lou agreed. "Where are Mick and Dr. Stenghal?"

"Right here," Mick replied as he burst through the door with another woman in tow.

Dr. Stenghal was tall and willowy, with silver hair coiled into a chignon at her nape and horn-rimmed half glasses perched on her nose. Beneath her white jacket, she wore hospital-green surgical scrubs, and Lou thought she seemed without doubt the most capable woman on earth. Her own worries eased considerably as a result.

"So, I hear you're about ready to send that little nipper on his way," Dr. Stenghal said with an affectionate smile.

"Any minute now," Emily affirmed.

"Well, then let's get you into the proper room. This is the labor room, in case you didn't notice. You can't deliver that baby until you get into the delivery room." Dr. Stenghal's smile broadened. "We do have rules in this hospital, you know. Rules that simply must be followed."

"Then get me out of here," Emily instructed on a shallow breath.

Lou watched as Dr. Stenghal wheeled Emily's gurney out of the room, noting how Mick held his wife's hand and murmured reassuring words meant only for Emily's ears. She allowed the group a substantial head start before she, too, exited the room. But where the others turned left for the delivery room, Lou headed right to while away her time in the waiting room. It would probably be a long afternoon, she guessed. She wished she had brought something to read.

She had a stenographer's notebook in her purse, she recalled. She supposed she could work on drafting a letter to the newspapers in Seattle and Phoenix in reply to their requests for interviews. But the idea held little appeal for Lou. The more she thought about leaving Washington—and Mason—the more depressed she became. But it would be ridiculous to remain knowing he felt no more for her than he did a number of other women. What kind of masochist would she be if she simply stayed in town waiting to be hurt some more? Life was too short to sit around mooning over a man, she told herself. Even if that man was someone worth mooning over. Still, maybe it wouldn't hurt to have a talk with Mason before she made her final decision. Maybe if they sat down to discuss everything that had happened between them recently, explored more fully all that had transpired on Sonora, maybe Mason might admit that there was a little more between them than just a sexual attraction. Maybe he would even admit that he loved her a little. Maybe...

Maybe pigs would fly, Lou concluded gloomily. She was just going to have to face the fact that Mason didn't love her the way she loved him. And to accept anything less than that from him would be to compromise her feelings. Frankly, Lou was tired of compromising, tired of giving more than she received. She wanted to have it all. And if she couldn't have it all, she resolved, then she would just have to settle for nothing. But at least *she* would be the one who made that decision.

The time dragged by as she waited for word from Mick about Emily's condition, and gradually she began to grow drowsy, leaning her head back against the wall and closing her eyes in thought. She didn't worry that something might have gone wrong during the delivery. She had been witness to enough births in Hack's Crossing to know that these things often took time, particularly with firstborns. She only hoped Mick didn't suffer some kind of emotional exhaustion as a result of his extreme concern for his wife's welfare. Lou smiled. What was it about men that simply prohibited them from believing that the women they loved were capable of taking care of themselves? She supposed it was something in their DNA, something that predated the dawn of civilization and would be around long after the modern world collapsed on itself. It wasn't that it was such a bad thing, she allowed, this protective streak that ran through men. It just tended to be a bit inconvenient most of the time.

"Lou?"

The masculine voice was familiar, but it took a moment to seep through the silver haze into which Lou had fallen as a result of her musings. At first she thought it was Mick who had come to tell her that Emily's ordeal was over, but when she opened her eyes and slowly focused them, she saw that it was Mason who stood before her in the waiting room. The first thing she noticed was that he looked more handsome than ever in the jeans and chambray work shirt that made the blue of his eyes appear even deeper. The second thing she noticed was that he also looked very, very tired.

"Mason?" she greeted him softly.

"I ... How's Emily?"

Lou told her heart to stop beating so erratically, told her lungs to take in air at a more sedate pace. Mason was only here because he'd somehow discovered Emily had gone into labor and was only concerned for his sister. His appearance had nothing to do with her own presence at the hospital, Lou assured herself. Nothing at all.

"She's fine as far as I know. Her contractions started about five hours ago. I would think it wouldn't be much longer now."

Mason nodded, but he was clearly still worried about something. Maybe there was a history of childbearing difficulty in his family that she didn't know about, Lou thought. Probably, however, it was simply that peculiar masculine protectiveness to which she'd been witness so frequently lately.

"Do you want to sit down?" she offered, indicating the seat across from her.

Mason noted her gesture, but took the chair immediately beside her instead, slumping into it as if his legs would no longer hold him. He ran his hands through his hair in frustration, folded his arms over his ample chest, crossed his feet at the ankles, stared up at the ceiling and sighed deeply.

"Lou, we have to talk."

Her heart skipped a number of beats at his quietly uttered assertion. "About what?"

"About—"

Mick came bursting into the waiting room then, his body covered in surgical green, a huge grin splitting his handsome features. "Lou, it's—" He stopped abruptly when he saw Mason seated beside her. "Mason, good. You're here, too. I wanted to be able to tell you both at the same time."

Lou and Mason had risen at Mick's appearance and now gazed at him expectantly, as if he held information that would end global strife forever.

"Well?" Lou prodded.

"Is Emily okay?" Mason asked at the same time.

"Emily is fine," Mick assured them with a vigorous nod. "Exhausted, but fine." His smile broadened to the point of becoming silly as he added, "It's . . . it's . . ."

Lou and Mason drew in simultaneous breaths as they waited for the news. "It's what?" Mason finally demanded.

"It's . . . twins," Mick replied.

"*What?*" the other two responded in unison.

Mick nodded proudly again, his chest puffing up three times its normal impressive size. "Twins," he repeated. "One boy, one girl. Both perfectly healthy." For a moment, his eyes adopted a faraway expression, and Lou thought whimsically that he was about to break into song. Instead, he only sighed and repeated, "Twins. Oh, boy. This is gonna be great."

"Whoa, whoa, whoa," Mason interjected. "It can't be twins. That's impossible. They always know these things ahead of time nowadays, don't they? They use radar or something to discover all that stuff, right?"

"Sonar," Mick corrected. "And yes, usually they know in advance if it's going to be twins. But Dr. Stenghal says they still get surprises every now and then. This just happened to be one of those times."

"Wow" was all Mason said.

Lou was a little more articulate. "Oh, Mick, that's so wonderful. Congratulations. When can we see the little tikes? When can we see Emily? You say everyone's all right?"

"Emily and I are a little stunned," he conceded, "but, yes, everyone is fine. The babies are . . . are just . . . It was so amazing, you know? I mean, all of a sudden . . ."

Mick took a deep breath and shook his head as if words could not describe his feelings. Lou smiled. She could only imagine what it must be like.

"Look, I have to get back to Emily," Mick finally concluded as he began backing toward the door. "She's in the recovery room...recovering. Me, I'm not sure I'll ever recover from this."

"We'll meet you back at the house," Mason said.

"As soon as we've seen the babies," Lou qualified.

When Mick was gone, Mason turned to Lou and frowned. "But we need to talk. And the hospital isn't the best place to do it. We'll come back tonight and see the babies."

"Mason, I've been waiting here over five hours for those babies to be born. I'm not going anywhere until I've seen them, and you can't make me."

Mason's eyes glowed dangerously with an icy fire. "You know what happened the last time you dared me like that," he cautioned.

Lou tried to ignore the pain that shot through her at the memory. "I remember too well. But this time is going to be different. You don't run my life, Mason. You can't make me do anything I don't want to do. And that includes leaving the hospital before I've seen the two newest additions to the Dante family."

"I bet I can," Mason challenged.

"I bet you can't," Lou countered.

"I can, too."

"You cannot."

"Can, too."

"Cannot."

"Lou—"

"Mason—"

They had nearly come nose to nose during their verbal parrying, and when Lou realized how close they were standing to each other, she jumped back from him. Mason noted her withdrawal and frowned, then relaxed his posture into a defensive pose.

"Why do we argue like this so much lately?" he asked her as he felt all the fight go out of him. "We never used to fight this way."

Lou shrugged slightly and suddenly felt very tired. "I don't know, Mason. Things have been different between us in a lot of ways lately."

He glanced up at her, and for a moment, Lou could have almost sworn she saw fires of desire flickering to life in his eyes.

"And that's just what we need to talk about," he told her evenly. "That and a few other things."

Lou's heart began to thump out an irregular rhythm. Don't hope, she instructed herself. Don't hope for anything. You did that once before and you wound up with a heart full of hurt. Don't want, don't wish, don't wait. Just tell him your intentions and make tracks.

"I'm leaving Washington, Mason," she whispered hastily, hardly able to recognize the husky timbre of her voice.

He waited only a moment, closing his eyes before asking, "To go where?"

"I'm not sure yet. Maybe Phoenix, maybe—"

"Seattle?" he asked roughly.

Lou felt her cheeks flame at his question, though whether the heat was a result of anger, embarrassment or desire, she wasn't quite certain. "You've been in my apartment without my permission again," she stated in clipped tones.

"I... Look, Lou, we need to talk," he insisted again.

"I think you said everything you needed to say the day you left Sonora," she returned.

Mason shut his eyes again, tightly this time, as if she had just plunged a knife into his heart. "No, I said the wrong things. I didn't say enough."

Lou emitted a single, humorless chuckle. "That's funny. I thought you said more than enough."

"Lou, please . . . Just give me a chance to explain."

She supposed that was the least she could do, she decided. After all, earlier she had been thinking the same thing—that they needed to talk, that maybe if they did, things might become a little easier to understand. She looked at Mason for a long time, wishing there were some way she could be sure that what he was about to say was what she so desperately wanted and needed to hear. If he was simply going to offer her rationalizations for behaving the way he did, for saying the things he had, she really didn't want to hear them. It would still all add up to the same thing. He would be explaining why he couldn't include her in his life, and therefore would be pushing her away. And if that was the case, she would still be leaving. Maybe it would be with a heart that wasn't quite so heavy, but what difference did that make when life held no joy at all?

"All right, Mason," she conceded. "We'll go back to the house and talk." She only hoped what he had to say to her wasn't simply an elaboration of the things she already knew.

Chapter Twelve

"Okay, talk," Lou instructed Mason immediately after he closed the front door of the Dante home.

He drew in a deep breath and expelled it slowly. She wasn't going to make this easy, he thought. Then again, could he really blame her for that?

"Can we at least sit down first?" he asked wearily, beginning to feel the strain and exhaustion of the past several weeks taking their toll on his body.

Lou shrugged noncommittally, but followed Mason as he went to the sofa and fell back onto it. Instead of joining him there, however, she opted to take a seat in the overstuffed chair beside the fireplace on the other side of the room. Not one to be put off by small rebellions, Mason rose and went to take the chair immediately opposite hers, fixing her with an intent gaze as he slumped down into it.

"Now then," he began. "What's all this about you leaving D.C. to move to another city?"

Lou took a moment to answer his question, and Mason noted that when she finally did, she wasn't quite able to meet his eyes. He considered it a very good sign.

"Paul had nothing but praise for my articles on Sonora," Lou explained. "I figured if that were the case, then the editors of other newspapers might find them equally impressive. I didn't see any reason why I couldn't look for employment elsewhere."

"That doesn't answer my question," Mason told her.

Lou sighed deeply, then brought her head up to meet Mason's steady scrutiny dead on. "I don't want to live in D.C. anymore," she told him simply.

"Why not?" he asked. "You've always said you loved it there. And now you've gotten promoted to the newsroom, a position you've continually told me is the job of your dreams. I'd think with a big change like that, you would be even more inclined to stay there."

"Some things have changed," Lou agreed. "But others haven't. The things I wanted most to see change, the things that were of greatest importance to me, have remained essentially the same. And I don't want to keep living in Washington knowing that's the way it will always be."

"What things, Lou?" Mason wanted to know.

But she only looked at him intently and didn't offer a word in reply. Mason thought he had a pretty good idea what she was talking about, at least he hoped he did. But he wanted her to be the one to describe it. He had done a lot of thinking during his brief vacations in Belize and Acapulco, and even more while he was riding out the rain with a band of half-serious rebels in the Central American jungle. Slowly he had begun to understand some things about himself he'd never been willing to consider before, and slowly he had begun to realize that he was desperately in love with Lou. But he wasn't sure how to tell her that. And he knew that she would leave him if he didn't.

"Look," he finally said, rising from his chair to pace the length of the living room. "I know that for the past six years, I've kind of treated you like a kid." Spinning quickly around, he qualified, "But for a lot of those six years, you *were* a kid, Lou. Which was why it was so hard for me to see and accept it when you did grow up. I'm sorry if I've been shortsighted and narrow-minded about that. You have to understand that I never meant to hurt you."

Lou listened closely to what Mason had to say, becoming more and more depressed as he spoke. He was doing precisely what she had feared he would do. He was going to justify his actions on Sonora, explain what his intentions had been, then try to make amends for the way he had behaved. He never meant to hurt her, she repeated numbly to herself. Well that didn't make it any easier to bear.

"Mason, don't," she pleaded with him quietly. "I know all that. You don't have to make excuses for what happened on Sonora. Believe me, I understand only too well how things progressed the way they did between us. You don't have to worry. You're off the hook. And once I'm gone from Washington, you won't have to look at me every day and feel guilty about having gone to bed with me."

"Guilty?" he asked, puzzled. "Why would I feel guilty about the greatest thing that ever happened to me?"

"What do you mean by that?" Lou demanded softly, afraid to let herself hope.

Mason shook his head ruefully. He was tired of taking the roundabout way to say what he had to say, and tired of hearing Lou disguise her own words. *Just say it,* he ordered himself. *Just tell her how you feel. Tell her that you love her.*

"I did a lot of thinking while we were separated," he said by way of a beginning. "And I began to understand some things about myself that I had maybe overlooked before."

"Overlooked ... ?" Lou said encouragingly.

"All right, maybe it was something that I consciously denied by refusing to think about it, burying it so deep inside that no one, including myself, would ever be able to detect it."

"Mason, what are you talking about?"

"I'm talking about needing people, Lou," he finally bit out on an exasperated sigh. "I'm talking about all those years, going back before I even met you, when I appointed myself as Emily's guardian, despite the fact that she claimed she didn't need one. While I was in Central America, I started thinking that maybe... maybe all that time I wasn't trying to take care of Emily because *she* needed *me.* Maybe it was because *I* needed *her.* And when she married Mick, I was—I don't know.... Maybe I panicked a little. Maybe I got scared. Of being left alone."

He took another deep breath and returned to his seat, leaning forward to take Lou's hand in his. When she looked into his eyes, they were warm and liquid and as blue as the summer sky, and Lou knew without question that what he was telling her was the truth. Her heart swelled with happiness, and her blood raced through her veins with a swiftness rivaled only by the spinning of her senses. Mason was trying to tell her she was important to him, she realized. He was trying to tell her that he needed her. But he wasn't telling her he loved her, she reminded herself sadly, feeling the emotions that had skyrocketed burst into so much nothingness at the realization. And that was the only thing that could keep her from going away. Before she could respond, Mason squeezed her fingers affectionately in his and began to speak again.

"So I latched on to you," he concluded in a quiet voice, "telling myself it was because *you* needed me, not the other way around. I haven't been watching out for you to prevent harm from coming to you. Well, not primarily. It's been to prevent you from leaving me, to keep you close by. I didn't want to lose you, Lou. I didn't want you to go away and leave me alone, too."

"Oh, Mason," Lou whispered. She reached out a hand to thread her fingers through his silky hair and pulled his forehead against hers. "I'll never leave you," she promised. "Not completely." Her next words cost her plenty to say, but she knew there was still no way she could keep living in Washington feeling the way she did about Mason. She had to leave. She had no choice. It would be too painful to remain. "No matter where I'm living, we'll stay in touch. I could never be separated from you entirely."

His eyes clouded over at her statement, and he shook his head in silent denial. "You're still planning to leave?" he asked, unable to mask the hopelessness he felt welling up inside him. "But you can't."

"I have to," she insisted, blinking back the tears she felt threatening when she detected the note of utter desolation in his voice that he did nothing to disguise.

"You don't understand. You might need me and want me, but you don't love me, not the way I love you. And I can't stay in Washington, working side by side with you every day, knowing you don't feel the same way about me that I feel about you. Needing and wanting is one thing, Mason. Loving is a completely different matter." Lou stared up at the ceiling in an unsuccessful attempt to keep the tears from spilling onto her cheeks. She strove in vain for a lighthearted tone as she added, "There's nothing sadder in life than an unrequited love. Songwriters stay in business because of it." She met his gaze steadily as she added, "I don't want to wind up looking beaten down and pathetic, Mason. And I don't want to wind up feeling that way."

This time it was Mason who tangled his fingers in Lou's hair and pulled her forehead against his. "No, you're the one who doesn't understand, Lou," he told her. "Over the years, especially lately, as I've seen you mature into a woman, with a woman's reactions and emotions, I've not only loved you, but I've fallen *in* love with you. The way any grown man loves a grown woman. No, scratch that. *More* than a man can love a woman, that's how much I love you. And if there's any way you might give me a chance to prove myself, well...I'd be very grateful."

"Mason, I—"

Her words were cut off before she could utter them, swallowed up by Mason, who took her lips possessively with his own. For a long time, he only kissed her, then when he couldn't stand the separation of their bodies any longer, he pulled her out of her chair and onto his lap. Cradling her head firmly in one hand, he circled her waist with his other arm and began to plunder her mouth more fully. When she was at the verge of tumbling over the precipice into sensual delirium, Lou felt herself being lifted into the air, not through any supernatural or celestial means, she realized dizzily, but because Mason was carrying her. He continued to kiss her as he climbed the steps to the upstairs bedrooms, entered the first one they came to, which fortunately just happened to be the guest room normally assigned to him, kicked the door closed behind him and lay back with Lou on the bed.

After that, things began to get a little hazy for Lou. When Mason finally stopped kissing her long enough to stare down into her face, all she could think about was how wonderfully attractive, how exquisitely sensual, how completely loved he made her feel. All she could do was marvel at how much she loved him in return. His eyes were lit with a heated desire she hadn't seen since their night together on Sonora, and her own body came alive for the first time in weeks. Instinctively, she lifted her fingers to the buttons of his shirt, fumbling to get them open, and pushing ineffectually at the softly worn fabric when she'd succeeded. Still looming over her, Mason shrugged hurriedly out of his shirt, then reached for her buttons. Lou lay still as he undid each one, sighing in delight when he spread her shirt open wide and went to place a kiss over her heart.

Her bra went next, Mason making short work of the front-closure clasp. The scrap of ivory lace was laid flat atop her shirt, and he lifted Lou up only long enough to pull them both from beneath her and toss them aside. Then he leaned in again, rubbing his naked torso against hers to draw a moan of deep longing from the bottom of her soul. Lou's hands spread open across the hot, satiny skin of Mason's back, pulling him closer to her, pleading silently for more. She felt his fingers wander up her rib cage, felt him place his hands firmly below her breasts so that the warm globes were cradled in the juncture of his thumb and index finger of each hand. When he could stand it no longer, Mason lifted himself away from her to cup his hands resolutely over her breasts, his ragged, heated breathing becoming as forceful and uneven as Lou's when he did so.

For long moments they lay entwined that way, getting used to the feel of having each other so close again. Then Mason rolled onto his back, bringing Lou atop him, sliding his hands down to cup over her derriere and pull her close. Lou gasped at the feel of him against her, so ready and anxious, and she let her own hand travel the length of his body to hold him in her palm. The gentle touch was Mason's undoing and he emitted a needful groan as he rolled over once more to help Lou get out of her jeans. She returned the favor by helping Mason out of his, and together they began to explore well-remembered territory to see if there was anything they might have missed the first time around.

A hot fever rose in Lou's body as Mason continued with his fervent caresses, and just when she was sure she would die from the heat of the fire, he claimed her body with his and slowly began to ease her distress. Higher and higher they climbed together, until they both exceeded every encounter they had ever shared together before. Even their night on Sonora had not resulted in the explosive fireworks they enjoyed now. Fireworks, nothing, Lou thought vaguely as they began to descend from the sensual peaks they had transcended. What they had just experienced probably boasted more firepower than World War III would need.

As she lay panting for breath and groping for coherent thought, gazing over at the man who lay equally breathless beside her, Lou wondered at what had just happened. It had been so much more than just a confirmation of the love she felt for Mason. As she watched him watching her with such obvious devotion lighting his eyes, she began to understand that it had also been his way of letting her know that the things he had told her earlier were true. He not only wanted and needed her with him, but he loved her, too. Loved her apparently as much as she loved him. The knowledge made her smile.

"Marry me," Mason said suddenly, urgently.

Lou's heart hammered in her chest. "Oh, Mason, are you sure?" she asked.

"The only thing I'm more sure of is that my life won't be worth living if you're not a part of it. The biggest part."

Lou pursed her lips thoughtfully, feigning worry. "You're sure the reason you're asking me to marry you isn't simply because you don't want to be left alone?"

Mason pulled her close with a throaty chuckle and placed a kiss on the top of her head. "Lou, the reason I'm asking you to marry me is because I love you more than anything else in the world. And no, frankly, I don't want to be left alone, but that doesn't mean I want to spend the rest of my life with just anyone. If I can't have you, I will be alone forever. Because there's no one else who could even begin to fill the void in me you'd leave behind if you went."

Without saying a word, Lou placed her hand over Mason's rough cheek and studied his expression hard. Then she began to smile again. The tired, frightened, painful looks she'd seen in his eyes earlier had fled, replaced by an expression of happiness and utter contentment. Lou knew she had been responsible for the change. And the knowledge that she could be of such a vital concern and influence in Mason's life now reassured her to the point where she began to feel as if nothing would ever go wrong again. The world was suddenly a perfect place. She felt like a woman who had everything she wanted, a woman whose heart, as well as her body, was thoroughly and completely satisfied. There was nothing that could make her get out of this bed, she decided as she stretched languidly and snuggled up closer to Mason. Absolutely nothing.

"I'm home! Lou? Mason? Is anybody here?"

Except perhaps the sound of Mick Dante announcing his arrival, she amended quickly as she tried to scramble out of bed. But Mason grabbed her wrist before she could flee and pulled her back down to join him among the tangle of sheets.

"You're not going anywhere," he told her firmly, laughing as she made awkward attempts to break free.

"But Mick—"

"Will understand perfectly well why I can't keep my hands off of the woman I love," Mason finished for her. "Hey, his wife just had twins, remember? I think that says a lot."

"But—"

"Ssh," Mason whispered with a soft chuckle. "He probably just forgot something and will leave in a minute. If we don't make any noise, he won't even know we're here."

"Mason..."

"Ssh..." he repeated. Then he added quietly, "Tell me that you love me."

"But you just told me not to make any noise," she whispered back with a mischievous grin.

"Then show me."

Lou's grin became wickedly licentious as she listened impatiently for the sound of the front door being slammed shut downstairs behind a departing Mick Dante. After a moment, when she heard that very noise, she proceeded to do exactly as Mason had requested.

The Fourth of July fell on a beautiful day that summer, breezy, sunny and hot, and perfect for a picnic at the beach. Emily and Lou sat on a yellow-and-green-striped blanket at the water's edge, keeping an eye on the collapsible playpen behind them, where ten-week-old Alec and Astrid slept peacefully, oblivious to the raucous cries of Mason and Mick playing volleyball with the Dantes' neighbors less than twenty feet away. Lou turned her face to the sun more fully and adjusted the straps of her flowered bikini in an attempt to prevent tan lines. What a great summer it had been so far. And it was only going to get better.

"So, you've got everything pretty well taken care of for the wedding?" Emily asked her, rubbing sunscreen over arms and legs that had already gone back to their pre-pregnancy shapeliness. She was wearing the gold maillot bathing suit Lou remembered from last year, looking every bit as firm and slender as she'd been then.

"Just about," Lou replied with a nod. "The caterer's still balking at the low total on the guest list, but I don't think it's going to be a problem."

"Oh, that's silly," Emily said with a wave of her hand. "Doesn't she know that small gatherings of friends and family make for the most intimate weddings? You remember how mine and Michael's was."

Lou remembered very well. There had only been a dozen people present, and it had made for a very special day, indeed. It was one of the reasons she and Mason had opted to go for a party of nearly the same size. That and the fact that now they were both working at the Central American desk at the newspaper and had to be ready to travel at the drop of a hat. She'd known there might not be time for any extensive planning.

But it would all be over in three weeks, she thought, trying to console herself. Or, more correctly, it would all be beginning. Lou smiled. She liked the sound of that. Over the past ten weeks, she and Mason had seen each other literally night and day. Together, they had convinced Paul Kelly to make them a team, and now they worked elbow to elbow at the paper. They'd also spent most of their nights either at Mason's or at Lou's, and had begun the exhaustive search for a home together in the Virginia suburbs. At first Lou had worried that in spending so much time together, they might wind up at each other's throats, arguing and bickering like two adolescents as they were wont to do when tensions ran high between them. Fortunately, they'd discovered a new way to deal with those tensions, but it had caused them to spend an inordinately large amount of time in bed. That, too, caused Lou to smile because it reminded her of the plans that she and Mason had made for the future.

They would spend the next six years covering stories for the newspaper, and then they would start a family. Lou had reasoned that such a time frame had worked well for Emily and Mick, and she had fantasized that maybe she and Mason would be lucky enough to have twins the first time around, too. Mason had gone white at the thought, had told Lou that maybe this family-planning business was best left for other people. But Lou had just smiled and assured him that everything was going to be fine, and that had been all Mason needed to hear.

It really was going to be fine, too, Lou realized as a sun-inspired lethargy settled into her bones and warmed her all over. Her grandmother Hattie Lofton had always assured Lou that someday she would have everything a sweet, gentle girl like herself could ever want. Lou smiled, inspecting the ring finger of her left hand where a pale blue stone winked happily at her in the bright sunlight. She wondered how Grandmother Hattie could have known.

"And just what, may I ask, is that smug little grin supposed to be about?"

Lou glanced up at the sound of Mason's voice beside her, and she scooted herself over to make room for him on the blanket. In his dark blue swim trunks and bare, bronzed chest, she thought he was without question the handsomest man on the beach. And from the looks she'd observed him receiving from other women all afternoon, she was well aware that she wasn't the only one in Cannonfire who felt that way. Now, however, Mason's effect on other women didn't faze her. In fact, she rather got a kick out of it. Because Lou knew those other women were only wasting their time. Mason loved her and no one else. And it would be that way forever.

"I was just thinking about Grandmother Hattie," she confessed. "I wish she was still alive."

Mason nodded sympathetically, aware that the only two people Lou had ever felt honest affection for in the mountains had been her mother and grandmother, both of whom had died while she was still a girl.

"She'd really like you, Mason. She'd say you were a scoundrel and a roué, but she'd be almost as crazy about you as I am."

He smiled at her knowingly. "And just how crazy is that?"

Lou threw both arms around him and kissed him hard on the lips. "I love you more than Alec and Astrid love those silly mobiles you bought them to hang over their cribs."

"Hey, there's nothing silly about Ninja Turtles," Mason told her self-righteously. "Those guys mean business."

Lou refrained from commenting, and said instead, "Did I tell you I got a postcard from Albert last week?"

Mason's head snapped to attention at Lou's announcement, and he eyed her warily. "No, you didn't. That guy isn't still carrying a torch for you, is he? Because if he is, I'm going to have to go back down to Sonora and—"

"He never carried a torch for me," Lou reminded Mason patiently. "We're just friends. In fact, he wrote that he and his ex-wife have been seeing quite a lot of each other, so... Maybe we won't be the only ones tying the knot in the near future. And speaking of Sonora," she added meaningfully, "are you ready to admit now that you were completely wrong about Marco Papitou and everything he stood for?"

Marco Papitou and his cabinet members had wasted no time in bringing reform to Sonora. In the two months since Lou and Mason had left the island, the government had freed a number of political prisoners, offering jobs to quite a few of them, and had announced plans for the construction of schools and hospitals all over the island, starting with the poorer communities inland. Tourism was up, and commercial trade had been established with several neighboring countries, including the United States. It appeared that Sonora was about to become a viable Caribbean nation. And with no small amount of pride, Lou reminded herself that she had been one of the first to point out that such a reality would someday occur.

"Okay," Mason conceded. "Maybe I was a little off base on that one. Your intuition and instinct might be just a tad more developed than my own in that respect."

Lou, Emily and Mick all stared at Mason's admission in disbelief.

"What?" Mason asked, puzzled. "What did I say?"

"Ego Man has spoken," Emily intoned with mock gravity. "And he has admitted to being outdone by his sidekick, News Woman."

Mason made a face at his sister. "What do you mean, 'Ego Man'? I don't have that big an ego."

"Oh, you do so have a big ego," Emily contradicted.

"I do not."

"You do, too."

"Do not."

"Do, too."

"Emily—"

"Mason—"

"Both of you!" Lou interjected with a laugh. "Stop that. You're behaving like children. Heaven knows you'd never catch me indulging in such adolescent behavior."

Mason offered Lou a dubious look and smiled. "No way, not you. You are a grown woman, after all. In fact," he added with a leer, "I think you're going to have to refresh my memory about everything that's involved in this grown-woman business, don't you?''

"Now?" Lou asked in a low voice, perfectly aware of the fact that Emily and Mick were eavesdropping on every word they said.

"Is that what you two were discussing that day the twins were born when I came back to the house to get Emily's slippers that we forgot to pack?" Mick asked mischievously.

Mason ignored his question and answered Lou's instead. "Now."

"Oh, Lou," Emily interrupted softly, tapping her discreetly on the shoulder. "You know, Michael's about ready to fire up the hibachi, and I just realized—silly me—that I left all the hamburgers and hot dogs in the refrigerator at the house. You wouldn't mind running across the street to get them, would you? I'd go myself, of course, but the twins..."

"You might want to take Mason with you," Mick added as he moved to set up the hibachi downwind of the picnic party. "There's a cooler full of sodas and beer, too. It might take you a while to find it, though, because I can't quite remember where I put it. You guys just take your time looking. It's going to be a while before we get these coals going anyway."

Lou looked at the other couple through slitted eyes, but they only smiled back at her with big, knowing grins. Before she could protest, she felt fingers wrap around her wrist, and Mason hauled her to her feet, tugging her along behind him as he walked toward the house across the street.

"You know, I think your sister and her husband are plotting something," Lou said suspiciously.

"Oh, you know them," Mason replied with an indulgent shrug. "They just want to be alone, little lovebirds that they are."

"Uh-huh. Sure."

"And speaking of lovebirds," he added, "wasn't there something you were going to tell me?"

"Like what?" Lou asked, feigning ignorance.

"Like how much you love me?" he suggested.

This time it was Lou who smiled knowingly. "Well, since we were headed back toward the house anyway, I kind of thought I'd just show you that."

Mason quickened his steps as he said, "Tell me anyway."

Lou yanked on his arm enough to stop his race to the house and pulled him back into the circle of her embrace. "I love you, Mason Thorne," she told him with every ounce of conviction she possessed.

He smiled down at her with eyes as blue and honest as the ocean behind her. "I love you, too, Lou."

She gave him a gentle squeeze before releasing him, then let him lead her toward the house once again. "You know," she said absently as they climbed the porch steps, "I think I'm going to like working with you, Mason."

"Yeah," he agreed, "especially on those assignments where we have to work up close."

Lou's eyes sparkled with fire, and warm laughter bubbled up freely from somewhere deep inside her soul. "The closer the better," she said as she stepped over the threshold and into Mason's arms.

His laughter joined with hers as he scooped her up and proceeded to climb the stairs. "Gee, I hope Mick didn't hide that cooler *too* well. We could be in here all afternoon."

"Forget about the cooler, Mason," Lou told him on a sultry sigh. "For some reason, I seem to be getting much warmer...."

* * * * *

Silhouette Special Edition

Commencing in May . . .

The stories of the men and women who ride the range, keep the home fires burning and live to love.

Cowboy Country

by Myrna Temte

Where the soul is free and the heart unbound . . . and the good guys still win. Don't miss *For Pete's Sake,* #739, the first of three stories rustled up with love from Silhouette Special Edition.

Silhouette Special Edition

salutes

MOMENTS OF GLORY

from Lindsay McKenna

In a country torn with conflict, in a time of bitter passions, these brave men and women wage a war against all odds... and a timeless battle for honor, for fleeting moments of glory, for the promise of enduring love.

February: RIDE THE TIGER (#721, $3.29) Survivor Dany Villard is wise to the love-'em-and-leave-'em ways of war, but wounded hero Gib Ramsey swears she's captured his heart... forever.

March: ONE MAN'S WAR (#727, $3.39) The war raging inside brash and bold Captain Pete Mallory threatens to destroy him, until Tess Ramsey's tender love guides him toward peace.

April: OFF LIMITS (#733, $3.39) Soft-spoken Marine Jim McKenzie saved Alexandra Vance's life in Vietnam; now he needs her love to save his honor....

"GET AWAY FROM IT ALL" SWEEPSTAKES

HERE'S HOW THE SWEEPSTAKES WORKS

NO PURCHASE NECESSARY

To enter each drawing, complete the appropriate Official Entry Form or a 3" by 5" index card by hand-printing your name, address and phone number and the trip destination that the entry is being submitted for (i.e., Caneel Bay, Canyon Ranch or London and the English Countryside) and mailing it to: Get Away From It All Sweepstakes, P.O. Box 1397, Buffalo, New York 14269-1397.

No responsibility is assumed for lost, late or misdirected mail. Entries must be sent separately with first class postage affixed, and be received by: 4/15/92 for the Caneel Bay Vacation Drawing, 5/15/92 for the Canyon Ranch Vacation Drawing and 6/15/92 for the London and the English Countryside Vacation Drawing. Sweepstakes is open to residents of the U.S. (except Puerto Rico) and Canada, 21 years of age or older as of 5/31/92.

For complete rules send a self-addressed, stamped (WA residents need not affix return postage) envelope to: Get Away From It All Sweepstakes, P.O. Box 4892, Blair, NE 68009.

© 1992 HARLEQUIN ENTERPRISES LTD.   SWP-RLS

"GET AWAY FROM IT ALL" SWEEPSTAKES

HERE'S HOW THE SWEEPSTAKES WORKS

NO PURCHASE NECESSARY

To enter each drawing, complete the appropriate Official Entry Form or a 3" by 5" index card by hand-printing your name, address and phone number and the trip destination that the entry is being submitted for (i.e., Caneel Bay, Canyon Ranch or London and the English Countryside) and mailing it to: Get Away From It All Sweepstakes, P.O. Box 1397, Buffalo, New York 14269-1397.

No responsibility is assumed for lost, late or misdirected mail. Entries must be sent separately with first class postage affixed, and be received by: 4/15/92 for the Caneel Bay Vacation Drawing, 5/15/92 for the Canyon Ranch Vacation Drawing and 6/15/92 for the London and the English Countryside Vacation Drawing. Sweepstakes is open to residents of the U.S. (except Puerto Rico) and Canada, 21 years of age or older as of 5/31/92.

For complete rules send a self-addressed, stamped (WA residents need not affix return postage) envelope to: Get Away From It All Sweepstakes, P.O. Box 4892, Blair, NE 68009.

© 1992 HARLEQUIN ENTERPRISES LTD.   SWP-RLS

"GET AWAY FROM IT ALL"

Brand-new Subscribers-Only Sweepstakes

OFFICIAL ENTRY FORM

This entry must be received by: April 15, 1992
This month's winner will be notified by: April 30, 1992
Trip must be taken between: May 31, 1992—May 31, 1993

YES, I want to win the Caneel Bay Plantation vacation for two. I understand the prize includes round-trip airfare and the two additional prizes revealed in the BONUS PRIZES insert.

Name _____

Address _____

City _____

State/Prov._____ Zip/Postal Code_____

Daytime phone number_____
(Area Code)

Return entries with invoice in envelope provided. Each book in this shipment has two entry coupons — and the more coupons you enter, the better your chances of winning!
© 1992 HARLEQUIN ENTERPRISES LTD.   1M-CPN